PERCIVIOUS

INSOMNIA

JJ Cook & AJ Cook, MD

 FriesenPress

Suite 300 - 990 Fort St
Victoria, BC, V8V 3K2
Canada

www.friesenpress.com

ISBN
978-1-5255-6544-1 (Hardcover)
978-1-5255-6545-8 (Paperback)
978-1-5255-6546-5 (eBook)

1. Fiction, Thrillers, Medical

Distributed to the trade by The Ingram Book Company

PERCIVIOUS (PER-SIV-E-US)

Noun

The ultimate in altruism. Self-sacrifice in order to benefit others with no regard to reward or reciprocity

CHAPTER 1

COOPER DELANEY
5:47 a.m.   Clock Tower Condo, NYC

COOPER RAN HIS HANDS THROUGH HIS DARK, WAVY HAIR AS the first rays splayed across his unshaven jaw, forcing him to squint against their indefensible assault. It had been three nights of the same dream. The same thing every time. What did his sister always say? The best way to end a recurring dream was to tell someone about it? It seemed so stupid in the light of day, yet so familiar and concrete while he slept.

Unfortunately, lingering in bed thinking about dreaming was a luxury Cooper could ill afford. Although he had been with Proteus for eight years, he still felt a pang of guilt if he showed up after his supervisor.

His military father had left behind a lasting impression; reflecting on one's dreams had not been part of the routine. There was no time for daydreaming either. In fact, it was entirely possible that his father would have tried to give orders as to when, how, and what the entire Delaney household dreamt had he been able to take control of both day and night. He would have come up with some military name for it, like twenty-four-hour mandatory dream compliance or some other crazy term. Cooper could just picture the daily dream schedule taped to the fridge for every day of the week, with each of their names at the top.

With a smile on his face, he lazily stepped his athletic, six-foot-three frame into the shower, laughing to himself about his father's response to his "dreams" about Hailey Swanson in the tenth grade. Hell, maybe the old man would have even approved had he still been around.

Cooper was a contradiction. His good looks should have been intimidating, almost otherworldly, but when he smiled, the warmth that radiated made you feel you had known him your whole life. He stopped conversations when he laughed—everyone wanted in on the story. In contrast, his default expression was a look of superiority, like he knew something you didn't even know about yourself. Fortunately, it was filtered by boyish concern and delight frequently enough that almost everyone found it impossible to dislike him. Luckily for Cooper, he had been born XY. Had he been female, there would be too many haters to count.

Walking into his office, he was surprised to find that the lights were already on. They were sensor-activated, which meant someone had come in looking for him. Cooper was disappointed. He was usually the first man in, especially on Monday mornings. His phone went off in his pocket. The text from Jon read: "Come upstairs once you get in."

Jon Cameron had been the director of research for five years before they met. Cooper's reputation, even as a student, made him top of the class and bottom of the recruitment list at the same time. He was all attitude, a class clown, but it was hard to argue with his grades. No one ever thought he would go on to save the world. Selling out to a pharmaceutical company seemed a perfect fit. Jon recruited him with an offer Cooper couldn't refuse; it had been all dollars and cents to him at the time.

Only lately had he started to wonder about the impact his "inventions" were having on society. We can't prevent cancer but we can father a child at ninety. Lately, he pondered the impact of selling out, how in most cases money and values sat in opposition—reluctant guests at either end of life's dining table.

Riding in the elevator to the thirty-first floor and walking down the glass corridor through the twelve-foot double-door entry was something Cooper had done only four times before. Usually for a promotion or bonus and only once to get chewed out. Today he felt the odds were in his favor. Since breaking up with his latest girlfriend, he'd spent evenings and weekends working on the most recent addition to the Proteus family instead. After months of testing, Noctural had become the forerunner as this year's drug of choice. A sleep aid with no side effects—no aftertaste, drowsiness, dependency, or reduced effectiveness over time. In phase-three trials, participants responded favorably, and shareholders even more so.

"Glad you're here. We have a problem." This was Jon's greeting from behind his new-age desk—a desk so oversized it fell beyond intimidating into the absurd, and then back again to intimidating once Jon stood up and started barking. He wasn't one for ergonomics or modest surroundings. The only things seemingly out of place were the three sheep sculptures standing in the corner.

Jon effortlessly dwarfed everyone; even Cooper was forced to look up at him, literally. Jon was overpowering and impressive rather than attractive or good-looking. People of either sex seemed to give way to his proportion, accepting the total package rather than carefully inspecting his individual features. Most people would describe him as handsome, yet piecemeal he was average, with deep-set dark eyes, thin lips, and a receding hairline. Jon was vain when it came to his hair. No matter how many times Carlos tried to blend out his grey, Jon would have none of it. The result was a LEGO effect. Jon's hair looked as if you could pop it off his scalp and change it up with a new color, if only you could reach his head.

Jon liked everything to happen exactly to plan—*his* plan, which meant grand, larger than life. Anything deemed impossible Jon made his mission to bring to fruition. If you needed a mountain moved yesterday, he was your man. No one could parallel his connections, track record, or funding. He had kept Proteus in first place for the past eight years, and in doing so, had made himself a fortune.

Now in front of him stood his rising star, the lead on his most promising trials, the real game changers. The kid was a cocky asshole with as much arrogance as brains. Jon had seen it all and was actually amazed by the kaleidoscope of individuals the field attracted. At the end of the day though, it was binary—all that mattered were the results. The packaging was just that, a simple amusement, especially in this case. Yes, that was it, he decided, he found Cooper amusing.

Cooper misread the hint of a smile that played on Jon's lips as sarcasm and was relieved despite the concerning opener.

"A problem? Whose ass needs saving? Bertram? Radcliff?"

"Yours!" Jon fired back.

Any trace of humor escaped his face and demeanor. Despite his appreciation of Cooper's intelligence, there were times when Jon wished he was one of the nerdy types he could depend on to be intimidated—one of the skittish introverts who would say something stupid and leave at the first chance. How was he going to get across to this kid that his arrogance would be the only thing holding him back? Cooper's misplaced confidence wasn't just a character flaw, it was an attitude that would eventually seep into his work. Perhaps it already had.

"You remember meeting Malcolm Schwartz at the centennial benefit last year?"

"Yeah, old guy, works over at Genetech."

"That 'old guy' is the head of genetic research. He's likely the smartest individual on the planet and laughs at us over here every day making our 'candy.' He has my utmost respect and trust, which is why, last week when he mentioned the chronic insomnia he suffers from, I offered him your 'wonder drug.' After he had the ingredients dissected and deemed safe for human consumption, he joined our trial."

"And the problem?"

"The problem is that it didn't work."

"That's impossible. It works. One hundred percent, it works."

"Oh, of course, my mistake. You're right. There must be something wrong with Malcolm. It couldn't be your test drug, still in trial."

"That's right, it's him. Not the drug."

A look of pain contorted Jon's face. The "simple amusement" had just crossed over to "insolent little shit."

"Just let me test him."

"I called you up here to get that drug back in the lab, not to test Malcolm. In retrospect, I should have called in Bertram or Radcliff to save your ass."

"Give me his number. There is nothing wrong with that drug."

Jon laughed. "You know, if it was anyone other than Malcolm, I would never do this. He is going to eat you up. . . ."

CHAPTER 2

CATHERINE DUMONT
6:59 p.m.   Mount Sinai Hospital, NYC

THE LIGHT AT THE END OF THE HALL WAS HER BEACON, IT always welcomed her home—a secret telegraphy developed over years of working together. If the reading lamp was on, regardless of the hour, the invitation was clear. Otherwise, she made her way down to the parkade alone. Pending weather made that soft glow even more comforting tonight as she began the 3.2-minute-walk past the adjoining offices.

She walked past each room filled with children's artwork, toys, and testing equipment. Her footfalls made little sound, disguised by the muted industrial carpeting; however, she always hesitated just prior to interrupting Will. Just watching him work was an exhilarating experience for her, impossible to describe or admit to anyone.

To everyone other than Catherine, Will Maelish would have been average looking at best, a four maybe. Five was a stretch. His hunched frame had surpassed thin to verge on anorexic. Will's salt-and-pepper hair left one to wonder what the original shade might have been. His sallow complexion was rivaled only by his sunken cheeks. His glasses hid dark circles beneath watery blue eyes frequently rimmed with red, due to the self-imposed late nights he spent at his desk. Will's work meant everything to him, and Will meant everything to Catherine.

Through her eyes, he became a glorious hero. In him, she could find no fault. In many ways, Catherine was the physical opposite of Will. She was a foot and a half taller and outweighed him by at least fifty pounds. Her untamed black curls had the run of her face, held back only by her reading glasses. Catherine's uniform consisted of floral-print maxi dresses—long sleeve for the cooler months and elbow length in the summer—which she alternated with the four pairs of shoes and sandals she owned in varying shades of black and brown.

"You heard the forecast for tonight?" Her question broke the silence, creating the familiar tension that hung in the room.

"Indeed. Looks like we are in for quite a storm."

"Are you finding any correlation between groups?"

"It's too early to tell," Will said, frowning. "But it looks like the numbers may be there to support our theory. The kids in group A simply do not show the regular symptoms leading up to the diagnosis, at least from what I am seeing."

"Let's say that the theory does hold some weight, and that what we are actually witnessing is an epidemic, not just a bunch of kids misbehaving . . ."

"Then we have to start searching for answers, Catherine."

CHAPTER 3

MALCOLM SCHWARTZ
4:45 p.m. Genetech, NYC

"DO YOU BELIEVE IN GOD, MR. COOPER?" MALCOLM'S DEEP voice echoed through the cavernous hall that connected his private lab to the general-testing facilities. He liked to play the acoustics to his advantage, especially the syncopated rap of his walking stick pounding against the marble floor. He embodied the troll beneath the bridge *"with eyes as big as saucers, and a nose as long as a poker."* His height together with his dark features, distinguishably teased white hair, and menacing demeanor had earned him a beastly reputation despite his age; few dared stray down his hall without good reason.

Jon had warned Malcolm of this one, of his arrogance but also his smarts. Regardless, this would be a quick and meaningless interruption, he assured himself. He predicted it would take about three minutes to scare the boy off.

"It's Cooper. Cooper is my first name."

"I see. Hell of a strange first name if you ask me. So, do you believe in God, Cooper?" Malcolm mustered up the most intimidating face he was capable of, one that punctuated his superior position and seniority within their world.

"No, I am a man of science."

"Lots of the best minds believe in a higher power, something larger than you and me. Perhaps not in a conventional God but in the existence of something beyond ourselves."

"Aliens? Parallel universes?"

"No, I mean unexplainable coincidences."

"There is always an explanation."

"Always?"

"Yes."

"Well, then, you will have no problem explaining the failure of your latest wonder drug," Malcolm said, watching for a flicker of shame to betray the confident set of Cooper's mouth.

"Let's talk about that. How long have you been taking Noctural?" Cooper replied without missing a step.

"For six weeks. I was excited to try it—not because I can't sleep. I can fall asleep without any issue. It is the *quality* of sleep that's the problem. I wake up feeling more tired than when I drift off. I need something that is going to really knock me out. When I mentioned that fatigue had become an ongoing problem, Jon invited me to try your Noctural. I declined, of course, because I loathe medication. Never use it. But the fact is that this has become a chronic issue. It started about eight months ago, and it just keeps getting worse."

"Are you taking any other medications?"

"No, not a thing. Not even coffee."

"Then it must be genetic variation."

"I know the odds of that. Please remember where you are, boy." Malcolm had grown tired of Cooper's arrogance, although he had to admit he admired his nerve.

"Maybe it's a Cytochrome P450 issue. The liver cells are packed full of enzymes responsible for metabolizing everything, drugs and toxins, including alcohol. Have you ever found that people can drink more than you despite similar height and weight?"

"Yes, junior, just whom do you think you are talking to? Any novice can identify P450. Don't you think it would have shown up a little sooner than age sixty-seven if that were the case?"

"Not necessarily. As you know, all of us change with time, especially in terms of our metabolism. I suggest measuring metabolic output as you sleep."

"A sleep test. Ha! Good idea. I'll remember my teddy bear and favorite pajamas. A colossal waste of my time."

"Humor me, sir. I would bet my life that you are just as curious for the answer as I am."

"Just make sure the bed isn't some gurney. If I actually can get to sleep, I want it to be a good one."

CHAPTER 4

SEAN IRWIN
10:57 a.m.   AMA Conference Center, NYC

PUSHING HIS WAY THROUGH THE SWARM THAT COMPRISED THE media gallery was easily the worst thing he had been made to do in his twenty-eight-year career. Sean's calling was research. It had always been research. It was his life, his passion. Until recently, he could focus exclusively on his work without interruption or compromise. He would never have guessed that this commitment would lead him astray.

Sean never dreamt that his success would create a frenzy, forcing him into a spotlight filled with people and professions he knew little or nothing about. Sean's immediate response was a bitter resentment of the attention, but he also understood the significance of his findings and accepted that he had no choice. The world deserved the truth, no matter how many times, voices, or languages it would take to deliver the message.

Identifying his colleague locked in what appeared to be a painful exchange with Mandolin Grace from the *Times*, Sean quickened his step. He hoped to save poor Barnett from her ceaseless inquisition.

"My apologies, Ms. Grace, I believe we are ready to begin. You will have to excuse us, my dear," he said politely, while quickly ushering both Barnett and himself through the perfumed-versus-sweat-enhanced crowd, and away from her machine-gun questioning.

"Your timing is impeccable as always, my friend," said a grateful Barnett. Despite their shared age, he had always relied on Sean to take the lead. Sean was the natural leader, with his slim, well-dressed stature and clean-cut sandy hair making him seem taller and smarter than he actually was.

Barnett knew he could never compete. Today would be no exception. He smiled to himself as they both made their way to the podium, glad to be the man behind the scene—a scene that had rapidly exploded in size and significance.

"Dr. Irwin, we are ready for you," shouted a close-shaven man with a headset; his words were barely audible above the deafening buzz. Sean glanced at Barnett. They shared a moment's recognition of fear mixed with exhilaration and perhaps a bit of sadness for what used to be a simple existence.

The room was packed, filled with everyone from physicians to astrologers, politicians to, of course, the media. As they both took their seats at center stage awaiting the introduction, Sean couldn't help but anticipate the inevitable response to their findings.

". . . without need for further introduction, please welcome Dr. Sean Irwin, pioneer of Human Pinnacle Theory."

CHAPTER 5

WILL MAELISH
10:38 a.m. Icahn Charter School, NYC

THE MODERN MERRY-GO-ROUND SPUN WITH SUCH SPEED THAT its primary colors blurred like a kaleidoscope. As Will approached, he could make out the tops of heads pressed against small hands, tight against the top bars. The slowly diminishing rotation had little impact on the screams and laughter exhaled by the ride's enthusiastic passengers.

He could not help the smile that started on his lips as he momentarily drifted back in time to his own early days. In contrast to both the children at play and the ones from the past in his head, he saw Albert Xavier, the boy he was looking for, sitting alone at the side of the school door's concrete steps.

Albert was small, pale, and fragile; he reminded Will of himself at that age. His slight build, blond locks, and haunted blue eyes made him a target for bullies. His ADHD didn't help. Perhaps the bond had stemmed only from being reminded of his own childhood, but there were times when Will felt it was something more. Albert had a way of connecting, a way of understanding other people that Will had never witnessed before.

Will walked on through the playground toward the young boy. Once it became obvious to little Albert that Will sought him out, he began to fidget slightly but managed to stay put. They had developed not trust but more of a pact over the past eighteen months. He would tolerate Will's requests, which he had learned were often followed with rewards, as long as Will didn't get too close and the job didn't take too long.

"How come you are over here on your own, Albert? Do you not feel like playing?" Will gently probed.

"I'm on a timeout" he replied. "I have to wait for the bell to ring."

"I see," answered Will, no stranger to Albert's socialization issues. "Well, I am here to ask for your help with something. You see, I am not quite finished with the work we started."

Albert turned up to Will with a look that melted his test-tube heart. Will wished he could do more to help him; it seemed almost cruel to run test after test, with his research findings being the only outcome. Perhaps his work would have an impact indirectly; he just feared it would come too late.

"Yes, you see I am hoping you will agree to continue on with our meeting time twice a week. It would really help me out. Do you think that would be possible?"

It saddened Will to think that Albert's mother had been too busy to schedule a meeting and instead had asked Will to meet Albert at school. It put Albert's teacher in an awkward position, but in the end she decided it was best to help the boy in any way she could. Will could feel her eyes on them as he sat next to the boy, the cold of the concrete seeping through his khaki pants.

"I'll think about it," little Albert replied, but his small smile betrayed his decision.

CHAPTER 6

MALCOLM SCHWARTZ
8:55 a.m.   Proteus, NYC

ALONE RAVEN SAT PERCHED ON THE OUTSTRETCHED ARM OF Sir Isaac Newton. Malcolm had been idly studying the statue as he waited to be called into the adjourning examination room. He couldn't help but think that Sir Newton was an ironic choice of subject for a courtyard statue—a fellow insomniac, nonetheless. He found the role reversal unnerving, he himself now the lab rat, and considered his participation in the sleep test a very poor decision, especially now, as he sat in his grey/green gown.

A muddy sky met the concrete spires of the Proteus research facilities. The overall scene from his perch was like a black-and-white movie. Figures in white lab coats against the bare pre-winter trees completed the setting for the film noir. A convincing return to the days of old was made possible by their timeless uniform. Those days were so much simpler, as time almost stood still when compared to the present. It was surreal that the view from his window would be devoid of any detectable color. He laughed (more of a snort) as it was, of course, the perfect scene to encourage his highly anticipated nap.

Malcolm Schwartz was a cynic. He had adopted then perfected this disposition over the years. He had experienced too many cases of inhumanity to believe otherwise, and so this attitude had migrated to all corners of his life. In almost every instance, he was not disappointed. From colleagues attempting to take credit for his work to the assholes that cut him off driving to both his ex-wives, he was rarely disappointed.

As such, he'd approached Cooper's request with a healthy dose of cynicism. The only reason he could not help himself from agreeing to the test was curiosity. He *had* to know. He had to know everything. He couldn't remember a day when he didn't want to know absolutely everything about everything, in detail. He found the world he inhabited fascinating. For Malcolm, it had always been filled with endless wonder and possibility. Wonder, possibility, and, unfortunately, people.

"Dr. Schwartz, have you completed the urine sample?" His assigned nurse broke his train of thought.

"Yes, it's there on the counter." Malcolm frowned. "Are we ready to get started then, or will we continue wasting time?"

"Right this way, doctor," she answered in a clipped tone, taken aback by his irascibility.

Malcolm made his way into the adjoining room. Walking through the freshly disinfected door, he observed the "bedroom," fully equipped with state-of-the-art sleep-monitoring equipment including an EEG. Counting all the wires made him doubt any sleep would be possible.

"Have we missed anything?" Cooper was sitting on an air vent directly in front of the window ledge at the far corner of the room. The lights were dim, so it was difficult to make out his expression, which Malcolm assumed was full of sarcasm.

"I'll take your lack of response as a no," laughed Cooper. Malcolm's hesitation had little to do with the state of the room. After being startled by the unexpected welcome, he was left wondering if Cooper would be running the entire test himself. He had fully expected to be in and out of the sleep lab with minimal interaction with support staff. A personal visit from Cooper had caught him a little off guard. It made him wonder about the importance of Noctural to Proteus. It made him wonder about the importance of this test.

"I'm just trying to determine how a pompous drug lord lurking in the shadows is supposed to expedite my trip to dream land," Malcolm replied.

"Drug lord. That's a new one. I like that." Cooper had to laugh. Malcolm's gruff demeanor just did not hold up in the hospital gown. He looked and sounded like some lost geriatric, angry with dementia. In contrast, Cooper was much more comfortable on his own turf. He was almost giddy, anxious to finish up this test and prove to Jon that the only thing wrong with Noctural was this old guy's failure to successfully swallow it.

"I know that you are anxious to get this over with, Malcolm, as am I. The EEG will monitor your sleep, so that we can detect your various brain waves before, during, and after. We will also be recording your oxygen consumption, and your breathing and heart rate in order to cover all the bases." Cooper didn't feel the need to go into any further detail. The look on Malcolm's face indicated that he was already insulted by Cooper's apparently condescending description.

"What if I don't fall asleep?" was Malcolm's only response.

"Why don't you let me worry about that?" Cooper shot back. He made a bet with himself that the old man's test would be over before the first round of the fight that night.

CHAPTER 7

SEAN IRWIN
12:15 a.m.   AMA Conference Center, NYC

"AT THIS TIME, I WELCOME ANY QUESTIONS—" BEFORE SEAN could complete his sentence, the room burst into a simultaneous roar, preventing his ability to decipher anything other than open mouths and waving hands.

He cleared his throat to shout into his lapel microphone from the podium. "For the sake of time, we will be taking a limited number of questions, beginning with the media."

Again, before he could finish the sentence, a familiar man rushed to the podium, press badge in hand. A half step behind was Mandolin Grace, aiming to overtake his lead if possible. The rest of them were not far behind.

"Rudy Mason with the *Post*, Dr. Irwin," shouted the balding reporter. Sean now remembered him. Just last week, he'd received no less than twenty emails and phone calls from Mason, requesting and then demanding an exclusive interview. The man had absolutely no compunction, regardless of the number of times Sean had explained the importance of a ubiquitous reveal. Under the circumstances, it was impossible to dodge him any longer, although he would have loved to ignore his onslaught of poorly researched questions had he the option.

"What makes you so sure your theory is correct, Dr. Irwin?" shouted Mason. "Throughout your presentation, you propose to have provided empirical data to support your findings; however, it's impossible to have—"

"Mr. Mason, I believe you have my email address." Sean's interjection was met with more than a few laughs. "I am happy to provide all the research methodology, outcomes, peer reviews, etc., that you may require. I daresay you will find them in complete support of my hypothesis. I will even venture a guess that the majority of your readers would be more interested in the potential impact than the mathematics justifying my argument, which again, I am more than happy to provide."

"Yes, Dr. Irwin, please tell us why we should care if, as a species, we have reached the pinnacle of our evolution, that we have all become the best we are ever going to be?" Mandolin Grace took her opportunity to interject, following Mason's scolding.

"There is not a 'best,' Ms. Grace," Sean responded. "There is no better or worse in evolution. When a species stops evolving, it is prevented from expanding its area of colonization, even though its environment continues to evolve and change. We have all witnessed the profound impact of climate change, for example. Nothing ever stays the same. If, as a species, we fail to adapt to our environment as it changes around us, we simply die out."

"What first triggered the notion that we have stopped evolving as a species?" Mandolin aimed to continue her lead, if possible.

"As far back as the Romans we have tested man's limitations. This evolved in the Olympics, and as in my swimming example, no records have been surpassed since Michael Phelps in 2008, no new hundred-meter sprint records since Usain Bolt in 2016."

"What is the most compelling evidence supporting your theory? I can't imagine you are able to hang your hat on the Olympics!" Mason was back on his feet.

"As my presentation outlined, it is not a single event that has triggered the findings, but the culmination of undeniable evidence that leads to this conclusion. We have uncovered a tipping point in a number of key indicators that are relied upon to monitor the development of our species, the evolution of mankind."

"Dr. Irwin, could you please review the indicators you outlined in the address, giving a simplified overview of each? Something that would speak to our readers at the *Tribune?*" Cole Matthews had finally gotten close enough to the podium to be heard. He hoped his polite interjection would be rewarded.

"Yes, Cole, I am happy to review. The lack of records being broken at the Olympics is self-explanatory. A more weight-bearing indicator is the results in IQ. Back as far as 2011, you will remember my reference to Victoria Cowie with a reported IQ of 162—above both Einstein's and Hawking's. Since that time, we have not witnessed a score higher than 130. In essence, we are looking at an extreme drop in intelligence, an actual cliff-like decline.

"The reason for IQ being such an important contributing factor is that we measure intelligence across cultures, economic, socioeconomic, as well as geographic categories. It alone should give us cause for alarm, due to the scope and length of time over which we have been collecting the data.

"It is also worth mentioning that, in 1940, an average of 91,456 more boys than girls were born in the US. Though not as prominent, this trend can also be observed worldwide. Over the last thirty years, we have seen the numbers spike by almost 467 percent. Fewer females available for reproduction is an indicator that we have not only plateaued but may also be starting a descent.

"Another contributing factor is that we, as humans, raise 95-99 percent of our young. In most cases, even the weakest of our species survives when compared with other mammals. This fact goes against natural selection, and although it provides evidence of our evolution in terms of compassion for each other, from a biological perspective, we are less intelligent, less evolved. Our altruism has become adverse instead of advantageous.

"Lastly, the evidence we have provided on cell count is arguably the most compelling. Currently the human body has between fifty and seventy trillion cells. We have observed a cap in cell production—a cap, and in many cases, an actual decline. There have been no changes, even minor advances, to our senses either, another critical indication of a human plateau for years."

Mason's interjection was loud and to the point: "So you expect us to believe we have an evolutionary crisis on our hands because we have a few less cells and most of us survive? To me, that sounds like we have reached a pinnacle, doctor, because we are no longer *required* to evolve. We are the apex predator at the top of the global food chain."

Sean's patience was wearing thin, but he reminded himself that, if Mason would ask this type of question, there would be others who would, as well. He had to hold on to the importance of the message. He needed patience. "Mr. Mason, I wish that were the case. I truly do. However, our habitat is not stable.

As you are a reporter, I am sure I do not have to go into detail on the various tsunamis, floods, ice storms, droughts, tornados, and hurricanes. It is apocalyptic, the changes to our environment, yet the species stagnates or wanes. There should be at least the smallest percentage of population responding to these crises, and yet there is none."

It was Ms. Grace's turn to interject: "In light of your findings, Dr. Irwin, do you have any idea what is causing our pinnacle?"

"Ms. Grace, that is where my theory ends. To postulate at causation would be a mistake for us all. Further research is required over a diverse group of specialties. My job is simply to sound the alarm bells and humbly offer any assistance to those who will take the next steps."

Sean smiled at the end of his sentence; it was a relief to use her question as an excuse to bring the presentation to its end and escape the spotlight—for now, at least. He would never admit it, but finding the cause and eventual solution were his true motivations. He had no intention of going down in history as the doctor who identified Human Pinnacle. He wanted more for himself.

While an announcement rang through the conference room that Dr. Irwin and his team would address further questions at a later date, a man at the back of the crowd removed his cell phone from his jacket. He stood buttressed against a pillar at the south side of the theater. There was no one standing next to him. He had attended virtually unobserved, other than by the event organizer who had scanned his invitation badge.

"Mr. Garland, you forgot to sign in, sir!" She had been looking for him since the presentation commenced.

Annoyance of billboard proportion eclipsed his face until he made great effort to recapture the serious indifference that typically reigned upon his features. Still without a title, Ray had been reporting to the directorate of intelligence for close to sixteen years. His job, as he understood it, was crowd control—on a global level, if necessary. He scouted out the significance of "research" such as this all the time, basically to gauge the level of interest and potential backlash from all the influencers, radicals, and crazies out there.

With the quick scrawl that impersonated his name, he reluctantly signed her form and immediately marched through the nearby exit, cell safely in hand. Could what he had heard today have any connection to File 710? Was it even possible?

CHAPTER 8

WILL MAELISH
10:35 a.m. Mount Sinai Hospital, NYC

THE SNOWMAN'S SILK TOP HAT LAY A FOOT AND A HALF FROM what had been his snowy head. They had witnessed his gradual decomposition in the week prior to the holidays, kept a silent vigil over his inevitable fate. Will never imagined his Dracula top hat from a Halloween past could have raised Frosty from the dead, or inspired enough singing from such tiny mouths to wake the same. The enthusiasm and energy of eight-years-olds at Christmas time was not to be underestimated.

With "Frosty the Snowman" still ringing in his ears, Will made his way to the makeshift lunchroom. The past three months had left him excited but apprehensive to start combing through the raw data. He started to unwrap his day-old veggie sandwich as he tallied up the findings in his head.

Out of the subjects they had selected for the study, just over 90 percent showed no change in symptoms. Ninety percent! He could not believe the results, but he had the data in front of him to prove it.

It was common knowledge that sleep deprivation was linked to about 50 percent of ADHD cases, so why did a powerful sleep aid like Noctural have little or no impact? It should show improvement on about half the participants, as previous studies indicated. The results made no sense.

After calling in a favor to use the drug on children, even though it was still in trial, he felt betrayed. Despite his good intentions, he knew they could be charged or worse, if the FDA would find out about it. It was never the parents. They would try anything to get their kids off these stimulants, which had been the cop-out of choice for the past eighty years. All they did was create mini-zombies in Will's opinion. Almost anything was preferable.

Therefore, a trial sleep aid was an easy approval from the moms and dads of ADHD kids. In something like 81 percent of cases, GPs were prescribing off-label use of sleep aids, approved only for adults, for children anyway. As usual, pediatrics got the shaft. It was well known that drug companies like Proteus were too cheap to run approvals for minors.

Will just couldn't believe the results; from everything Jon had said, they should have had a winner with this one. He thought it was perfect for his trial. Noctural would help him rule out other factors. It had seemed guaranteed to work. What a disappointment. It just didn't make sense.

CHAPTER 9

COOPER DELANEY

8:24 a.m.   Whistler, British Columbia

THE EARLY MORNING SUNLIGHT HAD A YIN-YANG EFFECT ON the cedar balcony slats. It painted the bottom half in orange fire while the top half was left in shadow. Neither being the true color. That was somewhere in between. Wasn't this true in life? Things were rarely what they seemed; all too often, the truth was lurking somewhere in the middle.

A train whistle blew in the distance, its bellow dampened by the marshmallow snow hanging on the pines alongside the tracks. The lonesome call managed to break his hypnosis on the balcony.

Cooper hadn't been able to cancel his trip. Skiing had become his favorite hobby. In actuality, it was the only hobby he had found time to retain with the demands of work.

He was up before everyone else, finding himself sleepless following the results from Malcolm's test. It just didn't make sense. Typically, during sleep, someone Malcolm's age should have been burning up fifty calories an hour, at most maybe sixty, in order to metabolize the drug. But 200 calories an hour? That was unheard of, completely unexplainable, especially during REM sleep. How could he be burning more calories while he was dreaming? There was just no answer for it. Cooper had the lab double and then triple check the results.

He could not escape the compulsion to find a quick answer. Cooper was driven to solve any problem that stood in his way. His devotion to being right was usurped only by the pleasure he felt in proving others wrong. And he definitely planned on proving Jon wrong on this one.

He startled a bit at the harsh rasping knock on the dehydrated-wood door to his suite. That knock could only be Sawyer, his roommate from college.

"Let's go already!" his ex-roommate yelled from the hallway. The phrase took Cooper back in time. Sharing an apartment through university bred familiarity akin to that of a family member. That knock meant either wake the hell up, you're late, or let me the hell in because I forgot my keys.

On the chair lift looking down to the slopes below, the fresh powder made Cooper itch to hit that first run. He loved the standing competition, especially for the first race of the day.

Sawyer and Cooper were adrenaline junkies. They both knew the risk of skiing out of bounds, but the virgin powder always got her way.

As Cooper looked down the mountain, he realized that skiing suited him the same way his work did. Both demanded that he see what wasn't there, anticipate the outcome, and trust his instincts instead of his eyes. It was ironic that he needed the hill to escape work. Work had no place on the mountain. On the hill, every thought left his head and all concentration went into staying on his feet while concocting a strategy to be the first man down.

They always started out with brief banter at the top of the back side of the mountain, both fully aware of what was next but relishing the camaraderie before the race began. As usual, Sawyer pushed off first, claiming his advantage. He argued that he was entitled to it as he stood a full two inches shorter than Cooper. As Cooper started out, he made a critical decision that he would later regret. In order to put the sleep test out of his head and guarantee the win for the coveted first run, he would head straight for the trees.

At first, he almost changed his mind. He hadn't skied in almost a year, and the extreme slope of the hill through the trees, disguised by the fresh snow, was punishing.

Sawyer must have slowed down a bit to look for him, because he could make out his red ski jacket bobbing through the snow at a tentative pace. Maybe he was rusty, as well. Cooper wasn't about to let it slow him down. He headed into the dense forest, determined to keep up his speed through the trees and surprise Sawyer at the bottom.

He kept his cadence natural, finally finding his rhythm and looking for the spaces between the pines. The hill had evened out a bit, and now that he could coast with the knee-deep snow to catch him on each turn, his mind started to drift back to the test.

There was no error; the machine was weeks old and the calibration was flawless. He had tested it multiple times prior and even once post-test. So, what was it? The old man wasn't running a marathon in his sleep. It was like he just started losing calories at an impossible rate in order to sustain normal energy levels—a rate not humanly possible in REM sleep. So *why*?

If loss of energy at this pace were normal, he would have a superhuman metabolism, like nothing anyone had seen before. Normally, the average caloric output during sleep was 0.42 calories per pound of weight per hour. Schwartz, at 220 pounds, should consume around ninety-two calories per hour while sleeping. The man would have to eat constantly, day and night, just to survive, which obviously was not the case. The energy loss at 200 calories per hour occurring during the period of REM sleep made absolutely no sense.

Had Cooper's mind not been racing to grasp any plausible answer, he might have registered the thunder of twenty feet of fresh snow collapsing behind him, a deafening roar so intense it was felt rather than heard. If he'd had time to react, he might have paid closer attention to how close he was getting to the trees, he might have tried to locate Sawyer or even call his name. As it was, there was only time enough to realize there would be no escape.

He saw the twigs before he felt the snow. The sensation overtook him. He couldn't breathe, and he couldn't stop. Intervals of snow and branches hit his face and scratched across his jacket. All he could think of was that he didn't want this to happen. He wanted it to stop, but his brain froze like the snow surrounding him, and he was unable to make any kind of reaction. He was an unwilling participant along for the ride.

This is what Alice must have felt like falling down the rabbit hole. The randomness of his thinking scared him. He realized it was completely out of shock. He was a human Plinko chip bumping his way down and down. His brain started to work again, and he realized he needed to do what he could to break the descent. The further he fell, the less likely his rescue would be.

He scrambled toward what he thought was a tree and felt a stabbing pain in his left leg. He tried to reach up with his hand to cover his mouth and the rest of his face that was exposed beyond the goggles and helmet, and then he heard a loud crack. He continued falling in total darkness. A branch in the upper boughs of the tree had given way and completed the work started by the avalanche, filling his snowy grave.

He was literally buried alive while still attempting to twist and flail in total darkness. Then it all stopped. He didn't know if he was alive or dead. He panicked and tried in vain to move, not knowing which way was up or down. He was terrified, and all he could think of was that he had to get out; he needed to get out fast. He felt his heart rate accelerate and his breathing become uneven. There was a ringing in his ears and then nausea. He had to slow himself down. He needed to regroup. Then a calm interrupted his panic—a calm that was all about accepting that he might not make it but he had to try. He was not going to be saved by staying put. He started talking to himself, only aloud this time.

"Cooper, you have to figure out your direction," he yelled to himself. His brain kicked in, and despite his pounding heart and the cold sensation that was coming over him, he moistened his mouth and let the saliva run down his chin.

"Ok, man, you are right-side up; that's a good start. You can do this." He talked to himself as if he were a child.

In total darkness, he tried to reach up with his arm, but it was no use. The fresh powder now formed a straightjacket around him. He was having a hard time breathing through the dense smell of pine and the suffocating pack of snow he was sandwiched between. He had never experienced such silence before. He lived in a world of constant sound, the ceaseless hum of existence. He had never realized how comforting the noise of life was until it was gone. He was shocked at his need to fill it in with his own voice.

He didn't want to die this way. He wouldn't accept that this was the end and made a huge effort to try to grab up at anything above his head. It was useless. Every time he tried to move, his leg would shout out in pain. He lost all grasp of time, not knowing if seconds or minutes had passed. He had no idea if he could keep breathing. He started humming. It sounded like someone else at first. A bone-chilling sound from a horror film, only he was the victim.

Panic overtook him and he tried to flail. With all the energy he could muster, he attempted to thrash out with all four limbs, screaming in time with his jerking motions. It was pointless; he was molded in the snow. He knew it was fruitless to struggle but guessed that everyone before him who had been caught in an avalanche had given it a try. So, he forced himself to calm down, again and again, succeeding briefly before the panic would build up again, like the water in the fountain in front of the Bellagio hotel. He couldn't keep surrendering to it; he had to keep his wits about him. *What would Dad do?*

Cooper wished he had paid more attention to his father's army stories, wished he had learned more from him rather than shutting him out. His dad couldn't help him now, and the thought of his family set off the jets in the fountain again. He felt tears against his freshly shaven face, caught up in the ski mask, reminding him that he was right side up. The strand of hope to the outside world up above his head became very thin; life above him would carry on as if he'd never existed while he suffocated in darkness alone.

He heard a familiar cracking sound, then felt a tremor run through the tree. Far above his head, the snow shifted, giving way to streams of light.

"Cooper!" shouted a familiar voice from some distance away. He remembered something about school days, and then suddenly it all flooded back. It was Sawyer. He had never been so grateful to hear his friend's voice.

"Help! Help me! Please, help me!" he shouted as loud as he could. The snow muffled his voice, and he heard his words come right back at him.

"Over here!" called another voice. "I see a ski."

"That's his!" shouted Sawyer, the panic in his voice mounting. "He must be down there!"

"Coop! Cooper!" he shouted. "Where are you?"

"Help! I am here! Please help!" Every time he shouted, it was excruciating, like a knife finding its way between his ribs. He felt disoriented but knew he could not give up now. He pushed forward with both arms so that he could throw back his head. He screamed. He screamed as loud and as long as he could while the knife twisted into his side.

"I hear him!" Sawyer's response fell like a euphonic wave down the tree well. Cooper thought that his voice alone could pull him from his tree-lined icy chamber.

"Cooper! Hang on! We are coming to get you!" shouted his friend. "I see the top of your helmet! You are about eight feet down!"

Cooper felt relief rush over him, and he was suddenly able to relax. Chasing the relief was the pain, and for the first time, he realized he was injured. His teeth started to chatter but not from the cold; he was well insulated, packed in the snow. Shock had now fully set in. He easily recognized the symptoms. Relief and shock, these were good signs, normal reactions to the situation. All of a sudden, he was Cooper again, the research star, one of the brightest minds in the industry. Perspective returned to what moments ago had quite possibly been the end of his life.

He wasn't out of the woods yet. He knew that a rescue could be difficult or even impossible, and that more snow could fall at any time, completely closing in his air space. Perhaps it was the contact with the world above, but he made the decision that he was getting out alive, no matter what.

He had never been a spiritual person, but he felt more alive now than he had ever felt. More aware of his surroundings, more apt to believe that anything was possible. It seemed cliché but in that moment he believed he might even have been spared for a reason, and immediately his mind turned again to the test. Despite his chattering teeth and the physical pain, he could not leave this dilemma behind. He had to solve this problem. There had to be an answer.

"Cooper, my name is Victor Maren, and I am with the hill patrol. Can you hear me?"

"Yes!" Cooper yelled as loudly as possible.

"We called in my colleagues to help dig you out. They are on their way."

It seemed like an eternity had passed, when it had been less than fifteen minutes from the time the snow had fallen.

It grew dark again as the shovels blocked the daylight momentarily. Victor was experienced at rescue, his calm voice reassuring Cooper that they were progressing toward him.

"Are you hurt?" Victor asked from where he had stopped a foot above Cooper's helmet.

"I think so, my side and my left leg."

"OK," said Victor. "I will try to attach the harness up around your shoulders and see if I can dig out your leg before we pull you up."

The thought of being yanked out of his grave was exhilarating for Cooper. The fact that it would create more pain didn't matter; he just wanted out. He felt Victor's arms digging out his torso and securing the harness around his shoulders. He felt Victor tug on the line, and his body pulled up slightly at the tension activated from the rescue team on the other end. He felt nauseated as the harness ripped him free of his snow-lined coffin. A stabbing pain in his leg shot through his body. Victor's position prevented him from stabilizing Cooper until he was yanked free.

"Fuck me!" Cooper cried out in pain.

"Sorry, man, I can only imagine how much it hurts. You will be out soon. You are doing great, just hang on." Cooper was getting annoyed with the cheerleading. He had never been in so much pain. He just needed to get out.

Once he could reach him, Victor moved over to Cooper's left side. His movement caused the snow pack to give way.

"You were lucky, man; we would have never found you. It's only because of your friend that you're alive."

Cooper sobered. He needed to get off the hill immediately. Despite the pain, his thoughts returned to Malcolm and the sleep test. The harness lurched as the uneven snow pack between the thick branches gave way. One more tug, and he would be free. As he felt the tension of the harness take hold, he had an epiphany. Just like he knew he would be rescued, as his limp body was pulled from the snow, he also knew that an outside force was what pulled the energy from Malcolm Schwartz.

CHAPTER 10

JON CAMERON
7:17 p.m. Proteus, NYC

HE HAD ADOPTED A MEDITATIVE STANCE WITH HIS ARMS crossed, legs apart. He stood about three feet away from the floor to ceiling window, just to the right of his desk. It was his tell, if anyone was around to witness it.

Jon was a collector. To his far right, gazing out the window with him, were three Lalanne sheep. Their dark black faces contrasted the snow-white wool stretched over their metal frames. The stewards of Jon's office, always at attention, like the queen's guard, loyal only to him, never revealing the lifetime of secrets they had overheard within the four walls.

Jon was also a collector of people. He never forgot a face or a favor. He had an uncanny ability to suspend people's judgment, creating an instant mirage of trust. People were quick to tell him just about anything, and if they weren't, he always knew exactly what to say to loosen their guard. If not, he knew what questions to ask, and if all else failed, he knew someone else who could get him the information required.

People and favors were Jon's currency, a currency much more lucrative than cash. He had built an empire on favors and secrets—favors, secrets, and lies.

What he hated more than anything was being in debt to someone, and today a debt that had been hanging over him since grade school had been finally repaid. It was cause to celebrate, and this is how he celebrated his arcane victories: alone in front of Central Park, looking down at the world below. He felt in control. From this height, nothing could get at him, not anymore.

Growing up poor had left its mark. It is impossible to forget where you come from; it defines who you become, for good or bad. Luckily for Jon, he was able to turn misfortune to his advantage. It motivated him to do whatever was necessary to propel him out of his circumstances as fast as possible. Unfortunately, his unwavering determination was met with more than a fair share of obstacles. For someone young and eager, with the best of intentions, he often found himself taking one step forward only to be shoved hard back into his place.

A soul less tenacious would have given up, especially after losing both parents—first his mom to childbirth and then his father to the bottle. His father never forgave Jon for killing his mom, and he reminded him of it every night after he finished a twenty-sixer of rye. It was Jon's bedtime story for eight years until, one morning, his dad just didn't wake up.

Without family or friends willing or able to take him in, he drifted from one foster home to another, never fitting in. He was either too smart for his own good, outwitting the abusive caretakers, or he was too good at school and would make his foster siblings jealous enough to make sure he left the nest early.

Around the time he was on his fourth home at sixteen years old, he'd decided he'd had enough and would go it on his own. But if he wanted to stay in school, he couldn't make enough money to afford his own place—not a place with an address, anyway. Without an address, he would eventually be thrown back in the foster pool. It was a vicious cycle.

So, he decided to lie about his age and room with some other prior fosters who had taken up in the projects. It was far from ideal, but at least he could be his own boss. It would have worked out for him too, but they wouldn't stay out of his room despite the locks, and everything he had made in six months went missing. When he accused them, so did his teeth.

He would never forget the day after, back at school, the nurse patching him up and then sitting alone in the cafeteria trying to figure out his next move. What could he do? He had nothing. No one. Just when it couldn't get any worse, the kid who would not leave him alone approached the table.

"What happened to your face?" Will Maelish asked.

"Beat it, unless you want the same," replied Jon. He really did not have time for this kid's stupid questions and lame stories today.

He got up to leave, really not sure where to go, and headed for the exit. He felt Will behind him at the end of the schoolyard and turned around.

"Why are you following me?" He looked down at the kid with as much contempt as he could manage through the pain and gauze.

"I don't feel like school today either," answered Will.

"So that's your plan? Just follow me around?" Jon laughed.

"Yeah, I guess," Will said, now unsure he had made the right decision leaving the schoolyard, despite his obvious adoration for the tough older boy.

Jon still wasn't sure why he didn't chase him away. It would have been for his own good. Maybe it was the pain or the fact that he really didn't know what to do next, but he just kept walking until they ended up at Will's place.

His parents weren't in a great situation. Will lived in the same neighborhood as Jon's last foster home. Will's dad worked the graveyard shift at the mall as a security guard, and his mom was a clerk at a clothing store. They didn't have much, but they doted on Will, their only child. He was everything to them. So when Will decided that Jon should be the older brother he'd never had, his dad didn't put up much of a fight, despite his wary look after taking in Jon's bandaged face.

Once his mom got home, they agreed to a night on the couch in the basement, which was a halfhearted threat at best. They all knew that he wasn't leaving any time soon. Jon could tell Will's parents were just praying that this wasn't the biggest mistake of their lives. He hated their charity almost as much as their pity but never forgot the debt he owed them. They all knew that he wouldn't have made it without them.

Days became years, and when he left for good, the only thing they asked is that he help out Will if he ever needed it. With an advanced degree in medicine and a promising career ahead of him, he couldn't have guessed what that would mean. Will tried to follow in Jon's footsteps but wasn't cut out for it; he just wouldn't admit it to himself. So, he landed where most of the strays do: in research.

Jon and Will weren't close; Jon was a loner and went his own way. Very few people even knew they had grown up together. When he got the phone call, he was shocked at first. But what could he do? He had to help. Just this one time, and then he would be finished with it. He could finally put the past behind him. Maybe.

CHAPTER 11

MANDOLIN GRACE

10:36 p.m.   David H. Koch Theater, NYC

SHE WAS LATE IN JOINING THE ARMY OF FOOTFALLS LEAVING the performance. The incongruous troops created a cacophony, which echoed through the expansive corridor. A single-minded mission, to exit as quickly as possible, kept everyone more or less in line, despite the deafening dissonance of multiple conversations alongside varying degrees of age, indulgence, and mobility. The rush to arrive was understandable, but the almost frantic panic to leave had always amused her.

Her season's tickets to the ballet were a frivolous expense due to the fact that she was often called away on assignment last minute. The performances she did manage to attend were treasured, and the opening night of *Giselle* was no exception. She had been watching Ines Stasevich's career blossom for the past four years, and tonight had been her best performance yet. Mandolin had squirmed in her seat throughout the entire second act, reliving her own fleeting moments on stage and dreams of becoming a professional dancer. Determination can only take you so far though in a profession heavily reliant on health and physique.

After the car accident, she had never been the same. She was reluctantly grateful it had happened at such a young age, so that she could quite easily transition to a new path. She was able to channel her disappointment and determination as a dancer to a career in journalism. It had served her well, and she was quickly making a name for herself as a reporter. She had a gift for being at the right place at the right time, alongside a steely will to get what she needed at any cost. She was almost impossible to avoid, using her stamina, persistence, and looks to open the doors or mouths she needed to unlock in order to get the story.

She had received the call following Dr. Irwin's address. Initially, she had chosen to ignore it. She fielded countless "leads" that promised a great story if she would only meet with them. She had learned through the years how to quickly weed through them; she could tell simply by the sound of their voice. But there was something about this guy that seemed worth checking out at least.

Armand Price, who had contacted her, was a respected physicist specializing in accumulated energy—in short, energy harvesting. All the big players relied on his expertise from IMAC to ARVENI, and even MIT. He seemed to be the go-to guy when it came to cutting-edge alternative energy sources and their viability. He had been in high demand for the past ten years. Global warming, climate change, and non-renewable resources were all the job security he could have ever hoped for.

Meeting him after the ballet was not ideal, but her flight to LA left tomorrow at 8:00 a.m. If she had to head all the way to the West Coast, she would at least make it worth her while squeezing in a shopping trip en route to her final destination. Between their schedules, this was the only time available. She'd insisted on a public place, especially given that he was a stranger, regardless of his credentials.

She would later lament her choice in seating. The Cellar was her go-to "meet the lead" lounge. Staff were efficient and knew her by name. She imagined that they treated all return customers the same, but deep down, she knew they appreciated her style. It was as if she were their ideal customer: the Cellar muse.

Mandolin was blessed with chameleon coloring. She could pull off pretty much any hair shade, from dark blonde to red to auburn to chestnut to raven. She was a wizard at creating a messy yet chic style with little effort thanks to her immaculate layers at $300 US per cut, complete with a daily dose of Dyson waves.

Taking full advantage of her luminous crown, she had perfected the hair toss. Mandolin remained poised and elegant while her hair morphed into Japanese maple leaves, like feathers blowing in the wind. Her lengthy locks slid strategically behind her slender shoulders and emerged as a billowing flag that drew males toward her and females away in equal proportion.

Introverted and timid by nature, she was forced to overcompensate, hiding her true self behind popular phrasing and a permanent unwavering smile as steadfast as armor. One had to observe with care to see the real Mandolin. Very rarely, she would reveal herself like a fairy or a phoenix. There would only be a glimpse, but it when it happened, people would realize they had witnessed something secret and very special. Something never meant for them. Something they would never forget.

The Cellar staff were hooked on her, and if she needed to excuse herself, they would ensure it happened promptly. She loved the Cellar's eclectic feel. The modern, smoky, old-world combination always set her at ease. The clean lines of the millwork juxtaposed with ornate seating. The ceiling-to-floor windows looking onto the street, reflecting the candles also nearing the end of their evening.

She perched on a leather stool at the window bar, far enough away from the entry that a conversation could be carried on with ease, yet close enough that she could easily manage an escape if necessary. As she got settled, she mentally forged through the highlights of Dr. Irwin's address. Was Human Pinnacle Theory just another buzz for academia? She would have written it off entirely if she had not witnessed the composition of the attendees herself.

It was the representation that nagged at her. It was not the usual crowd. There were too many new faces representing too many interest groups to believe that nothing was up. She recalled his words: *"Nothing ever stays the same. If, as a species, we fail to adapt to our environment as it changes around us, we simply die out."* She had a tendency to drift off in this place, usually called back to reality by the arrival of her guest. But not this time. It was the scent of burning flesh that brought her back to her surroundings.

In horror, she looked down to witness her beloved, limited-edition Prada slowly roasting on the tea light. What had been a somewhat questionable decision, to meet this source, now became an infinitely disastrous one. How could this be happening? Baby-soft aubergine calf skin melted and charred to a tobacco-brown scar directly beneath the handle. She felt nauseous from not only the smell but the sight. To make matters worse, her guest had arrived and was being led over to her by the hostess. She could barely manage an outstretched hand, and her cold greeting all but stole what little resolve the gentleman had mustered to make his way across the bar.

She looked him over. "You aren't Armand Price, are you?"

The man, bald and in his early fifties, was visibly shaken. His body shook nearly as much as his hand. His eyes widened, and he began with a stammer, "N-no . . . but I work with him."

She rose to leave, livid with herself at entertaining this lead. Mandolin vowed never to let it happen again—double vowing never to sit next to an open flame again. But then the man did something that surprised her: he moved out of her way with his head in his hand.

She assumed he would grab at her, ultimately chase her down. There was something in his desperation that held her attention, despite the catastrophic end to her evening.

Once he realized she was still standing beside him, he turned to her almost dumbfounded, blurting out, "I think what we have going on would interest you."

She literally rolled her eyes at him. If for no other reason than needing a drink at that point, she sat back down and ushered him to the chair beside her. Halfway through a thirty-five-dollar glass of Bordeaux, she let her lead, aka Dr. Peter Camberg, start talking. Until the wine took hold, she berated, then scolded, and then actually threatened the man for pulling this type of stunt.

He took it considerably well in her opinion. He didn't seem a stranger to being put in his place, and seemed quite comfortable taking ownership of his attempt to deceive her. His remorse was impossible to ignore, and with the wine's abetment, her mood toward him mellowed.

"Are you familiar with energy harvesting?" he asked.

"No, but I am sure you are more than qualified to give me the Coles Notes on it." *Great!* she thought, as she drank in the Bordeaux. She primed herself. This late night was just about to become an early morning.

"Energy harvesting is the process whereby energy is captured and stored from external sources. To date, we have made small steps. Examples are solar power, wind energy. . . . Biomechanical energy harvesters are currently in use. For example, I am powering my cell phone with a device strapped around my knee." Dr. Camberg pulled his suit pants taut to his leg so that she could see the outline of the device. "We are on the cusp of being able to provide clean, reliable energy to the masses, but what limits us is the cost associated with large-scale generation."

He continued. "Irwin's measures are what stuck with me. How records were no longer being broken, IQ scores have stagnated, and the lack of increase in human cell count."

Mandolin's senses tingled. So, he had also been at the presentation. She suddenly realized the impact of her aggressive nature in questioning Irwin: It had created the perception that she was an expert in his field, which was far from the case.

"Irwin thinks it's a human condition, and I say it's bigger than that. I say it's energy," Camberg continued, oblivious to her lack of concentration.

She interrupted him. "So, we are declining as a species due to lack of energy? That I believe, Dr. Camberg. Yes, I am exhausted just listening to this." Her annoyance was slowly morphing into sarcasm.

"Please, just hear me out. When I saw the persistence in your questions to Irwin, I knew you were the right person to bring this to. I trust you, and what I am about to say is completely confidential, but we are on the edge of changing the game. Answer me this: What is the most efficient source of energy?"

"Solar power." Her guess was only to placate him—to put an end to this grueling evening. She was barely following him at this point. She wanted to go home and mourn her bag, burned and scarred beyond repair. Her glass stood empty, but the way she kept looking at her watch prevented the server from risking a top up.

He shook his head. "The human brain—human brain waves, to be exact." Camberg became animated, attempting to win her over. "The human brain is astoundingly efficient. IBM's Watson, the supercomputer that defeated Jeopardy champions, required ninety IBM power 750 servers, generating more than sixteen terabytes of RAM. The average human brain typically functions on twelve watts—a fifth of the power required by a standard sixty-watt lightbulb. The more intelligent the individual, the less power required. We are still infants when it comes to this, but to harness organic, intelligent energy, the most efficient energy source in existence, would propel our race beyond imagination."

She could hardly believe what she was hearing. "So, what you are suggesting is that we should start harvesting people's brains?" This was a nightmare she prayed to wake up from.

"Please don't insult me." He looked at her with a new set of eyes, like he had been cursed at. It was obvious her last remark had disappointed him. At a loss though, having lied to gain her audience, he decided to continue. "We have already taken small steps in determining a process that could potentially capture and store intelligent energy. If we were successful in this endeavor, we could power whole cities, perhaps even countries."

"OK, so what does this have to do with Dr. Irwin's address?" She was too tired to care any longer. None of this was coming together for her, and the thought of an early morning flight made her weary.

"Well, don't you see, Mandolin? *They* already beat us to it." Dr. Camberg looked pointedly up to the ceiling, clearly trying to implicate extraterrestrial involvement.

Mandolin's head snapped up, despite the wine and fatigue. At first, she thought she had misunderstood—hadn't heard him correctly. She could not believe he was saying this straight faced. She would never forgive herself. The anger she felt at allowing this man to dupe her was quickly replaced by fear, realizing that he was probably insane.

"Thank you for your time, Dr. Camberg. You understand, I have an early flight tomorrow." As if on cue, the waiter arrived, bill in hand. She signed and rose to leave.

"Please, I understand how unbelievable this may seem, and I fault myself for the rushed explanation, but if you would just—"

"Good night, Dr. Camberg." With that, she left him in his seat to stare after her. Mandolin clutched what was left of her coveted bag close to her chest. She realized just how vulnerable she truly was. Her thoughts returned to the ballet; at this moment, she envied Giselle's fate. How foolish she had been to believe in the intentions of others, or to believe that her instincts were flawless. They had let her down terribly tonight. She would never let this happen again, although she instinctively knew that she was already in over her head.

She would need to talk to Jack about all this, which was bittersweet—bitter in the sense that she already owed him so much that she lived in fear of what she would have to do if he ever asked for repayment, sweet because he probably already had a solution for her. Yes, she knew full well that Jack would sort all of this out for her when she saw him tomorrow. He would help turn the tables to her advantage as he always did. Whenever she was in too deep, she could always count on him. While making her laugh, mapping out next steps, and easing her fears, he never let her falter. Yes, she owed Jack very much indeed.

CHAPTER 12

COOPER DELANEY

10:23 a.m. Willows Beach, Victoria, BC

THE SOUND OF SEAGULLS. IT WAS THEIR WINGED APPLAUSE and salty cries that confirmed he was home. The chill from the damp ocean air and the gulls' lonesome calls were all the welcome he required. After the accident, there was no question—he was forced to take a few months off. For someone like Cooper, who never used a sick day that was not self-induced, it was a lot to adjust to. But after a week in hospital and his release in a wheel-chair, he realized nothing was going to mend overnight. There was no magic pill this time.

"Cooper, you have to stop pushing yourself!" As the words left her mouth, he was limping on one crutch through the foyer toward the chesterfield. His mother's mantra hadn't worked when he was growing up, and it definitely would not work now. Being sprawled out across the tartan sofa was like going back in time. The entire house was a shrine to their family's existence—frozen that way since his father died.

Richard Delaney had been a solider, and a good one by any measure. He was decorated abroad prior to returning to Canadian soil. His father was proud to serve, but all that glory came at a price. Horrid nightmares and bouts with depression stole away many a carefree moment growing up. His mother calmed the waters; she always did. Her family was part of Victoria's founding history dating back to the 1840s. Their Oak Bay residence had been handed down through four generations on her side. Looking back, he did not fully appreciate the sanctuary of that house. How important it had been. The design of the horse hair carved moldings, the eyebrow attic window, the panes of stained glass, and the all-important creak of the floorboards. A smile pulled at his face as he remembered that they had betrayed him more than once as he attempted to sneak back to bed in the early morning hours. It was all etched in his memory. He knew every inch by heart.

To be home was a huge comfort. He hadn't realized just how much he missed the place, how this house, this street, even the sound of the ocean were so much a part of him, it was woven into his DNA. Things stood still on the island, long enough for that sparkly emerald moss to fix itself to anything immobile. He had always feared that, if he stayed too long, he would suffer a similar fate. His home town belonged to newlyweds and the nearly deads—luckily both of which excluded Cooper

Day after day, mother and son made their way down to the beach. She plagiarized a crawling pace so he wouldn't feel rushed on his crutches. Together, they limped down to the end of Dunlevy at Willows Beach. He remembered himself as a boy, running as fast as he could down this same street to get to the water. Growing up on the ocean never leaves you, or so they say. Even in Manhattan, his runs always seemed to lead down to the Hudson. Perhaps the water would always be in his blood.

Chessboard under her arm, she led them in silence toward their newly found driftwood table and chairs. The logs had come to rest in a surprisingly comfortable configuration. The pair sat for hours, genuinely happy to continue this seemingly never-ending game. While Cooper had inherited his nerve from his father, the family all agreed his mother had bestowed his brains. Hers was the first face that welcomed him to this world, and to his relief, the one he woke up to in the hospital after his accident. They had pumped him full of so many pain meds that he drifted in and out of consciousness for the first couple of days. Once he finally did come around, he was in shock all over again, reliving every sickening moment of the avalanche and his painful rescue. Her face let him know he would make it; she alone created the stillness he needed to push through.

The accident had caused a femoral fracture to his left leg and three broken ribs, among additional scratches and bruises. The good news was that he would fully recover, the bad news was that it would take six to eight weeks. The broken ribs were worse than the leg; every breath hurt. The mechanics of respiration demand no attention until one breaks a rib. Every short inhale and exhale created a macabre symphony of ripping and tearing.

Painkillers could only do so much, and could only last so long. There was no way around it—he was in for six to eight weeks of pain. He had little success with his argument when the doctor insisted he travel back home with his mother until he recovered. He tried everything to convince them he was fine, that it was not a big deal. He was frantic, now more than ever, to figure out the mystery behind Malcolm's response to Noctural. He was absolutely desperate to uncover why the man was burning calories in REM sleep at an impossible rate. He could not rest until he figured out where the energy was being absorbed and how it could be explained.

If Jon had not stepped in, revoking his access to the office and insisting he take the time off, he would have paid someone to carry him back to his desk. At least he had remote access and could work from his bed. No one could stop him from proving not only to Jon but also to Malcolm that he had been right all along, there was nothing wrong with Noctural. He knew that for a fact, just as he knew that he would figure out what happened during the sleep test. Now more than ever he was haunted by one question: Where was the energy going?

"You will never guess who I ran into this morning." His mother's steady voice broke through his pool of thoughts like a tidal wave. Cooper mentally staggered back to his perch on the log, sitting across from her. The chessboard patiently awaited his return as the waves rolled into the shore, lulling him back to reality.

The dumfounded look on his face revealed that he obviously hadn't heard a word she had said. Exasperated, she widened her eyes and emphasized each syllable carefully,

"Alicia Christie. You do remember Jack's mom, don't you?" She was beginning to wonder how much of what she was witnessing in Cooper was due to the recovery from his accident and how much was due to his being totally self-absorbed. In the week that had passed, she had found that she was incapable of separating him from his laptop and cell phone. He only surfaced for food and the toilet—each being tied to the other, reliable necessities of existence. Showers had definitely become optional. In her opinion, he was absolutely possessed by his work. She had never witnessed anything like it, other than the behavior of her husband.

Now there was a name Cooper hadn't heard in so very many years. Listening to it roll off his mother's tongue did not seem to do it justice. A flood of summer days flooded through him, chased by every wicked rite of passage young men can conjure. He and Jack had been as close as brothers, possibly closer, if that were possible. If someone had asked back then if they would ever part ways never to speak to each other again, he would have laughed in disbelief. He wouldn't have thought it possible. However, once he started med school, everything (including family) had fallen by the wayside. Cooper had realized his personal ambitions had come at a price; it wasn't till much later that he knew just how high.

He rolled his rook through the thumb and forefinger of his right hand as he relived the best and worst of Cooper and Jack episodes like a movie in his head. It swallowed him up as he drank in the same crisp ocean air from so long ago.

"Yes, of course, how is she?" Cooper finally stammered to the impatient glare from his chess rival. It was just like going back in time. Her expression was the barometer on which he based all right and wrong. The majority of the time it had reflected the level of wrongness. Some things would never change.

"She is well," came her chirp of a reply. And then, after some hesitation, "She asked about you. Thought you may want to get in touch with Jack, so she wrote down his number." Her voice trailed off as it always did for requests that were not to be ignored—requests that were not really requests at all, but highly recommended suggestions that she would champion for months at any given opportunity. It was unlikely that Mrs. Christie had done any such thing, at least not without a suggestion from his mother. He laughed to himself at how transparent one's parents were and had always been.

"Why are you laughing? Really, Cooper, it is so very sad that you lost touch with everyone you knew."

"Yes, yes, OK! I will call him." He would say anything to avoid the lecture that would ensue. Truth be told, he could not imagine calling up Jack out of the blue. It just wasn't in him. And he wasn't the Facebook type.

CHAPTER 13

JACK CHRISTIE
9:38 a.m.   Habit Coffee, Victoria, BC

IT WAS JUST AS JACK LIKED IT: HE HAD THE UPPER HAND. STANDING third in line at the eclectic coffee house, he was almost certain now that the cripple at the counter, checking out the barista's ass, was Cooper. He hadn't thought about his old best friend in forever, until his mother mentioned running into Fran Delaney. Word travelled fast on the island.

"I had a speech for your funeral all planned out," Jack called out from the back of the line, "but it looks like you survived."

Cooper's hand fumbled with the coffee Ashley had pushed seductively toward him with her name and number written on the sleeve, but you would never know it from Jack's vantage point. Even though Cooper's left leg was killing him because he refused to keep track of when to take his next hit of meds, his back and shoulders did not move, deliberately still despite the attack. He just straightened slowly and began to turn around as calmly as possible given the crutches. Years of competition in med school, and the pool of piranhas he called colleagues in R&D had created survival instincts that never slept. Any show of surprise was a sign of weakness.

"You must be disappointed. If for no other reason than you would be missing out on the free funeral lunch by the looks of you." Cooper's words were cutting, but when their eyes met, it was like going back in time. When you share as much as these two had, more days and nights than could be counted, words had little meaning, even after all the time lost in between.

They caught up quickly, as men seem to do. Stuck to the facts. The real stories were set aside for later during drinks.

Cooper and Jack made their way over to the Bard and Banker. Cooper's crutches and the extra pounds Jack carried compounded by the sunshine falling on their faces demanded a saunter at best. The background music to their reunion featured a mix of seagulls against a legion of buskers. Only on Government Street did one hear a different song on every corner.

They were seated in the McKinnon Snug area at the Bard. The high-back stools suited Cooper, as it was easier to perch than sit down with his injuries. They decided on scotch, despite the fact that it was early afternoon. They had a lot of ground to cover and needed to get past any awkwardness.

Cooper and Jack were always destined to end up boyhood rivals/best friends. Both gravitated to the roll of nerd disguised as class clown, each daring the other to ever-greater acts of insubordination and heights of academic achievement. They truly brought out the worst and the best in each other, until they graduated and went their separate ways.

They relived the past with feigned surprise. Both of them felt obligated to play along only to be polite. In actuality, it was an exercise of filling in only a few blanks. As much as each party would like to pretend they knew nothing of the other's existence over the years, their mothers would not allow a total separation to occur. Few family dinners could be counted where the respective best friend's name was not mentioned.

Sadly for Jack, his star had not risen in line with Cooper's. He'd left high school on equal footing, if not at an advantage to Cooper. His passion for facts and fairness fueled his obsession with law. He was the only student in his class to be accepted to study at Harvard in his high-school graduating year. His IQ was Mensa league, and if he read something, it stuck—word by word, page by page. Where Cooper had to earn his grades, Jack was blessed with a flawless memory. He graduated summa cum laude from Harvard Law.

Jack had been at the top of the hiring list and head-hunted by top-ranking firms. Six months into an associate position had him drinking from breakfast till bed. Pre-Wall Street crash, he spent twice as much time entertaining than advising. For many clients, he actually was their best friend in every sense of the word, and Jack fell easily into the lifestyle. That was until the bottom fell out five years later, and all of a sudden, at a big firm where millions were being lost every hour, there needed to be a fall guy.

Jack took the blame for a huge fraud scandal that left the firm, the client, and Jack in peril. He never recovered. The only thing he managed to keep up was the drinking. Everyone knew his story, and despite his opprobrium, they still respected his mind. He knew a lot of people and had made a lot of important contacts, but his reputation was ruined and he would never practice law again.

The thought of a new profession terrified him. He went back to Harvard, the last place he had felt valued, and registered at their journalism extension school. That was where he met Mandolin. He would never forget the day he first saw her. He had been beaten and still in disbelief that he was signed up for journalism after being at the top of his game only a year earlier. He had trouble concentrating on the lectures, which bored him. Every night, he went home to drink alone. She was the only person who penetrated the self-destruction he had created.

She was beautiful and vibrant. What she might have lacked academically she made up for in perseverance. He had never witnessed anyone fight for what they wanted like her. Everything had always come easily to Jack, until it didn't. Then he was unable to recover. He was absolutely defeated after being fired.

Mandolin made it her mission to know everyone in every class. That was the thing that drove her: other people and relationships, and how everyone was connected. He was the smartest guy in class by far. She needed help. She had the looks for TV but needed to move up the ranks. What she lacked, Jack made up for.

How unfair life had been to him. He meets the girl of his dreams after losing everything, his career, self-control, and waistline. In terms of his looks, the only things Jack had retained from his childhood were a thick head of reddish-brown hair and sparkling blue eyes that danced as he laughed. Jack's laughter could fill a room and empty a glass. He was a people pleaser, with a smart remark or funny story for every occasation and occasion.

When it came time to find a job, recruiters had been grateful for a double major from Harvard. Jack was easily the most over-qualified journalist at the *Colonist*. Returning to the island had not been an easy decision, but after an attempt at the *Times* in NY, working side by side with Mandolin, constantly running into all of his old colleagues, he went back to the bottle, hard. Regardless of her attempts to keep him out of trouble, he just couldn't stay sober, and after four months, he was let go for the second time. Back home away from it all, he could lay his demons to rest. He could lean on family when he needed to and was able to supplement his meager income as a local journalist by consulting to a few of his old clients, who felt he'd gotten the short end of the stick, and some other acquaintances he wished he had never met.

The one advantage to Jack's position was his ID. He could gain access to just about any conference anywhere. No one really seemed to care where he was from. They just saw five letters: P-R-E-S-S.

Beside his position at the *Colonist* and his contract work, Jack focused a significant amount of his attention on following Mandolin's career from afar. He often helped her win important stories, championing her causes. If he were honest with himself, he would have to admit that he lived through her success. In his mind, it was shared.

He had a gift for finding the truth, getting to the heart of the issue. He made complex issues simple. There wasn't much he couldn't get a hold of. His low-key position was a perfect camouflage. No one ever suspected him, and his credentials always got him where he needed to go. He had an uncanny knack for disappearing into the millwork. Disappearing like a shark. No detail left his steel-trap mind. Despite the alcoholism, he remained as sharp as ever.

Jack may have won Harvard, but Cooper won ultimate class clown. All through medical school in Toronto, his pranks were notorious. His doctor/firefighter third-year class calendar was legendary. Nothing was sexier than med students with their shirts off, or so they told themselves. One thing the boyhood friends had in common was a penchant for excess. Cooper drank like a fish and partied like a rock star. He chased the next party and the next girl, weekend after weekend.

During the weekdays, he was all business. He'd had to study his ass off to keep ahead. Looking back, he wasn't sure how he'd managed to pull it off. After his MD, he'd stuck it out to finish his PhD in pharmacology. Graduating top of his class, he had his choice of drug companies, although his reputation as a smart ass and his attitude had conservative companies crossing him off their lists.

Competing offers came flooding in from cutting-edge big pharmas, but he'd had his heart set on Proteus for years. Jon had started courting him in the second year of his PhD. Cooper's reputation, as well as his grades, had caught Jon's attention. He wasn't the typical hire. The kid had reminded Jon of himself. Ten minutes into their initial meeting, each knew it wouldn't be the last. Jon couldn't remember ever having drinks, let alone drinks till 6 a.m., with a potential hire.

It was odd timing, the way their paths had converged. Just as Jack was making his exit, Cooper made his entrance. All the way from West Coast Canada to the big Apple, and then in Jack's case, back again.

Ironically, both were now back where they had started, albeit for very different reasons. Jack wasn't sure why, but he held off until the last minute to tell Cooper that he was meeting a colleague that evening. He hadn't thought their drinks would stretch into the evening, or that they would really have much to say to one another. To his surprise he was actually enjoying their trip back in time, and reluctant to bring the chance encounter to a close.

Cooper would have left as well, but the scotch and their candid conversation kept him in his chair. If he was truthful, he was also curious as to what Jack's colleague would be like. Jack had taken such a different path from his own. Cooper's co-workers were grown from petri dishes, each one nerdier than the next.

When the waitress came by to ask if Cooper wanted another drink, he looked over at Jack, hesitating for a moment. Then their eyes met in what was a bit of the challenge from days past, to which Cooper answered,

"Sure."

CHAPTER 14

MANDOLIN GRACE

6:36 p.m.   Bard and Banker, Victoria, BC

THERE WAS NO QUESTION SHE WAS HOT. BUT WHAT IMPRESSED Cooper was her oblivion to the heads she turned as she walked through the public house. The reaction her presence evoked from the male persuasion was lost on her, taken for granted because it had begun at such a young age. He wasn't expecting NYC for at least another week, and here she was, coming to him.

She wore a new crepe cocktail dress, from her quick stop in LA just hours before, which said, "Business . . . but maybe not." Mandolin couldn't help but notice that the black Lanvin stood out in consummate contrast to the hippie-inspired attire draping her counterparts. Life's greatest cruelty: attractive women never reap the rewards that grace attractive men. And so began her exhausting ritual of winning over the waitress.

"I really like your earrings," came Mandolin's overly loud compliment as she was escorted to her seat in the McKinnon Snug section between Jack and Cooper, the recently reacquainted best friends.

In response, the young girl smiled up at Mandolin with her whole face. Mandolin hadn't seen someone smile like that since grade school. As the waitress left to have her order of Taylor 30 filled, Mandolin became keenly aware that she was no longer at home. Here, she had no need for the Lanvin dress she wore as armor in NYC.

As she scanned the crowd more closely, she was reminded of the voile sundresses she had worn as a child and experienced a pang of regret that today nothing in her closet even came close. She wondered if that girl was lost completely, or if it was possible to resurrect her if only for a Sunday afternoon. With that thought, she made a mental note to go dress shopping immediately upon her return.

"Mandolin, I'd like you to meet my boyhood nemesis and best friend, Cooper Delaney." Jack's face was still red from receiving her warm-hello embrace.

"Pleased to meet you," came her strong reply and even stronger handshake. Cooper had never liked women who shook hands like men. They always seemed to have a feminist chip on their shoulder and some personal agenda for the evening. He prepared for her to monopolize the conversation and visibly tried to appear as physically comfortable as possible within the constraints of his injuries.

Mandolin would have none of that. She started doing what she did best: getting his story. That meant question after carefully designed question, to the point where the inexperienced Dr. Delaney would soon be divulging his company's Christmas-party mishap. Jack sat back with an ever-widening grin, knowing exactly what she was up to and proud that he had taught her so well.

After the torrid account of his accident, Mandolin was up to date. She now had the Coles Notes version of Cooper's existence. He was a perfect stereotype, the alpha male: cocky, with confidence verging on arrogance, looks to match, and just enough sophistication to get laid in NYC. She guessed correctly that he had come by it the hard way, especially meeting him here in his hometown. This place was like going back in time, like stepping into a poorly curated local museum forced upon you by your parents on yet another summer vacation.

She could feel her guard slowly fade away in spite of herself. It was impossible to stay sharp in a place that lulled you into submission with Irish folk tunes and turn-of-the-century décor. Working antiques surrounded her, and she suddenly felt like the outsider she was.

Yes, everything about Cooper fit the bill; he would have fooled her completely but she caught him off guard when she led the conversation away from his parents and his dad's death and back to his latest drug, Noctural. He was vulnerable, if only for a moment. She instinctively knew that he wouldn't admit it, but noticed him squirm slightly and was pretty sure something was up. There was something he didn't want to tell her—something she was now driven to find out.

". . . and you are incapable of actually taking this time off, I see." Mandolin ended the conversation, as he reached once again for his cell.

He smirked as he declined the call from the lab. He would have to call them back tomorrow. Besides, he hadn't yet re-mastered his habitual pacing back and forth during office calls, due to the crutches. Being laid up made him realize how the pacing was really part of how he worked. He needed to be free and moving around in order to think clearly, it seemed. He hated being in this condition, especially being here with Jack and Mandolin. It felt like everything he told them was a half-truth.

He usually led conversations from a position of strength. Recounting the story of the last few weeks made him hate his situation even more, as it drove home Noctural's failure as well as his miscalculation on the slopes. Perhaps he was slipping a bit, or maybe being back in this sleepy town made it even worse. That seemed more likely, somehow. All of a sudden, he felt claustrophobic. As he looked around, he wondered just how bad things must have been for Jack to have returned for good.

Wallowing in self-pity made him miss out on Jack and Mandolin's discussion. Once he resurfaced, he realized that he would have to work his way back into the conversation on his own merit. His moment in the spotlight was over.

"So, you were there!" Mandolin exclaimed, ready to chastise Jack. "Why didn't you come find me? I can't believe you just left without a word!" He had attended Dr. Irwin's presentation. Following the recent coverage surrounding Human Pinnacle Theory was definitely on Jack's radar, not only for Mandolin's sake but for one of his client's, as well.

"You seemed to be doing just fine on your own, love," Jack said. Watching Mandolin monopolize the few questions Dr. Irwin would allow at the press conference had been satisfying for him. She had already created a reputation for getting the story and was becoming well known within (as well as outside of) industry circles. Jack knew Mandolin's career would be rewarding not just for her but for him, as well. He just wasn't certain this would be her big break. Human Pinnacle Theory could definitely solidify her future, but there were so many missing pieces. It touched so many disciplines that Jack was having a hard time wrapping his head around it all, let alone determining how best to guide her through the minefields the findings had divulged.

Cooper tried his best to feign interest as Jack and Mandolin discussed the finer points of the arguments Dr. Irwin had presented. The whole thing sounded like philosophy to Cooper. He dealt in reality, with science, where things were black and white. Where he could always find the answer, the *right* answer—the only one that made sense. He kept looking at his watch, wondering if he should make an excuse and leave, as he was now completely excluded from the conversation with only his cell for company.

"Can you believe he lied so that I would agree to meet with him? And then, on top of it, after three long hours of trying to convince me that I should overlook his betrayal, he turns out to be some fanatic? I couldn't believe it. I even had him checked out, and he does indeed work directly with Armand Price—one of the most respected physicists in the world. His work is groundbreaking. Should I reach out to him and let him know that Camberg is a nut job?" Mandolin had become quite animated, reliving the meeting with Camberg. It still upset her that she'd met with him in the first place.

Jack shook his head. "Never reveal your source, Mandolin, you know this. You never know if you might need him, regardless of how crazy he may seem."

For a moment, she considered the confidential path their conversation had taken and glanced up at Cooper.

Jack noticed her hesitation and immediately answered her question, "Not to worry, Mandolin. He's been playing Tetris for the last fifteen minutes."

She reached across the table and grabbed Cooper's cell before he could stop her. Sure enough, Jack (as always) was right on the money.

"So, tell me about accumulated energy," Cooper said. He saw through them, attempting to talk above his head, boring him with their academia on this latest "theory." He decided that he would use being dressed in a T-shirt and ripped jeans, limping around on crutches, to his advantage. He wasn't Proteus's rising star for nothing. He'd won his graduating class gold medal with grades that had still never been matched. Their little theory was child's play for him, or so he told himself.

"Accumulation of energy is the storing of energy by various means," replied Jack, amused to see his old/new best friend had rejoined the conversation.

"What type of energy?" asked Cooper.

"Anything." Jack began his explanation in his best grade-school-teacher voice. "Electric, wind, solar. More traditional methods include—"

"Yes, OK, I don't need a science lesson from you of all people. So, we are discussing energy accumulation from traditional sources." Cooper's patience was wearing thin with this meaningless discussion. He needed to get back to Proteus and figure out why Noctural had failed. He was desperate to get back in the lab.

As a result of the accident and the time away from work, he had started to doubt himself. He must have missed something. He needed a new angle. Perhaps the Malcolm Schwartz test should have included viral abnormalities; there was a remote chance that he could have accelerated caloric results due to a virus. It was rare, and the testing would be difficult, but it was possible . . . maybe. But deep down, he knew he was wrong. Even if he did manage the approval for the testing, and was able to coerce Malcolm back to the lab, he knew it would be negative. It just didn't make any sense.

"Not necessarily traditional," interjected Mandolin. "Energy could come from anywhere. The physicist I met with had a contraption strapped to his leg." She finished as she stifled a yawn. The flight and the time change were catching up with her. It was 3 a.m. back in NYC.

"Well, in that case, I will fire up a hamster-wheel farm, and we'll all be multi-millionaires," shot back Cooper, though he softened it with a grin.

Mandolin yawned again. "I think I'm done. It's past my bedtime, and I've boarded three flights this week. It was nice to meet you, Cooper." She didn't have the energy to keep up further banter with Jack's doctor friend. It was obvious that his entire existence began and ended with Proteus and his latest invention. She admired his ambition but was growing tired of his attitude. She did feel for him though. He was lucky to have survived the avalanche. Very lucky, indeed.

"Of course, Mandolin," Jack said. "You must be exhausted. Do you need a cab?" He rose to see her out.

"No, I drove straight here from the airport. I'm parked just outside." It was her first time to Victoria, and she hadn't realized they were meeting only blocks away from her hotel. She was actually feeling weak as she stood up to leave.

"Great, you can give the cripple a ride home!" Cooper said, inviting himself with an entitled look on his face, daring her to refuse him in his time of need.

Mandolin returned an amused glance, and rolled her eyes. Apparently hopes of falling into bed at the Empress Fairmont without interruption until at least noon the next day would have to be delayed. Self-drive had effectively killed the intoxication excuse—something she still had to remind herself of from time to time. Mandolin hugged Jack goodbye and said she would call tomorrow to make plans to continue their discussion. Cooper and Jack shook hands and managed a man-style hug, promising to keep in touch.

Jack watched as the pair hobbled toward the door— Cooper on his crutches and Mandolin exhausted, wearing four-inch Gucci heels. After all these years, despite the injuries, Cooper was leaving with his girl. He laughed and shook his head; time for another drink.

CHAPTER 15

JON CAMERON
7:58 a.m.   Proteus, NYC

HE WATCHED THE TRAFFIC BELOW, TWISTING AND TURNING through the snow melt. Slush lined the sidewalks and streets from the heavy snowfall they had received the night before. Through the delivery drones periodically obscuring his view of the street below, he witnessed NYC's finest attempt to clear an accident involving a delivery truck and a taxi cab. Horns echoed in protest as drivers still clung to hopes of making it to work on time. Manhattan rush hour was chaos. You think they would have figured out a better system by now. Rats still chasing the cheese. He pondered the sentiment. What did that make him? King of the rats, perhaps. Jon laughed at that. He'd been called much worse.

His cell went off at exactly 8 a.m. EST, just as Cooper had promised. He felt for the kid. Jon was on the verge of calling it quits with Noctural. Malcolm's results coupled with the expense of manufacturing the drug had led Jon to place it on the back burner in the Proteus kitchen. With Cooper away, he was even more inclined to search for some greener grass in R&D. However, he had learned patience over the years.

On more than one occasion, he'd found himself a contender in a nasty fight with the competition. No sooner would he abandon a drug in trial than a bastardized version would be released by a competitor. Noctural was groundbreaking in the insomnia arena, an issue that had become near epidemic over the last ten years. He had been on the verge of trying it himself prior to Malcolm. Still, he had shareholders to answer to, and that left little room on the roster for a drug that was failing trial.

"Still working from home, I see," Jon said as he answered the call of his boy wonder. He didn't fault Cooper for the failure of the drug. Not every drug could be a winner. What was more important was how he recovered. Cooper either fixed it or moved on with something bigger, something better. What Jon could not tolerate were excuses. He detested the stalling and whining so many of them displayed when told to shelve their latest project.

Jon understood the hours that went into development but abhorred the attachment his staff sometimes fell victim to. These drugs weren't children, for God's sake. He would never understand it, perhaps because he was too far removed from the process and because his job was to focus on the bottom line, which left little room for attachments of any kind. He had two failed marriages to prove it.

"Yes, quite literally, I'm afraid. Sleeping in my childhood bed nonetheless. It's killing me, Jon. I would give anything to be back in the lab." Cooper didn't realize just how much he desperately missed work, the office. Hearing Jon's voice, despite being miles away, made him realize he even missed Jon.

"Soon enough," Jon answered. "You are back next week, right?" Jon didn't want him pushing himself. He reviewed the reports from IT and knew Cooper had been logging in full-time hours for the past four weeks.

"Listen, Jon, I know Malcolm's results were not what we expected but—"

"Cooper, I'm going to have to stop you right there." Jon wasn't going to give Cooper the chance to disappoint him. Instead, he conferenced in his long-lost brother (of sorts). "Will, are you there?"

He liked the element of surprise. It also saved him what would undoubtedly be a long drawn-out debate with Cooper about why they should continue the testing, how if he just had more time he could explain the results of Malcolm's sleep test, blah, blah, blah. Well, Jon was hopeful that he had done Cooper a huge favor, at the same time somewhat expunging himself of the debt he owed to Will.

"I'm here, Jon," came Will's stiff reply. Will hated conference calls; he never knew when it was his turn to speak.

"Great, thanks for joining us," Jon answered. "Cooper, just so you are up to speed, I brought Will in to further test Noctural with his research participants." Jon wasn't about to go into any details. He was too anxious to have Will share the results.

"And what research participants might those be?" asked Cooper. He couldn't believe he had actually thought he had been missing Jon a second ago. Cooper wasn't keen to be ousted. He was seething. He would never forgive Jon for making decisions regarding the trial without telling him. How dare Jon blindside him this way. Cooper didn't care if he was on the other side of the world, or if he never walked again, he was not about to let anyone mismanage the fate of his drug.

He knew the stakes were high and that Jon needed him to formulate the outcome required to release the drug from Proteus, pre-FDA approval. He just didn't know how to convince Jon that there was more to the story, that there was something going on with the drug that just didn't make sense. He wondered how he could possibly convince Jon, when he didn't have an answer himself.

"Our research consists of thirty enrolled participants diagnosed with ADHD." Will felt sick as he spoke; he couldn't believe Jon had set him up this way. Obviously, nothing had been shared with Cooper.

"Will, my name is Cooper Delaney, the lead on the drug at Proteus. So, if I am understanding you correctly, you have administered a sleep aid, still in trial, to participants most likely using some stimulant medication. I assume these are adults, not children. Please, tell me they are not children." Cooper's voice grew louder and more agitated as he spoke.

Jon spoke up. "Cooper, you know as well as I do that the drug is safe; its effectiveness is the only thing in question."

"Cooper, it's Will. None of the participants use drugs of any kind to treat the disorder. All have opted for behavioral therapy." Will stopped talking, wishing for death. Betrayed by Jon, he didn't know what to say or how much to reveal.

Cooper couldn't believe it. They were feeding a test drug to minors. He wasn't sure what to say. This was beyond what he thought Jon was capable of, and he'd had first-hand experience of the worst of it. He was tempted to report them both to the FDA but didn't want to risk losing his own job, which he had been away from for six weeks already. He couldn't imagine why Jon would have agreed to this: it didn't make any sense at all. Proteus had all the resources, testing facilities, and backing required to put the drug through its paces. All his questions and anger aside though, he had to admit he was curious as to the results.

As Jon sat back in his chair, a smile touched his lips. Now that all this unpleasantness was over, they could get to the purpose of the conversation: to see how the drug responded with these kids. Part of the reason Jon had agreed to the trial was that testing with drug-free minors held even more weight than most adult test groups. The testing was more reliable, as participants' entire medical history was less than ten years, versus thirty- or forty-year-olds taking God knows what for God knows why.

"Please go ahead, Will. What did you find?" Jon wanted to make a concrete decision on this drug today, one way or another.

Will's response was dead pan; his throat was dry and he had a ringing in his ears. "The results are inconclusive. Noctural had a significant impact, but on fewer than half the participants. The remainder showed no improvement at all."

Will could feel Cooper's betrayal and hated Jon for it. Why did it always have to be this way with them? He should have known better. It was incredible, something to admire on a certain level, how Jon could retain the upper hand even when making good on a favor. Will never had the stomach for this type of thing. His passion was helping people; it was the only thing that drove him. He was the type of guy who cried at the sad parts in movies without fail, no matter how many times he watched them.

Will might feel like shit, but Cooper was pissed enough to come through the phone had it been possible. He wanted to kill Jon, and Will for good measure. Thanks to his father, he had learned how to redirect his insuppressible temper into something more socially acceptable, albeit frightening enough to (more often than not) leave him victorious.

Jon was disappointed but relieved that he could move on. "So, I guess that settles it. Cooper, first thing when you get in next week, come straight to my office so I can sign off on the post mortem. I have a new—"

Jon never got a chance to finish his sentence. What happened next pushed him back into his seat. Not much surprised him after forty-plus years. He thought he had seen and heard it all. At first, he thought it was Will, but then as the laughter and clapping rose to a crescendo, it was evident that this level of insubordination was not something of which his kid brother was capable. There was no way he had the balls.

"Well done, my friend! Well done!" The clapping continued, and now whistling joined the macabre applause as Cooper continued his rant.

Jon knew Cooper was pissed. If he was honest with himself, in Cooper's place, he would have been pissed as well.

Jon began the canned speech he had crafted over the years, filed away under "drug-trial termination." He was disappointed he had to resort to it. However, he was still in a tailspin following Cooper's display. Not sure how to proceed, he fell back on an old fail-safe. In retrospect, he knew he would regret being thrown off his game, knew he would replay this one over in his head later tonight, with a comeback he felt better about.

"Look, Cooper, I understand you have worked on this for months—"

"Save it!" Cooper shouted into the receiver. "I'm not interested in hearing your bullshit."

Jon wasn't about to tolerate being cut off twice, even if it was Cooper. He was just about to put Cooper in his place but stalled with the thought of Will still on the line.

His hesitation gave Will just enough time to take the floor. "Look, Cooper, I am so sorry. None of this should have happened. I was so anxious to make a breakthrough with these kids. I really thought I was onto something."

"You *are* onto something; my boss is just too stupid to see it. You send me the data on the participants who responded as soon as you hang up from this call. Write down my email. It's cd@proteus.com." Cooper was in the driver's seat now.

It was Jon's turn. He could feel his tie cutting into his neck as he literally shook his head, glaring in anger at the conference speaker.

"Godammit, Cooper!" He started out on a rampage that might just end with Cooper's termination. "You listen to me—"

"No, you listen to me!" Cooper screamed into the receiver. "You go behind my back with a trial that, if leaked to the FDA, would potentially land your ass in jail, while I recover from what could have been a life-ending accident, and you think I am going step aside and let it happen? If you think I won't take this to them, please believe me when I say I will not hesitate. But you should know this won't be the only thing I report!"

Jon went from hot to cold. The color left his face, and for the second time in one day, he was pushed back in his seat.

"What are you talking about?" It was a moot question. Jon knew he knew. But how? He felt sick.

"I hoped I would never need to use this, but you are leaving me no choice."

Cooper knew this was over. He had won, for now. He also knew that Jon was not the type to let this go, and that his days at Proteus were now numbered. The bond they had forged was now severed, despite all the shared victories. It would never be the same.

Will was left to break the never-ending silence. He considered just hanging up, but his incompetence with the conference hardware made it only wishful thinking.

"OK, Cooper, I will forward the results. Please confirm once you receive them." These were the last words to be recorded on the call.

Silence prevailed—the only indication that Jon had folded for the time being, leaving Cooper the underdog victor, with a shaky winning hand.

Alone in his office, with the call over, Jon turned to his bottom desk drawer that housed his emergency scotch then he turned to the sheep. "Where the hell were you?"

CHAPTER 16

MANDOLIN GRACE
8:37 a.m. Oak Bay, Victoria, BC

SHE WITNESSED A CRUTCH MORPH INTO A BASEBALL BAT AND hit a home run with an empty coffee mug. Mandolin immediately regretted her decision to return Cooper's wallet, which she rightly assumed had been not-so innocently forgotten in her rental car during the ride home the night before. Now she swayed, standing on his childhood porch having reached out for the doorbell, instinctively recoiling with the sound of the cup reverberating off the adjoining wall.

She was definitely having second thoughts now and felt nauseous as a blend of salt air, aged wood, and fresh coffee engulfed her. From where she stood, she had a front-row seat to the Delaney kitchen through the carved, turn-of-the-century screen door.

A moment earlier, she had lingered, deciding to take in the surroundings uninvited. She loved the character home. In her opinion, just the right number of original fixtures had been retained. Without question, the furniture needed updating, and a fresh coat of paint was long overdue, but with her eye for design and attention to detail, this place could be as stunning as she predicted. Pity she would never have the chance.

At the top of a long list of impossibilities was the fact that she couldn't stand this sleepy city. She was itching to get home. Mandolin couldn't imagine living anywhere but Manhattan. Her trip to visit Jack would not be repeated—it would be the first and last. She concluded that their time together was much more enjoyable when he came to her.

Standing there on the porch confirmed her decision never to return. How had she strayed so far from what she had intended: meeting Jack and getting back home as quickly as possible? Yet here she was, loitering on Cooper Delaney's mother's doorstep, returning the wallet to a fellow New Yorker who had been a stranger just hours before. If it wasn't for Cooper's chance run-in with Jack, they would have never met.

He definitely was not her type. From what she could tell, he would be far too much work, although she had to admit that she did find him slightly amusing, if she allowed herself to ignore his arrogance. One thing they had in common was that they both loved NY. From what she could surmise, he was dying to get back, as well. She couldn't help but feel for him. Evidently, he was struggling. If she had to guess based on her interrogation last night, she would bet it was his work.

After Cooper's display, ringing the doorbell did not seem the appropriate means of announcing her arrival, especially as she knew he could hear her from where he stood. Now that he appeared to have composed himself, the likelihood of him noticing her seemed too high to risk an escape unseen. Barely fifteen feet away, with nothing but a screen door between them, he gripped the back of a kitchen chair. The brooding expression on his face seemed permanent.

"Yeah, I miss NY coffee too, but try to hold it together," she taunted from the front porch. "It's only another week."

Embarrassment betrayed his features as his head spun in her direction, his hands tightening on the back of the chair, but it was only for a moment. His recovery was impressive, even to her.

A smile immediately devoured his face. "Back so soon? To what do I owe a second visit in twenty-four hours from the lovely Ms. Grace?"

"Really, Cooper, you have nothing better than this?" Mandolin held up his wallet and pushed open the door. He seemed to deflate slightly, presumably disappointed that she was unwilling to play along. "Although it would seem that you are too distracted to focus effectively on anything else at the moment." She paused and deliberately took in the shattered cup and punctured wall.

"Yes, well . . . as you can see, it's been a shitty start this morning, so I'm glad for the diversion. Glad you weren't too busy with your 'stories' to return this to a helpless invalid." He limped over to her, supporting himself on the kitchen entryway, exploiting his injuries as an excuse to stand much too close to her, making sure to take her hand along with the wallet in his own, before finally reclaiming his decoy.

She felt like rolling her eyes but was far too curious as to what had set him off.

"Not so helpless, are you?" she said, with a look that suggested he had been unsuccessful with his shameless maneuver. "So, what could it be? Money? An unfaithful lover? I am guessing it's work. After such an outburst, I would presume you would want to provide some sort of explanation." Surely, he would cave now that she had deflected all his advances.

A flicker of humor touched his lips. It was his turn now. "Really, Mandolin, I can imagine you must feel horrible for me in this situation, but there is no need to stay and feign interest. I am sure you and Jack are extremely busy. Unless, of course, you have your own motivation for coming all the way back here to give me something you could have easily passed on to him. We are 'best' friends after all."

In a second, he had turned the table and made her feel like she was the one who was stalking him, just when she thought she had prevailed. Perhaps more credit was due than she had initially awarded him.

He could see she was running the odds of what the rest of their relationship would be like, if there was to be one at all. He was pretty sure he had her attention and had to admit that she definitely had his. He self-diagnosed his attempts to entertain her as a reflex, something he would continue despite himself. It was unnerving that she could allow him to forget, even momentarily, what was quite possibly a career, or even a life-altering, exchange with his boss.

Next to chess, Cooper loved poker, perhaps it came first. He considered himself a poker psychologist. People were easy to read. He was rarely surprised or disappointed. In fact, after the exchange with Jon earlier, he might have considered going on tour.

"You had written me off from the start," he said, "so you let your guard down. That's how I beat you."

"Beat me?" Mandolin gave him the look reserved for the junior assistants who took it upon themselves to rearrange her schedule without consulting her.

"Yes. Right now, you are wondering why you lost the upper hand in our little exchange, and while it bothers you, you can't help respect the fact that it happened. Admit it, you might even like me. At the very least, it is killing you to know why this cup is in pieces on the floor, so I think I will just keep that to myself."

Cooper's candor surprised even him. He just couldn't seem to help himself, having not taken such pleasure in insulting a female since grade school. In fact, the whole exchange had become very much that: a grade-school crush. Why do boys of any age exert physical dominance, like pulling the proverbial pony tail of the girl they like, instead of swallowing their pride and just admitting their attraction?

Cooper's mind reading had Mandolin rolling her eyes for real this time. She wasn't about to concede defeat to this circus act, despite the fact that it was killing her not knowing what had caused his outburst. Mandolin was not about to give up; she never left empty handed. Obviously, he was enjoying this, so why not let it go on long enough to find out the story?

The lie left her lips more quickly than her head had time to work out the details. "Yes, well, Jack is waiting for both of us at Murchie's. He has a lead that dips itself in your world, so lucky for you, our time together isn't over just yet."

He directed as they drove down the streets of his formative years. One block looked older than the next. It was like slowly driving back in time. She felt like she was in one of those Christmas-scene miniatures, minus the snow. Why was she bringing him along? She needed to come up with something fast. She and Jack were about to review the inquiries following Irwin's presentation, and as far as she knew, they had nothing to do with pharmaceuticals. What should she say?

"I take it you both enjoyed the 'ride' home last night?"

Mandolin winced at Jack's greeting from the corner table. She had been so preoccupied with an excuse for Cooper's attendance that she'd discounted the impact of them showing up together after just meeting the night before. Judging by his adolescent smile, Cooper had not.

She liked the way he kept her on her toes, challenging her to turn the tables in her favor once again. How had this sleepy little place conceived a soul like Cooper, or even Jack, for that matter? More importantly, how had the two of them managed to escape?

"Really, Jack? You disappoint. You were the one who suggested consultation with a medical expert on the Ophelia Sasaki lead." Jack was one of the few individuals aware of the classified evolutionary research Ophelia conducted, and the implications of it falling into the wrong hands.

"I thought you meant Cooper," she continued, "as you brought it up in front of him last night." Mandolin was surprised at how easily the false accusation materialized. It was usually Jack who saved the day.

The rolling stone Cooper had launched seemed only to gain momentum now, catching Jack up in its path. Mandolin, now too engaged to quit, instantly regretted using Jack, but felt helpless from her position. Saving face seemed of utmost importance with Cooper standing beside her.

It was Cooper's turn to be impressed. She was a worthy opponent after all. As such, he would humor her and play along. Truth be told, he hadn't heard much of what she and Jack had exchanged the night before. He had been deep in his third game of Tetris when the Sasaki lead was discussed. What made it even more fun was that Jack would have known all along. Yes, all of a sudden, the exchange with Mandolin took on a whole new meaning, and the childhood competition between the two men resurfaced.

"Yes, Jack, I have to admit I thought the same. Only too happy to help old boy." Cooper winked at Jack in place of punctuation, and now Jack was the one left feeling helpless as their rivalry was resurrected from the grave.

As the three sat together, Mandolin providing the notes from her discussion with Dr. Sasaki, no one would have guessed at the significance of the meeting. No one, including the parties involved, would have speculated that their discussion would initiate events that would change our world forever.

CHAPTER 17

RAY GARLAND

1:00 p.m.   J. Edgar Hoover Building, Washington, DC

THE DIRT UNDER HIS FINGERNAILS WAS ENOUGH TO DISTRACT him as he sat at the far-left end of the boardroom table. His place was unofficially reserved, always at the right hand of Carl the EAD (executive assistant director), in order to field any of the unsavory questions that may arise. Today, by the looks of things, that would not be the case. Since 9/11, these joint FBI/CIA meetings had been made mandatory, each one more painful than the next.

"Ray, anything to report on the Human Plateau Theory release?" Katelyn's shrill voice cut straight through his train of thought from the opposite side of the table, a dull razor on chapped, dry skin. They both knew she addressed him directly, instead of engaging Carl, only to annoy him. Both knew he despised the CIA involvement, and both knew that she exercised her senior administrative position only to piss him off. The worst part was that it worked. Every time he shot her a look to kill, Katelyn successfully defended the assault with a broad, condescending smile—every . . . fucking . . . time.

Today, he didn't give her the satisfaction of actually witnessing her Cheshire grin. Instead, he turned toward Carl as if he had posed the question. He rolled his head to look at his friend of thirty-five-plus years, sitting beside him. Carl shared a pained expression with him, as if to say, *"I know, buddy. It sucks, man."*

Ray and Carl had ridden the ranks of the FBI hand in hand. Ray had found his niche in the field, to no one's surprise. Diplomacy and management were lost on him. In contrast to his friend, he embraced the crucible of his training. His operative personality matched his physical strength, and he embodied the look of a solider, from uniform-like clothing to crew-cut hair.

Carl was better suited in the tower. His strategic mind was unparalleled in Ray's opinion, and together, they were a formidable duo. Although their wings had been clipped in order to limit their power in an organization rich in bureaucracy, they had had enough wins to maintain a high degree of autonomy—the thing Ray valued most.

He had met with Carl the night after Dr. Irwin's presentation to discuss the potential link to File 710. It was a long shot, but Ray had a sensitivity to these things. Almost forty years in the field had gifted him quite literally with a sixth sense. It was uncanny. He just *knew* things, as if he saw them with his own eyes. Since the Human Pinnacle Theory release, his spider sense kept nagging at him; this one just wouldn't leave his head. He had witnessed it before with the ISIS attacks: just too many coincidences, too many things pointing in the same direction. The world operates safely in natural chaos. The minute it begins to organize, something goes awry.

He would never share intel with anyone other than Carl. Carl was the only one he trusted. He could tell him anything, knowing that what he confided would never go any further. Carl had his full confidence, which did not come easy. Ray was a skeptic and a loner. His job suited him perfectly. If left alone, he could bring down the house singlehandedly. He was decorated and a legend in his own right. But he didn't get there by making friends. Come to think of it, Carl was probably his only friend, and he debated whether Carl would concur. No matter, he was as close a confidant as Ray needed. Work, personal life, and everything in between could be discussed at the surface. No small talk, no banter, no birthdays—a perfect friendship with the lowest possible commitment. It was ideal in Ray's mind. It was absolutely perfect.

File 710 was FBI folklore, a fairy tale of sorts. It was quite possibly the most clandestine FBI file, and only a handful of individuals were aware of its existence. The file had been assigned no fewer than thirty-nine official names in fewer than five years, in order to protect it from discovery by outside sources. The FBI had enough difficulty keeping track of the names, and those privy joked about the absurdity of the change in handle over the years, especially for a file so obscure.

As the story/file/theory went, there is (or was) reason to believe that life on earth was much more sophisticated than any of us had been led to believe prior to our beloved dinosaurs' mass extinction. The file's abstract suggested (as unbelievable as it would seem) that the dominant life form on earth had reached a level of sophistication that allowed them to not only detect but survive what we currently know as extinction level events (ELEs)—not just cosmic impacts but precipitous, extreme changes in climate responsible for mass extinctions.

Our ancient humanoid cousins participated in advanced thinking, modern ideas, and space travel long before our primate ancestors existed. Unfortunately, an ELE was predicted (now labeled as the Paleozoic Extinction Event–the Earth's most severe known extinction event to date), and despite best efforts by the leading thinkers of the age, it was determined non-survivable or alterable, and therefore, our ancient cousins came to the unfortunate conclusion that, in order for their species to survive, over 99 percent of them would have to perish. The ultimate in altruism.

According to File 710, they had left behind what would today resemble a DNA time capsule, literally a genetic roadmap to recreate the species, all packaged up in an extremely tidy, incredibly efficient viral vector. Prior to the pending ELE, they had buried the capsule 400 miles beneath the Earth's surface, at coordinates near the current-day Baltic coast. The capsule was compromised as a result of the disturbance of a massive water reservoir due to the tectonic activity that ended Pangaea 300 million years ago.

After the Cretaceous period began, volcanic activity subsided, and the fertile waters recovered our ancient life. The viral vectors—perfect tiny packages as they were with their DNA wound like an infinitely small ball of yarn, complete with the entire genome of our ancient advanced relatives—found their way, through logarithmic chance, via the primordial seas into primitive bacterial life. Subsequently, the viral vectors unwound their precious foreign cargo, and evolution accomplished the rest.

We were all taught in middle-school science class that boys are XY and girls XX. However, according to the file, a Z chromosome existed: an ancient remnant of our advanced ancestors. It precipitously inserted itself into our genetic code those millions of years ago, following the premature rupture of the DNA capsule, and as the file reports, actual DNA proof can be found in a small number of our current population.

The Z chromosome is extremely, extremely rare, occurring in literally one in a billion individuals. Darwinism at its best, modern-day humans morphed into a reflection of these ancient beings, conceived in the earth's watery womb. As our species evolved, the Z chromosome was selected against, and it became almost impossible to identify an individual with this DNA signature unless one deliberately tested for it.

All of this may have gone completely undetected; however, the bill mandating DNA typing in the fight against ISIS brought the theory to light.

Following the deadly Imam Sadiq mosque bombing, Kuwait's decision to instate mandatory DNA testing for all permanent residents as a counter-terrorism measure inadvertently set a new standard in 2016. Subsequently, all G20 countries followed suit that year, despite human-rights concerns.

Billions of dollars and countless hours of testing promised a global united force against terrorism, protecting every American. The fringe benefit that no one anticipated was the "alleged" discovery of the Z chromosome, detected for the first time on Earth. As the file/theory divulged, we were not alone. We never have been.

For those who subscribed to this lost file, our ancient hominid cousins left long ago to ensure their survival in the face of Earth's potential demise. Ultimately, the "ET (extraterrestrial) File" was the only name that really stuck. It was the science-fiction file that got resurrected any time an alien sighting or scare surfaced—an event that had never occurred during Ray's tenure. Not until recently.

For Ray, who was quite likely the world's greatest cynic, the whole idea was laughable. When Carl asked him to investigate Dr. Armand Price, he fully expected a case of potential terrorist involvement in the advancement of energy harvesting. As the world moved away from finite oil as our primary source of energy, which had incredibly lasted a century, wars were waged on an economic field where financial institutions were the kings in the sandbox. The real heroes would be the scientists and engineers who came up with the next big fuel source. Solar, wind, water, nuclear . . . everything was on the table. Including the interesting new concept of intelligent energy, founded by Dr. Armand Price.

According to Price, the most efficient energy source is the human brain. His study of the accumulation of intelligent energy was still in its infancy, but it had caught the attention of the super elite, the handful of organizations or individuals not only interested but able to dictate our collective future. While the world patted itself on the back for nugatory advancements such as self-driving electric cars, in actuality, alternative energy did very little to improve our situation. Simply put, we were substituting one pollutant for another.

In contrast, Price's work, the harvesting of intelligent energy, completely changed the game. It literally had potential to free the world from dependency on external resources. In essence, we would use our large mammalian brains to power ourselves and everything we required for existence. His promise was a world free of dependency on oil, gas, electricity, or ultimately anything that required mass accumulation, distribution, and a carbon footprint.

As is often true, history repeats itself, and whether prediction or promise, many souls invest themselves in the status quo. For Price's protection, he was currently under twenty-four-hour surveillance due to the multiple attempts on his life. In fact, all members of his team were on surveillance as well. The stakes were high. The only one Ray was having trouble locating was a Dr. Camberg, who in the midst of the initial threats had been terminated by Price himself. Dr. Price had been forced to disassociate himself as quickly as possible from Camberg's hypothesis that intelligent energy harvesting was not only possible but already in existence. The problem was that, according to Camberg, the process took place outside our atmosphere.

Price did what any respectable scientist interested in protecting his reputation would do. He fired Camberg, discredited his findings, and went into hiding of sorts. To the best of Ray's knowledge, Price was under protection from a number of different agents representing numerous groups, and the FBI watched him to keep track of who he retained communication with as much as who tried to kill him.

Now, as events would dictate, the ridiculous File 710, aka the ET File, had intersected with the rantings of the ill-fated Dr. Camberg, whose squeaky-clean resume and track record in one of the world's most pivotal areas of study were the latest things keeping Ray up at night.

Ray's best and admittedly only friend delivered a blow to his forearm that woke him out of his trance.

"Ray? The release?" Katelyn plaintively reminded from her side of the table.

"No, ma'am, nothing to report," he said from the hot seat, mustering up his most defiant glare. He didn't have many, but in this case, his silence was a response he would one day come to regret.

CHAPTER 18

COOPER DELANEY
6:50 a.m.   Proteus, NYC

THE CLOSED OFFICE DOOR DID LITTLE TO STIFLE THE CLIPPED staccato of Maggie's heels as they stabbed at the Carrera tile floor. Cooper's secretary had worked for him for the past six years. She was his New York mom, and she usually left him alone unless she sensed he was "out of sorts." At times like this, she morphed into a mother bear, pacing his door until she reached her little cub in distress. All the women in his life eventually wanted to take care of him; he seemed to attract the "mothers" of the world. That was until Mandolin Grace, whose response he admittedly found a bit puzzling. Especially as he was surely at his most mothering worthy, sporting the crutches post-accident.

In all fairness, he hadn't really "attracted" her, so to speak. Reflecting on their two meetings, he had to admit that not once had she really tried to fuss over him; if anything, it was the opposite. He sensed she considered him a worthy opponent, which suited him perfectly. In fact, the last thing she brought to mind was a mother, which was definitely a good thing. As he sat at his desk, it would seem she was the only thought capable of distracting him following the six-week leave.

Cooper felt like the world had turned upside down while he was back home recuperating. He was at his desk by 5 a.m. the day of his return, determined to secure "first man to the office" advantage. Being away for a month and a half left Cooper feeling vulnerable, especially in an industry as competitive as pharmaceuticals. He felt as if he had been away for a lifetime. Immediately following the exchange with Jon, he no longer had access to development files, save Noctural, and that was only because he was blackmailing Jon in order to get at them.

Jon would feign a new security policy or some bullshit like that, but they would both know he planned to keep Cooper under thumb until he could devise a "mutually beneficial" arrangement for his exit. Cooper knew he had to fight to maintain his offensive position and push as hard as he could while he held the upper hand. From his experience with Jon, this would not be long. So, despite the sick feeling that engulfed his stomach, he would ride the elevator up to Jon at 7 a.m. sharp and take on the old man face to face, come what may.

First off, he had to sneak past Mama Bear, who would no doubt do her best to keep him safely recuperating in his office, so Cooper waited for her bathroom run, which should come any minute. He had never met anyone who peed as much as Maggie. Although he had been scheduled to return the crutches last Friday, there was no way he was going to give them up prior to his return to work. He was not above working the sympathy angle, or any angle available, given the situation with Noctural. Defending his work would likely cost him his job, but he felt compelled to continue and uncover what was causing the inconsistencies in the testing, regardless of the expense.

He had never been this reckless. He had been cocky and arrogant. Absolutely. But if a colleague had made the moves he had made in the last couple weeks, the old Cooper would have laughed in their face. Why would anyone jeopardize the sweet gravy train this industry provided? He had always thought that there was nothing that could ever motivate him to rise against the machine, and yet here he was: the proverbial black sheep.

He told himself that it was his ego that would not let Jon win, but deep down, he knew that wasn't true. Jon had always won despite Cooper's opinion, one way or the other. That was why he and Jon worked so well—they were always aligned on the things that mattered most, until now.

Reminding himself to get down to the task at hand, Cooper pushed up on his good leg and steadied himself with the crutches, by habit now more than necessity. The stopwatch on his phone reached 12.48 minutes of unpunished tile, and Cooper felt safe to peer out the door.

"Thought I was in the can, didn't you?" was Maggie's greeting, as she sat perched on the corner of her desk, heels in hand.

"You think I'm not onto you, love?" She waved the Bordeaux-colored pumps up under his nose, making quick work of the space between them as she crossed the tile in her bare feet.

Despite himself, he softened toward her, a smile replacing the shock in his expression that had first betrayed his feelings.

She smiled widely back up at him and hugged him as tightly as her fifty-eight-year-old, four-foot-eleven frame would allow. Maggie excelled at office politics, shoe shopping, and hugs, in whichever order was required.

"Glad to see you in one piece, Coop!" she said, following up the accusation with her initially intended greeting. "And I'm not the only one. Jon has been lost without you." Her raw laugh filled the hallway, a tattoo of her days as a smoker.

Cooper's smile drifted away. He knew better. He knew much better.

His deflating face was not lost on her, and Maggie thought better than to ask. She didn't want to know the specifics, and something about the look on his face made her glad she probably never would.

"Speaking of Jon, I need to see him first thing." Cooper weighed the odds of an escape now that she was on to him.

She shot him a look as if to say, *You have got to be kidding,* but then caught something more in his expression that instinctively told her to let him go. If she thought it was his painkillers, or lack of them, she wouldn't have held back, but he honestly seemed fine, other than the crutches and that look like someone had just driven over his new puppy.

"Go get him, boss! You've been milking this accident long enough, I'd say." She laughed again, determined not to let him see that she was more worried about him than ever.

Another half-hearted smile softened his face as he limped away. Limping in to see Jon was not the vehicle of choice. He expected no sympathy from his boss. Not now. Not ever again.

The steel elevator doors opened to reveal Jon's receptionist glancing up at him. Her expression was a fraction less sharp than usual, and she invited him to take a seat. Maggie had obviously called up here immediately following their exchange. He had never witnessed Daphne offer anyone a seat, and the unadulterated, pristine white leather of the waiting area ottoman was all the proof one required of her unwelcoming demeanor.

"He's not here yet," she offered. It was the best Cooper could have hoped for.

Cooper made himself comfortable, reaching for his cell so that he could respond to a couple new messages. He startled slightly as the twelve-foot elevator doors began to open. He could feel his pulse quicken as he over-ruled the immediate dread of seeing Jon. It would be the first meeting in person since their face-off on the conference call last week.

Daphne's head shot up at Will with a look of disdain. At least she had received a warning call about Boy Wonder coming up from Maggie, but a second unscheduled visitor first thing Monday morning was far too much.

"Can I assist you?" she hissed from behind her carbon-fiber desk.

This was the Daphne Cooper had grown to love. He assumed that his hunch about Maggie's call to whitewash his arrival had been correct.

"I'm here to see my brother, Jon Cameron," Will said. He held his ground— at least he thought he did. Although they shared no biological connection, he could barely remember a time when he didn't consider Jon his true brother.

From his seat at the ottoman, Cooper couldn't have been more surprised. In all the time they had spent together, in and outside the office, never once had Jon mentioned a brother. Even if he had, Cooper would have never guessed this slight, hunched, balding nerd type was Jon's sibling. Not in a million years!

By this point, Cooper was literally hanging off the edge of the ottoman like a never-blinking gargoyle, curious to learn even the slightest detail about Jon's brother.

"I'm sorry I've never had the pleasure." Daphne's response was guarded, equally skeptical that this waif of a man before her could be related to the Proteus resident giant.

"Sorry. I'm Will, Will Maelish, with Icahn." He was starting to lose his nerve to confront Jon face to face.

Cooper shook his head. The Will from the conference call was Jon's brother! That was all the introduction he needed. "Will, I'm Cooper. Cooper Delaney." This was so much better than running into Jon. Now he had Will.

Daphne had never witnessed anyone navigate crutches like Cooper, as he literally exploited them to his advantage, propelling himself toward her desk.

"We met on the conference call last week. You are testing my drug, I believe." Cooper towered over Will as he shifted one crutch to join its mate under his left arm, holding out his right hand in order to complete the preliminaries. He had fully mastered the crutches, making them seem effortless, more like an accessory than an aid.

Whatever courage Will had mustered now completely dissolved. He had soothed himself during that damn call with the fact that he didn't have to sit across from Cooper, and he had come up here today to demand that Jon rectify the situation, so that he never would. Yet here he was, larger than life, crutches in tow, looming over him just like Jon had, so many times before.

"Good to meet you." This was the best Will could come up with as he shook Cooper's outstretched hand.

"You and I have a lot to discuss, my friend. So fortuitous running into you this way. Just think of all the time you will save. No need to reply to the twenty-something emails I forwarded, outlining the development and testing last week. Perhaps it is easiest if we head straight to the lab. Jon is obviously not here yet, and I can show you firsthand the issues we've run into." Cooper had secured his lead and wasn't about to let go.

Before Will could protest, Cooper ushered him into elevator and pushed the button to close the door. The crutches actually seemed to enhance his agility, like a third appendage of sorts. He offered a wave to Daphne, and they exchanged an understanding grin before the elevator doors closed. Jon would never be the wiser of his unsolicited guests this morning.

If there was one thing everyone acknowledged about Jon, it was that he didn't like his schedule interrupted; he called the shots, he made the summons, and if there were to be surprises, they were to be at his discretion.

CHAPTER 19

MANDOLIN GRACE
2:18 p.m.   Lenox Hill, NYC

HER LANDER BLUE SUEDE GUCCI FLATS RESTED IN FRONT OF the petrified wood stool that graced the entryway. From the sofa, it looked like an advertisement, something warm and lux, offset by an object of equal appeal but the opposite composition. In this case, the wood's glossy, uneven patina, exhibiting every possible shade of black and white, allowed the delicate suede, crystal-toed slippers to reflect themselves in a mirror created over millions of years ago.

There it was, Gucci and a stump, both getting even better with age, one made by man and the other by nature. Or was that true? What was deemed man-made? A better question may be what was not? So much was so blurry. We had effectively taken over this planet, but was it for the better? Billions of years of evolution and what have we aspired to?

A caffeine-rich society competing for the lives our parents never had. First-world residents living in an insulated bubble, but if you really got into it with people, everyone was a little scared that the bubble might burst at any moment. Good and bad, right and wrong became more and more difficult to navigate. In fact, just about everything had taken rest in a sea of grey, including Mandolin's chance meeting with Cooper.

They had exchanged numbers prior to saying their goodbyes to Jack. It was hard for Mandolin to leave Jack behind. She remembered his wide smile as she put on her coat and hugged him farewell, his attempt to drown out the emptiness she felt, knowing she would be on her own again. He was always a phone call away, but it was never the same as when they had worked together in the city. She truly believed he belonged back in NYC. That sleepy hollow was no place for Jack.

It was definitely no place for Cooper either. They must have been handfuls in their youth. She could feel the rivalry between them. Mandolin had to admit it was amusing to watch the two of them jockey for the upper hand in almost every exchange. It was endearing to her. Mandolin could almost picture them growing up. She could see some of Cooper in Jack, small comments he had always made; now she knew where they originated. They were more like brothers than friends. It was sad that they had drifted apart, and she smiled slightly, thinking she had played a part in bringing them back together.

The contents of her purse spilled on her lap, some landing on the floor, as she extracted all the evidence of her trip to the coast. She turned Cooper's card in her hand and wondered if he would keep his promise regarding Dr. Ophelia Sasaki. Leaving the meeting, they had agreed that he would liaise directly with this source.

Ophelia's specialty was the study of the evolutionary phenomenon called natural selection—in short, genetic mutations/evolutionary traits that were advantageous in one time or place, which become obsolete in another. She was investigating why some traits break down quickly while others take longer to erode.

According to Sasaki, numerous cases of trait loss spanning over 150 years of research illustrate that evolution is not always progressive; unique evolutionary rules are followed when an organism loses a trait versus when an organism acquires it. According to her research, traits that are expensive to the organism to maintain are discarded more quickly. Most interesting was her finding that a relatively small number of genes could be capable of even the most significant evolutionary trait loss.

Sasaki's interest in Dr. Irwin's address was palpable; however, the insistence that her research was key to determining cause is what placed her at the top of the list of potential sources to meet with. While this was definitely not Cooper's specialty, his PhD and research expertise made him an excellent prospect to weed out Sasaki's claim and relevance.

Mandolin planned to set up a meeting once Cooper had a chance to review Ophelia's research. However, she had no idea how long it might take him, especially given that he was returning to what appeared to be a volatile situation at Proteus following his accident.

Although she was having difficulty admitting it, even to herself, Cooper was limping his way into her thoughts more frequently than she would have liked. She was grateful for his help and felt a camaraderie between herself, Cooper, and Jack that would typically take years to attain. If it had been that simple, all would be well; however, a competitive undercurrent and Cooper's blatant advances made a strictly working relationship impossible. There was always the underlying suggestion of something more.

She didn't like the potential impact on her relationship with Jack either. She could tell it put him on edge, but it was his willingness to play along that surprised and annoyed her in equal parts. He seemed all too happy to fall in line, competing for her attention. She needed Jack and did not want to rock the boat, especially for someone like Cooper—someone so full of himself. Jack meant the world to her, and Cooper, in her opinion, looked out for Cooper first.

Mandolin prepared herself to be more strategic with him in the future. She chastised herself for so easily falling into his games, and promised to refrain from being caught up by him next time they met. She pushed away the hint of anticipation at the thought of seeing him again. It was rare that someone she just met would instantly take up a role on center stage in her life this way. Something told her that this was just how it was with Cooper. He was either everything or nothing, and had left behind more than one broken heart.

She would have none of it. On the cusp of what was quite possibly her biggest break—a career-changing story—she was not about to fall prey to Cooper Delaney (a predator on crutches nonetheless). She would make sure she took exactly what she needed, while seeming to play along with his not-so-subtle advances. She decided that placating Cooper was definitely the best of all possible plans. He would never be the wiser, too caught up in his own story to consider that she might have an agenda of her own. This thought brought a vainglorious smirk to her face, just as her robotic personal assistant entered the room to retrieve the discarded items from her handbag and return the

Gucci flats to her closet. Her dependency on him outweighed the fact that the assistant was probably the ultimate big brother, collecting the most intimate evidence of her existence imaginable.

The more she considered it, the more her plan just made sense. She and Jack would focus on the details of the leads and how the story would unfold, and Cooper would be the puppet, filling in the blanks where required—in between games of Tetris, of course. She liked the thought of her and Jack pulling the strings, using Cooper as they saw fit. She was sure Jack would feel the same, and her smile grew.

Now the only loose end that kept nagging at her was Camberg. It was his look of desperation as much as his fanatical ranting that stuck with her. With so many potential leads to follow, she wondered why he would enter her conscience at all. Perhaps it was that he worked with Armand Price, one of the most well-known and respected physicists on the planet. She was tempted to reach out to him. Did he know about Camberg and his crazy theory? Surely he would want to know that his colleague was impersonating him, hoping to gain audience for something so ridiculous. Maybe that was what bothered her most: He had seemed lucid and believable. She physically shuddered at the thought of their meeting and how vulnerable she had been.

Perhaps that would set her at ease, reaching out to Dr. Price regarding Camberg directly. She was on the verge of pulling up his number when Jack's words echoed in her head: *"Never reveal your source, regardless of how crazy they may seem."*

CHAPTER 20

WILL MAELISH
7:12 a.m.   Proteus, NYC

IT TOOK WILL BY SURPRISE WHEN THE ELEVATOR DOORS OPENED to the Proteus parkade.

"Odd place for your lab," Will said, hollowly. He felt sick. He was being abducted by a man he was never supposed to meet, and a kidnapper on crutches at that! At this moment, he hated his brother like never before.

"You think you and your big brother are the only compadres capable of a coup?" Cooper wasn't sure which of them was actually the older sibling, but at this point, he didn't care.

"Which one's yours?" he continued, as he scanned the cars, looking for a Prius or Civic.

"Really, Cooper, there is no need to see me out, I am happy to leave—"

"Oh no, you aren't going anywhere without me. We are taking a little field trip to your lab—not mine." Cooper was satisfied with the look on Will's face following his announcement. Why was it so enjoyable to shock this guy? Cooper loved it. He could do this all day long. He wondered if Jon felt the same, if he enjoyed running Will's show.

Cooper chastised himself as Jon's thoughts or feelings should be of little concern to him now, as he had gone far beyond insubordination to kidnapping of sorts. *Well, fuck Jon, this was his fault anyway.*

Cooper no longer had access to anything other than Noctural files, and it stood to reason that Jon shouldn't wonder where he was or what he was working on. There was nothing else he could be doing. Jon had set it up so that he really had no choice. One could argue that Jon should actually applaud his initiative. Visiting an offsite test lab really was above the call of duty.

As Cooper shook his head, he couldn't help the villainous smirk that spread across his face.

"Glad you find this amusing." Will was pissed now. It didn't happen often, but this young kid calling the shots was taking its toll. "What are you hoping to gain from this, Cooper? I can send the results to you in any format you wish." As soon as the words left his mouth, he realized they had fallen on deaf ears. Once Cooper made up his mind about something, he followed through. Cooper was more like his father than he would ever admit.

"You and Jon test my drug behind my back, and now you want me to trust your results? I don't think so, my friend. It's my turn now."

Cooper was eerily comfortable in this role of mock abductor. It made him wonder what else he was capable of. Uncovering the truth behind the perceived failure of Noctural had forced him to embrace traits of his character he usually kept hidden. It was surprisingly easy to acknowledge that it felt good to stir what he had always suppressed.

They pulled up to the Mount Sinai hospital security gate. Will fumbled with his ID tag. His pusillanimous demeanor was beginning to annoy Cooper. After the hour-long car ride to Will's lab, he was finding it verged on defiant— a passive aggressiveness that Cooper found immensely irritating. Perhaps his new-found love of hostage taking was beginning to wane. Or perhaps the longer Cooper spent time with Will, the more he was reminded of Jon and Jon's inevitable response to this stunt.

As they pulled into Will's spot, Cooper was still lost in his own thoughts. Will interrupted them. "Now what, Hauptmann?"

Cooper rolled his eyes at the reference and held out his hands for Will's keys. Will led the way to his lab, and swiped them in through the east-lot entry. They walked together down the uninviting corridor that led to his office. The looks the pair aroused from his colleagues made Will uncomfortable. He was not accustomed to the attention, and considering that he was now a hostage, he became even more nervous.

In contrast, Cooper would have been disappointed by an absence of second looks, especially from females. He effortlessly filled the hall with his height, crutches, and ego.

Will opened his office door with yet another swipe, and then settled behind his faux-steel desk. It was economy modern—a perfect fit for his institutional position.

Cooper propped himself as comfortably as possible on the small chair in front of Will's desk. He had taken for granted the bespoke furnishings at Proteus. The hours he'd spent at Hudson's personally selecting them for his own office were all but forgotten.

"Let's look at which of the kids it's working for and for which ones it's not." Cooper's instincts told him that his best chance of identifying the reason for the drug's inconsistencies would be found with these kids.

"We administered Noctural to thirty test subjects over a six-week period," Will said. "Another thirty made up the control group. The testing was overseen by myself and my colleague Catherine Dumont. All results were recorded by myself and Catherine, and the drug was administered by either her or me in a controlled environment. There are no errors. I stand by the results implicitly."

Cooper was impressed by Will's passion, and from a cursory glance at the data Will had presented to him, he could see that he'd also had some cash behind him. Undoubtedly some, if not all, came from Jon via Proteus. It crossed his mind that this was likely not the first time.

"I need to run my own tests on these kids, especially the non-responders." Cooper ignored Will's reddening face. He was oblivious to how he had offended him, how deeply Will believed in his work, and his debilitating obligation to help others. He needed to make a difference, especially for these kids.

Cooper misread his lack of response as defiance to his plan. "This one, Albert Xavier." Cooper demanded the info for the first non-responder on the list. He wanted to start on the testing immediately.

Will was seething. "These are children, Cooper, you cannot—"

"Yes, that's right!" Cooper was up from his cheap metal chair, wielding his crutch in a show of force. "Children you have been feeding an unapproved drug to for the past six weeks. Let me remind you," Cooper growled, "you are not in a position to refuse." Cooper was now towering over Will. His six-foot-three frame dwarfed Will, and reminded him of Jon.

Will was not giving up. "These kids all have ADHD. You can't subject them to undue stress—"

"Look, Will, I want the info for all your participants. Send it to me right now, and I will contact them this afternoon to set up the testing at Proteus. Explain that it is imperative that they comply. Tell the parents it will impact their kid's benefit from the drug. Tell them whatever you need to in order to get these kids to my lab." As soon as the words left his mouth, his brain started protesting the rash demand. Kids at Proteus would raise every kind of suspicion.

He was prevented from further second-guessing himself when the phone rang. Will picked it up out of reflex. It was a welcome distraction from this nightmare with Cooper.

"It's for you." Will passed Cooper the phone. The smug look that took hold of his captive's face meant it could only be one person. Now the real fight began. At least Cooper had the study and subject info in hand. He had what he needed, which was also enough to bury Jon—and Will, for that matter—with one call to the FDA.

Cooper took the phone from Will and pressed the speaker button. He knew Jon would censor himself on speaker, especially when he had no idea who besides Will and Cooper might comprise the audience on the other side.

"Jon, good to hear from you. We have just finalized plans for Noctural testing to resume this afternoon. Of course, we will move the study over to Proteus, so that I can oversee it personally. I trust you will want our underage test subjects provided with the highest security, so I encourage you to reserve the Upton Wing for exclusive use over the next two weeks." Cooper's heart was pounding and his knuckles went white as he gripped his crutch.

"You will live to regret this, Cooper. I have finished better men for less," Jon replied in a voice devoid of the malice he felt.

It was all the consent Cooper needed for now. He knew better than anyone the price he would eventually pay.

"Yes, Cooper, you *will* live to regret this." Her words punctured the silent, tension-filled room like a siren, startling both men.

It was Catherine, Will's protector. She had worked by his side for over seventeen years. She loved Will. It was something even Will could not deny. However, it was not meant to be, and that was OK. At least she told herself it was.

Regardless. Will was her man here at work, and these kids were the closest thing to children of her own she would likely ever have. No one was going to touch a hair on their precious heads unless they came through her, especially not Jon. Not Jon *or* this kid. She had only heard the last few minutes of the conversation but had put enough together to deduce that further testing at an offsite location was in the works, and she would have none of that, at least not without her involvement. She was curious as hell as to why the drug produced these inconsistencies, but would not agree to finding the answer at the expense of these kids, *her* kids. Cooper had no right to be involved from her perspective, but she guessed that the drug was his creation, judging by his demands for further testing.

Will's response was weary. "Cooper, Jon, this is Catherine. My partner." He pictured this day being over, as he fell back into his favorite chair in front of the TV in his living room.

"Excellent," Cooper said. "I believe I have assembled my test team. I will expect you all at Proteus, Upton main-floor lobby tomorrow morning, selected participants in tow. It's been a pleasure meeting you both in person like this. Makes the work so much more enjoyable. Pity, Jon, that you aren't here to join us." With his last remark, he ended the call.

Will looked up at Cooper in disbelief, and Cooper smile broadly. "Now, my good friend, I will need a lift back to Proteus."

As he crutched toward the door, he held out a hand to Catherine, which she ignored. He shrugged and substituted a wink instead, signing off on his first foray into hostage taking, pirating information and exploiting minors. He assured himself the best was yet to come.

CHAPTER 21

RAY GARLAND
4:45 p.m.   Musée d'Orsay, Paris

HE LIKED TO STAND BEHIND THE CLOCK AT THE MUSÉE D'ORSAY. It was quite literally a window in time that reminded him how quickly it passed. The iron arms stretched out high above, inviting him back to the city of lights, which the clock's face framed below. This was Ray's fourth trip to Paris, and every time, he hoped it would be his last. Following the ISIS bombings, Paris had become a work destination, a city he would have never sought out on any other terms.

D'Orsay just prior to closing was perhaps the only place he could get away from the streets bustling with tourists and take in the city on his own terms—one of the few places where he could collect his thoughts. It was both private enough to meet uninterrupted and public enough to keep just about anyone he might need to meet with in check.

Somewhere down there amidst over two million Parisians, and almost six times as many tourists was Dr. Camberg. Ray, along with his newly assigned sidekick, had been tasked with finding him. Jaxxson Clive was this one's name. Jaxxson was his first name. For real. Ray couldn't believe it, although very little surprised him anymore. It was always the same, only the names changed. Ray was responsible for breaking in the new superstars; only the best were placed with him for a year, and then they were good to go.

He was infamous with the newly baptized recruits. Legendary, really. They hadn't even started training until they shadowed Ray. As unbelievable as it was, they came in only two varieties: the ones he had to keep close and eventually save, and the ones that went on to be heroes. Ray didn't worry about the 10 percent that would do well. He worries about the 90 percent that would flounder and make his life miserable.

"I am so tired of never, ever meeting someone as good as me," he had lamented to Carl.

"Maybe someday," he sighed. You think the Academy could have figured out a way to send him the heroes even 50 percent of the time, but the truth was that none of them knew until the recruits hit the ground. In all his years, he had never been able to come up with an algorithm to predict success. Neither had the academy. It was truly amazing; even those who became stellar trainees often buckled under the weight of responsibility as full-fledged agents.

Jaxxson was not off to a good start. It was ten minutes past 17:00. Ten minutes too late. Ray's phone went off in his pocket. He reluctantly answered, bracing himself for the excuse.

"Ray! It's Jaxxson. I've been waiting ten minutes for you." Jaxxson had deliberately waited the full ten minutes to call Ray, despite the waitress insisting that the Café Campana was now officially closed. She had fought with herself, tempted to say something coy like *"J'espère que vous reviendrez bientôt!"* knowing that he would never understand and might ask for the translation.

In the end, she had chickened out. It just was not the way of the Parisian female, despite the fact that his broad shoulders, sandy hair, and the cavernous dimples on either side of his smile set him apart from the rest of the crowd. In the end, she settled for *"Pas mal du tout pour un Americain,"* to which he could only shrug and shake his head in reply.

Jaxxson wanted to make sure Ray was officially late. Ray's sparse instructions and use of military time left little question as to who would be in charge. Jaxxson was almost giddy to have caught Ray up on something as unforgivable as being late to his own rendezvous.

"Funny! I've been doing the same." Ray was just about to tear a strip off the kid when he realized it actually may have been his fault. He detested the restaurant at the entry on the fifth floor—detested it so much that he forgot it housed the second eye of D'Orsay. The turquoise modern chairs were as ridiculous as they were uncomfortable, and absurd orange metal sculptures, which were apparently meant to separate the patrons, looked like miniature playground climbing bars. The old school deli tables, which would have otherwise won him over, had a permanent layer of grease left behind by over three million visitors per year. All in all, Ray preferred to stand.

"Why don't you make your way down the hall to the actual meeting place, the one where I have been waiting for you. Perhaps the Impressionist artwork along the walk over here will inspire you to make a better impression next time." Ray wasn't about to admit his fault. Had Jaxxson been more astute, he would have asked which clock. No, this one was definitely not off to a good start.

Disappointed, jet-lagged, and now hungry from the smell of quiche and pasta lingering in the air, Jaxxson wove his way through the last tourists of the day to the beginning of the famous Impressionist paintings.

He had never been one for the finer things. Acceptance to Quantico had been his dream since childhood; he had made little space in his life for much else. Jaxxson was what his parents had raised him to be: a stereotypical, God-fearing Confederate, and he could not have been happier to oblige. It seemed that he was a perfect fit, just what his parents and the FBI had ordered.

He was reluctant to waste time now that Ray had decided it was his fault their meeting had been delayed. He made his way past Renoir and Monet at an insulting pace, even the uncultured masses vying for selfies beside the priceless works were perturbed at his apparent disinterest. However, the dancers caught his eye. He had always fancied ballerinas—their existence and trappings the polar opposite of his own. Their grace and elegance were timeless, captured by Degas, and still relevant today even if appreciated at the most basic level possible.

Ballerinas soon gave way to turkeys, something with which Jaxxson was much more familiar; Thanksgiving was almost as big as Christmas at the Clive residence. His mother hosted their large extended brood every year, and the multigenerational feast seemed to get more lavish as the numbers grew. His stomach growled. He could almost taste her sweet potato casserole as he rounded the corner to find Ray standing square in the center of the second eye.

The latest candidate approached. His swagger was unmistakable and something he would likely lose by the end of the trip. That was Ray's prediction anyway, and he was usually right. Jaxxson had a military build, similar to Ray back in the day, but he had way too much attitude in Ray's opinion. He shook his head as Jaxxson confidently thrust an open hand toward him, initiating a handshake and deliberately flexing his forearm at the same time.

"Ray Garland, it is truly an honor, sir." Jaxxson did little to contain his obvious excitement at meeting Ray and reaching this coveted milestone with the FBI. You would think he was meeting Walt Disney by the enchanted grin that spread across his face. It made Ray feel equal parts nausea and contempt. He made a mental note to bring up this babysitting routine with Carl upon his return. Ray was getting too old for this.

"What is Camberg's location?" Ray decided to get straight to it. The sooner the wheels fell off this forced partnership the better.

"Our intel has him staying at Hotel Fauchon in the eighth arrondissement," replied Jaxxson, visibly disappointed that pleasantries had been cut short, as his large, warm brown eyes fell and he subconsciously retracted his bottom lip.

Ray looked across the Seine in the direction of the hotel through the clock face. "Well, Jaxxson," Ray replied with the best southern drawl he could muster, mimicking the boy's accent, "Time is ticking."

Ray had left his unmarked Audi A1 across the river—parking on the left bank anywhere near D'Orsay had been impossible. He was in disbelief at the car Interpol had supplied him. It was easily the smallest car he had driven. Ray hated driving in Paris. He had been honked and cursed at more times than he could count, trying to navigate the streets for parking, and had finally given up, leaving the car across from the US Embassy, taking his chances half in and half out of a tow-away zone. One more reason to hate the intolerable city of lights.

As they strolled across Passerelle des Arts, Ray snickered at the plethora of locks embracing the iron safety rails. An old man approached with a collection of them for sale. After taking in Ray's scowl, the Parisian lock barista immediately reconsidered.

As they made their way through the Tuileries, Ray started to sweat. Record highs had the city at a scorching thirty-four degrees. He had never been so thankful for trees. He had to admit that he did appreciate the perfection of the garden—man's domination over nature. It struck a chord with him, as keeping order had been his life's work.

Jaxxson was starving. It was hard to pay attention to Ray, as all he could think about was the smell of food wafting over to them from Café des Marronniers. His stomach rumbled so loudly it caused Ray's eyebrows to raise. Once again, he was reminded to bring up this babysitting with Carl. As they approached the end of the garden, a fairground materialized, sabotaging the elegant garden of past kings.

The fair was completely out of place, pretty much identical to any county fair in North America. Jaxxson couldn't help but think of home, watching the children laugh and scream on the Ferris wheel and the Free Fall respectively. Some things were universal.

"Hey, Ray, let me buy you an American cheeseburger!" Jaxxson couldn't take it anymore, the smell of burgers pushed him over the edge. Ray was about to refuse, but Interpol's tracking of Camberg didn't have him back at the hotel for another hour or so. He gestured to Jaxxson to hurry up. The truth was that Ray could already taste the carnival burger as his mouth began to water. The jet lag was starting to get to him too. At his age, the time change was inhumane. Ray could go without sleep or food, but not both.

They walked the tree-lined edge of the garden, burgers in hand. Neither had much to say between bites, trying to avoid pedestrians on foot, bicycles, and kick scooters. Both of them took note of the WWII commemorative plates on the garden wall, reminding them of their oaths to defend their country.

They crossed the hectic Rue de Rivoli, coming up to the uninviting, gated United States Embassy in order to retrieve their vehicle. It had not been by chance that Ray had decided to park it as close to home as possible.

They continued down Rue Saint-Florentin. Jaxxson, grateful for the Parisian take on a burger that now lined his stomach, became captivated by the aroma from the garden restaurant Le Florentin. As it called to him, they crossed the street to the car, his unrelenting appetite echoing his impressive stature.

Jaxxson barely fit in the German car. Ray actually laughed out loud as he tried to make himself as comfortable as possible. Ray started the vehicle and they joined the back-to-back traffic that lined Rue Royale, thankful that they were close to the hotel and still had thirty minutes until Interpol's ETA.

Camberg had fled New York once the FBI began their investigation of Armand Price. Armand had made it clear that he did not stand by Camberg, and Camberg knew it. The new energy discovered, and his crazed prophesies, together made him a security threat. Once Armand cut all ties with Camberg, Camberg left the country. The only reason they knew of his whereabouts was because security at Paris-Charles de Gaulle airport had recognized him. Ray wondered why Camberg would have taken a commercial flight. For someone who was supposedly so smart, it was a really, really stupid move.

They sat parked in front of the Fauchon L'Hôtel entry. It was an interesting choice for a physicist specializing in accumulated energy. The glamourous five-star hotel promised a stay full of luxurious indulgences and was apparently a favorite among fashion-scene editors. Perhaps it had been deliberate—the last place he would be expected to stay pre-Paris fashion week.

Ray was not known for his patience. He gave Interpol a full fifteen minutes to respond, and in the absence of hearing back from them, decided to proceed on his own. His reputation could easily afford him the transgression. As they entered through the front gold-framed glass doors, they were greeted by a bellman in black, with fuchsia-striped tuxedo pants. Ray shook his head, smiling to himself. *Only in Paris.*

Both Ray and Jaxxson were ushered to the library, where macarons waited patiently on small, glass-covered cake plates; it appeared there would be dessert following the burgers, much to Jaxxson's delight.

Ray refused to waste a minute more. When the concierge approached to ask if they had a reservation, he made it clear he was with the FBI, working directly with Interpol, in search of a Dr. Peter Camberg. While the concierge searched the list of guests, Ray retrieved a recent photo of Camberg from his phone. It was likely he had used an alias for the reservation. Ray would have had the name, had he waited long enough for Interpol's update.

She nodded to him that, yes, she recognized Camberg, and in fact, he had just retired to his room about ten or fifteen minutes earlier. The boutique hotel had only fifty-four suites, and the staff prided themselves on providing exceptional service, which meant catering to each guest individually.

Upon review of their identification, she provided Ray and Jaxxson with skeleton swipe cards that would grant them access to Camberg's room, 7/03, as well as any other room on the property. Cards in hand, they set out on the hunt. They made their way around the corner to the small double elevator bank, and as they waited for their ride up, Jaxxson couldn't resist a famous Fauchon caramel, housed in glass resting on the console table in front of the elevators. Not unlike the macaron, it was the best he had tasted in his life.

As the elevator reached the seventh floor, they were greeted by an asymmetric black-and-white striped carpet, rectangles and squares alternating with a random stripe of the Fauchon pink. Ray felt dizzy just looking at it, and had to wonder if the rooms would be just as gaudy.

"Peter, we know you are in there. My name is Ray Garland. I am with the FBI. Open up." Ray banged loudly on the door, which had a privacy tag. With no response, he struck the door again repeatedly, this time with the outside of his clenched fist.

"Peter, open up!" Ray called again in vain, as he reached for his swipe card. "Look, Peter, I have a key to your room, and I am going to use it. Interpol is working directly with us to bring you in. We have a warrant for your arrest, and we also suspect you are in danger. Please open up." Ray waited half a second more before swiping the card and entering the room.

At first it was difficult for their eyes to adjust to the dark hallway leading into the room. To the right was a full-length, modern, brass-framed oval mirror, suspended from floor to ceiling. In front of them stood a small, well-appointed armoire with glass doors. In between, Peter Camberg lay collapsed on the charcoal-black herringbone hardwood floor that camouflaged the color of his blood as it silently left his body.

"Jesus!" This was all Ray could muster as he knelt down to check for a pulse. There wasn't one to be found, but his body and the blood were both warm and wet. They had been only minutes late.

Ray and Jaxxson heard a door open to the next room. They looked at each other and both instinctively started out into the hall. Maybe, just maybe, the assassin was still here.

A lean, dark-haired male in bellman attire walked purposefully down the hall. Ray and Jaxxson followed him, finding it odd that he would remove his cap and not turn to cater to the two apparent guests. Ray and Jaxxson picked up their pace, and in response, the bellman's brisk stride morphed into a run. He never bothered to look behind him as he sprinted past the elevator banks. Ray and Jaxxson watched him from the full-length windows overlooking an exterior courtyard as he darted through a staff door in the hallway just past the elevators and onto an exterior balcony, seven floors above the courtyard floor.

Without hesitation, the man climbed out onto one of the modern wooden slats, which straddled the aligned balconies joining on each floor. It became his makeshift ladder as he tried to make his way toward the ground.

Ray nearly lost his breath as Jaxxson pushed him out of the way, leaving him to stagger behind as his protege followed the steps of the suspect at a sprint. He also swiped through the pink door labelled "staff," and was out on the balcony just in time to see the bellman drop to the sunroof on the second floor, then slide to the courtyard cobblestones below. Knocking over pots and upending tables, the suspect finally regained his footing, then ran through the courtyard exit to the sidewalk facing Place de la Madeleine.

Jaxxson had never lost a foot race, not once all through grade school or college, not once in the academy either, and he wasn't about to lose this one.

Ray stood still in disbelief, after having watched the suspect slip and fall through the air some four stories to the second-floor sunroof, with only glass and iron support beams to break his fall, and knowing that this was the path Jaxxson would soon follow.

"Christ!" Ray uttered aloud just as the elevator arrived. He pushed past the fashionable hotel guests and pressed the button for the ground floor at least ten times. The perp would have some means of transportation. and Ray needed to get to his car ASAP so they wouldn't lose him.

What Ray missed on the elevator ride down made the seventh-floor hotel guests he had pushed out of the way scream, and the hotel staff passing through the second-story sunroom—a sunroom that had become Jaxxson's makeshift stuntman net—recoil to safety.

Jaxxson heard and felt the glass crack simultaneously. The fractured sunroof could not support a second impact. Shards of glass flew up around him, slashing through his pants and cutting his arms and hands as he grabbed for the iron support rails that had framed it just moments before.

He hit the ground running, the glass somewhat breaking his fall. Despite the lacerations, he pressed on, pushing staff and patrons out of the way as he followed the hallway beside the kitchen. As he ran past the rose-gold counter and fuchsia chairs, he recalled that the restaurant was attached to the Fauchon patio at the front of the hotel. The staff did not have time to react as he drew his gun and made easy work of the space between the restaurant entry and the landscaped private décor of the patio, which was protected by glass fencing and perfectly sculpted boxwood hedges.

He sprinted to the patio entrance to find the perp had just started his motorcycle. The suspect looked directly back at Jaxxson from amongst a thick collection of bikes, lined up in disjointed rows across the street from Fauchon, and lamented the time he had wasted rifling through Camberg's belongings.

With little thought of his injuries due to the adrenaline coursing through his veins, Jaxxson raced over to a Ducati owner innocently admiring his own ride.

"FBI!" Jaxxson shouted at him as he grabbed the man's key and pushed him out of the way in order to mount his ride.

Starting the Ducati sounded like lighting a match in stereo. He had always dreamt of riding one, but had somehow never pictured it under any of these conditions. Foreign country, assassin chase, and confiscated from the owner were circumstances not even a thrill seeker like himself could have imagined.

"I got you!" Ray shouted from his open car window as he followed Jaxxson. Interpol was live on his monitor, with feed on his car as well as the perp's bike and now Jaxxson's Ducati on the screen. They were tracking the two bikes via satellite and had let Ray know they would transmit to him directly.

Ray cursed himself for being only minutes late to save Camberg. It was just another example of how he should never rely on someone else. Ray hated being stuck in the Audi, despite the fact that it was turbo-charged and flush with state-of-the-art tracking equipment. He wistfully looked across the street at the Tesla dealership, wondering why Interpol hadn't set him up in one of those.

Jaxxson winced as shards of glass cut down further into his palms as he gripped the handlebars. He followed the perp, still in his bellman attire, down Rue de l'Arcade, flying past architecture a thousand years old, made new with sale signs and delivery vans. He passed a storefront, Pressing de la Madeline, and the name of his baby sister interrupted his thoughts.

He immediately pushed Maddy and her accident from his mind. He needed to compartmentalize everything in order to catch this guy, regardless of the cost. As the bikes split the narrow street, they were engulfed with a silvery haze brought on by the billowing exhaust, made darker still by the height and the endless winding rows of the giant buildings, which seemed to make way just enough for the speeding motorcycles racing at their feet.

Interpol announced that the perp had been identified as Asad Jamali through the hotel's security cameras. According to Customs, he was allegedly a well-connected official on an extended business visa working at the Saudi Embassy in Paris. Interpol was concerned that his next move would likely be to head to the embassy, based on the direction he was heading, so they planned to cut him off.

Jaxxson cursed as the cobblestone streets shook the bike despite the state-of-the-art shocks. Passing Hôtel Bedford, he briefly looked back over his shoulder to see Ray far behind him, desperately trying to weave his way through the thick traffic. If Jaxxson had not confiscated the bike, they would have already lost this guy; hopefully, Ray would remember this.

The uninterrupted length of Rue de l'Arcade allowed the bikes to pick up speed. Ironically, time appeared to stand still as they passed the Montblanc store. Ray watched the tiny bikes far ahead of him make their way toward Saint-Lazare train station.

Jaxxson wasn't prepared for it. In order to follow the assassin left on Rue de la Pépinière, he was forced to turn against traffic up onto the sidewalk, almost taking out the customers dining at La Cour de Rome. Chairs, tables, and people scattered as the bikes claimed what had once been theirs.

From behind, Ray looked down at his screen to see the bikes racing past the station as they took a right on Rue Joseph Sansboeuf against traffic.

Interpol announced, "We have him blocked at the corner of Rue de Laborde, between Laborde and Rocher."

Asad swore to himself. He should have known better. He had been trying to reach Khalid's guy since he left the hotel. Why wouldn't they pick up? To make matters worse, up ahead, he could see the Interpol blockade.

Asad tried again, yelling into his earpiece, hoping his voice would overcome the crescendo of his engine mixed with the cacophony of the streets of Paris, "I need to abort the plan for the embassy! I am going to try to lose them at the river!"

To avoid the Interpol blockade, he broke right on Rue du Rocher, again on the sidewalk in front of the Allegria pasta bar, as people desperate to avoid the screaming bikes pushed each other out of the way.

Asad needed to divert Interpol and hopefully lose his tail in the process. He knew just the place. He stayed on the sidewalk and turned slightly onto Rue Pasquier, crossing Boulevard Haussmann, then ducked into Square Louis XVI through the swinging gates. The tree-lined park was overgrown; branches escaped the wrought-iron fence with tree tops rising above the elegant lamp posts. Like a mirage, it seemed to appear out of nowhere, and it welcomed weary travelers, many whom had given up on their Paris destination for a moment's rest. Fortunately, most of them were seated as Asad's tires pelted them with sand from the pathway.

The old man was a stickler for time and always locked the park's Rue des Mathurins entry gate at half past eight. A second set of screams rang through the air as Jaxxson followed suit, scaring the hell out of patrons yet again. The old man hurried to chain the gate, having witnessed Asad's assault on the park, only to have it pushed back hard against him as Jaxxson screamed at him to get out of the way.

Jaxxson startled himself at the anguish in his own voice, still in pain from the openly bleeding lacerations from his fall. In close pursuit, he followed Asad's path down the sidewalk, carefully avoiding the metal safety rods. He crossed Rue des Mathurins, following the perp left on Rue d'Anjou. They both flew past the red doors with the lion knockers at Banque Palentine.

Jaxxson, desperate to make up the time he'd lost at the park, recklessly picked up speed, taking a right on busy Boulevard Malesherbes. As he analyzed the chase, he observed that the perp continued to favor the sidewalk. Jaxxson heard the screams and watched helplessly as Asad pushed a pedestrian out of his way down the Malesherbes–d'Anjou parking entry, where he fell some six feet to the pavement below. He felt sick not being able to stop, but the sound of the Interpol sirens now in pursuit gave him solace.

Keeping to the sidewalk, both bikes flew past the Hyatt Paris Madeleine on the right. Jaxxson was now only seconds behind Asad.

"Fuck!" Asad swore, and quickly took a left on Rue Roquépine, as Interpol had once again blocked him up ahead on Boulevard Haussmann in front of the Saint-Augustin church. At the end of the street, he almost dropped the bike by a bad patch, as he wove against traffic. He had to keep his cool, his tail was gaining on him.

On Ray's monitor, both bikes turned left on Rue d'Astorg speeding with traffic. With Jaxxson close behind, Asad took a right on Rue de la Ville-l'Évêque, careening against traffic and sticking to the cobblestone sidewalk.

Jaxxson followed Asad, speeding to the right at the intersection at Place des Saussaies keeping to the sidewalk through the roundabout. They both veered left on Rue des Saussaies against traffic, arriving at the French Ministry of the Interior, Place Beauvau. Flying past its golden gates and two armed guards, Jaxxson could afford only a quick glance at two backpackers crossing the street, Canada flags emblazoned on their packs, and for a microsecond, was reminded of home. Almost.

Startled by the policemen, Asad cut through the opening in the chain-link fence heading left, only to be startled yet again by a horse rearing up from a tourist carriage at the sound of his bike. If only he could have made it to the Saudi embassy. Where the fuck was Khalid?

They sounded like two hornets in battle as Jaxxson and Asad passed by Palais de l'Élysée. Unfortunately, the guards at the French presidential residence were contacted by Interpol too late to intercept them, and consequently the chase continued through the Champs-Élysées, where both bikes were flanked by the Arc de Triomphe to the right and the monument Place de la Concorde to the left.

Asad pushed on Avenue de Marigny to the Seine, in hopes of losing Jaxxson at the water. The Ducati roared as it closed the gap, speeding past the Grand and the Petit Palais. As the chase continued, the bike stayed true to its reputation for endless adrenaline, as it allowed Jaxxson to position himself immediately behind Asad on the Alexander Bridge.

Finally, Asad got through to Khalid directly. "Asad, come to the airport. We will get you out of there, my friend. You just need to lose them."

Jaxxson reached for his weapon, now confident that bystanders would not be in the line of fire, only to lose the shot as Asad took a sharp left after the bridge and navigated down the steep stairs to the waterfront like a stunt man. He hoped to lose Jaxxson by taking another quick left underneath the bridge, continuing down the Promenade des Berges-de-la-Seine.

Jaxxson was respectable on a bike, but stairs were something he had never attempted under perfect circumstances, let alone a chase scenario. He finally made it down only to hear Asad race away toward Pont des Invalides, yet another bridge that crossed the Seine. He opened up the Ducati to full speed, passing Fluctuart gallery and the Bateaux-Mouches, closing the gap between them once again.

Ray, being followed by the National Police, drove procession style down the side ramp to the Pont des Invalides road. Asad heard their sirens, and in response expertly negotiated his ride back up the stairs, taking the lead far ahead of them in order to secure the fastest route to the airport. Jaxxson stayed close behind Asad as he navigated the same stairs, admitting to himself that going down was much better than going up.

The bikers kicked up dust around them on the sandy path, passing a playground with a single, lonely red slide, avoiding pedestrians and Segways, this time making easy work of the small stairs required to gain entry to the pedestrian access of Pont de l'Alma bridge. In sight of the Eiffel Tower, they crossed the bridge to the Place de la Reine-Astrid intersection, where Asad took the roundabout, with Jaxxson in tow, heading straight up Avenue George V.

Two bikes, one Audi, and three Interpol marked cars sped down Avenue George V past Balenciaga, BMW, and Bvlgari, taking a right at Champs Elysées and careening around the Arc de Triomphe.

The cavalcade reached their second roundabout in front of the Palais des Congrès, and followed the bikes toward Neuilly sur Seine. "He is obviously headed to Charles de Gaulle Airport," Interpol blared over Ray's earpiece.

"No shit!" Ray shouted back to them.

Jaxxson followed Asad through the multiple freeway tunnels. He knew he had to take him down before they got to the airport. As he entered the last tunnel before Charles de Gaulle, it was as if they entered the twilight zone instead of Tunnel du Landy. Interpol was one step ahead and had remotely taken control of all vehicles within the tunnel, shifting them to the far-left side of the underpass.

Jaxxson grabbed his gun as Asad raced ahead into the dark, open mouth, as the evenly spaced lights at the top of the passage walls blurred at the speed. Jaxxson had a clean shot, so he aimed to bring the guy down, not kill him. Pain from the lacerations made him flinch as he tightened his grip on the right handlebar, as the Ducati shook at the speed.

He hesitated, especially as he was forced to shoot with his left, because of the Ducati's controls. This would be his first kill if he aimed wrong. Suddenly, Asad's bike reared up and he fell to the ground. It was all Jaxxson could do to avoid being taken down in the process, like a Tour de France domino crash.

Jaxxson slowed his bike and circled back to find Ray and Interpol already standing over Asad, guns holstered. As Jaxxson reached them, he took in Asad's vacuous expression and the tell-tale smell of bitter almond—textbook signs of cyanide poisoning drilled into him at Quantico. He vowed this would be the first and only race he would ever lose.

Ray walked over to Jaxxson. "You did good, son. He gave up. He knew he was never going to make it."

CHAPTER 22

COOPER DELANEY
8:49 a.m.   Proteus, NYC

CHIMES FROM THE PLETHORA OF INCOMING EMAILS FILLED HIM with dread until her name caught his eye. An email from Mandolin under any other circumstance would have monopolized his day, but as he was discovering, romance was low on the to-do list of abductors.

He literally had eleven minutes before his test subjects arrived, and likely eleven seconds before his secretary Maggie paged him again. Kidnapping Will had been easier than organizing testing for these kids. He would have thought state-of-the-art facilities that brought to market thirty-plus new drugs a year would be available to him at a moment's notice, which was typically the case, but without Jon behind the scene clearing the way, it was next to impossible. He never fully appreciated how easy Jon had made his life, not till now, and he would likely never experience it again.

Focusing on the irrevocable disaster the relationship with his long-time mentor and friend had become would not serve him at this moment. If his accident had taught him anything, it was that falling down a rat hole of catastrophic thinking would get him nowhere. He believed this to be true for everyone. We all stand alone against our darkest thoughts; those who rise to the occasion believe, despite the reality of the situation. With the results of his test drug still haunting him, Cooper had no choice. He felt compelled to find the answer and knew these kids were at the root.

From the doorway, speaking in a deliberately over-exhausted tone, Maggie said, "I think we are ready." The strain of the last few hours had made this her worst morning ever. She had called in every favor she was owed to get the testing arranged, and the truth was she didn't know how long they had until Jon would shut them down.

She realized her days at Proteus were now numbered alongside Cooper's, but she had been looking after him for so long now that he was like a son to her. Cooper was lucky she had enough to retire on—more than enough. Shares in the company had tripled her annual wage for the past ten years. For her, it had never been about the money; she loved her job, and she genuinely loved Cooper. He was the son she'd never had, and she wouldn't leave him. Not like this.

Anxious parents wiped at little noses and tugged at little hands. The all-glass-everything foyer to the Upton wing looked like it had been invaded by an army of baby "Thing T. Things." The expression on the receptionist's face betrayed her, and anyone could guess she wouldn't have been surprised if the real Addams family showed up next.

The madness was not lost on Cooper, and once again a wave of panic at this surreal situation engulfed him. The realization that this was his own doing followed, and that come what may, he was going to have to see it through. He just hadn't prepared himself for the swarm that thirty participants and their angry parents created. Just as he stepped forward to introduce himself, Maggie stepped in and saved the day for the hundredth time.

"Moms, dads, or guardians and kids, if you could please follow me." Her assertive tone gave nothing away; no one would have guessed that a child had never set foot in this building and that the testing they were planning over the next few weeks was not only illegal and unethical but could potentially be shut down at any given moment.

"Please do not forget your waivers and be prepared to present your ID once we reach the seventh floor." Maggie led the group like a tiny drill sergeant toward the twenty-foot bank of elevators. The large doors opened, and the entire group was able to make their assent in just two of them. Cooper and Maggie exchanged looks of disbelief just before her group's door closed between. Standing alone in the lobby, Cooper knew he could never repay her, but he also knew that she knew it, too.

"So here we are, Dr. Delaney, at your disposal." Sarcasm dripped from Catherine's voice. Cooper was grateful that Will and Catherine had arrived after the group had already headed up to the test floor. Regardless of the obstacles this morning, they had still managed to pull it off. Maggie had been wise to orchestrate a staggered arrival of parents and kids first, and these two troublemakers afterward. At this moment, she was the best thing that had ever happened to Cooper.

"Excellent timing, my friends." Cooper turned toward them with his brightest smile. "Everyone is upstairs waiting for you. We are all very excited to begin."

Catherine's face soured as she glanced over at Will with a look that clearly said *I told you so.*

They rode up to the seventh floor in thick silence. Cooper had hit his stride and was already choreographing his entrance. Maggie would have these kids eating out of her hand. All he had to do was win over the parents. For the first time this morning, he was actually excited about the next two weeks of testing, if only Jon stayed out of his way.

"Good morning, everyone. Thank you so much for meeting us here today. My name is Dr. Cooper Delaney, and I will be the lead on our testing over the next two weeks. My colleague Maggie and her assistants Marcus and Rosemarie will be here to help every step of the way. We are very excited to be working with you and your children in this state-of-the-art facility to study a drug that has the potential to change their lives. We welcome your involvement and want you to know that you are invited to stay on location throughout the weeks to come. However, as mentioned in your overview material, we will require you to remain outside the drug administration and testing areas. Do you have any questions?"

"I want to know why this is necessary." The anger in Mrs. Pearson's voice rang through the near-empty test lobby. Her son, Bryce, had been involved in the test group since inception, and she was anxious to see some results from all the hours she had invested in this process. "Will and Catherine have been doing an excellent job, and I really don't see the need for this."

In a split second, Cooper decided to use Will and Catherine to diffuse the situation. "Yes, you are absolutely right. They have both done an excellent job.

Further testing is only required to confirm what they have already identified. Will, perhaps it is best if you explain?"

Cooper gestured for Will to take the floor, and despite Will's half smile, he managed to gain the group's confidence in under ten minutes. Perhaps there was more to Will than Cooper had given him credit for, which to this point, had been very little indeed.

Maggie led the extended group on a tour of the facilities, and as they made their way down the corridor, Cooper could hear them laughing in unison. He felt invincible. This was working out better than he could have hoped. As he headed to the elevator to retrieve the testing notes from his office, his phone went off.

It was a text, with an attached picture. "Do I have your attention now?"

The pictured showed perfectly naked, perfectly pedicured wet toes protruding from the rim of a modern, egg-shaped white tub. Mandolin had given up on a response from Cooper to confirm their meeting with Sasaki that night, and had resorted to male Morse code to get through to him.

"Yes, Mandolin, you definitely have my attention now," Cooper said out loud to the empty room. His role of abductor perfected, it crossed his mind that he should seriously consider a new victim.

CHAPTER 23

OPHELIA SASAKI
6:04 p.m.   Champagne Bar, The Plaza, NYC

THE TOURISTS CRISSCROSSED OUTSIDE THE STONE-FRAMED window, fighting to get ahead of one another. After a while, they seemed to become a single mass, just a blur of movement to Cooper's eyes as the dance continued. He had arrived on time, evidently expected to secure one of the few available tables, despite the fact that he was not, nor had he ever been, a guest at the hotel.

The issue of gaining entrance past the front guards without a room key and taking priority over the hordes of tourists would not have even crossed Mandolin's mind. She would simply use her press ID or flirt her way in. Cooper, on the other hand, was forced to attach himself to a group of young females returning from a shopping spree next door at Bergdorf's. They were only too happy to oblige, and all three accomplices now sat at the bar toasting him with the fresh drinks he had promised in return for their assistance smuggling him in the front entry.

She was late, as usual. In Cooper's experience, women used this stereotype to their advantage, and Mandolin Grace was no exception.

He didn't wait long. She entered the lobby with her Asian counterpart in tow. Ophelia Sasaki bridged the gap between research and runway. Her glossy jet-black hair paved an enticing strip between her porcelain shoulder blades.

Full lips defied an ultra-feminine nose and chin. The pair appeared to have come directly from a Testino shoot. Cooper stood up to welcome the duo, and looks of disappointment crossed the faces of his fellow male admirers.

"I see you have made a full recovery." Mandolin was unaccustomed to his full height. As much as the crutches had made him seem vulnerable, they had also disguised his true size. He now towered over her, despite four-inch Valentino heels.

"Dr. Ophelia Sasaki, this is Dr. Cooper Delaney. As I mentioned, Cooper has been testing a new drug, Noctural."

Mandolin had to fight the urge to roll her eyes as she watched Cooper take Ophelia's hand, setting out to seduce with an overwhelming smile and gesture that virtually lifted Ophelia into the seat beside him.

"So, how is it that a beautiful woman such as yourself feels she holds the key to uncovering why we are all on a crash course to destruction?" Cooper didn't waste any time, and he would soon discover the same was true of Ophelia.

"So, how is it that a pharma pirate would assume to denounce my findings?" The look on Ophelia's face seemed to depict disdain or annoyance or maybe both.

Mandolin bit her lip. She was pissed at Cooper. If Sasaki walked out on this meeting, she might never get a second chance, and both she and Jack were convinced Ophelia was critical to the story.

"Ophelia, please forgive me, I failed to properly warn you of Cooper's condition. A chronic case of Peter Griffin meets Casanova."

"Nonsense, I think the good doctor and I will get along famously." Her tone swung in an instant, and while Mandolin was relieved, she was not one to sit in the passenger seat. She would make sure she hung onto this interview tightly.

The hour passed as Mandolin took notes and the two doctors discussed the finer points of their respective research. At times, Mandolin was convinced they shared specifics on testing methodology more to impress than was actually required, and she became listless with the shop talk. It was time to reign in the conversation, which bordered on flirtation.

Surprisingly, it was Ophelia who led the way, with Cooper only too happy to oblige. Ophelia always seemed to give the impression that she knew something you didn't, just by the look on her face.

Cooper noticed Mandolin's unrest and took it upon himself to redirect the conversation. "Ophelia, I have to be honest, I do have one issue." He now had the attention of both women at the table. "If what you hypothesize is true, and instead of losing ground, we are actually only discarding traits unnecessary for our evolution, then why the stagnant IQ scores? Why are we not getting smarter?"

"What makes you think IQ scores will be the best measure of our future intelligence, Cooper?" The smile on Ophelia's face indicated that she was only too happy to defend herself. "Is it that difficult to imagine that we may have the potential to eclipse standardized testing? Is it impossible to fathom that we may evolve into beings more advanced than we are today?"

Mandolin's hair stood up on her arms, and she felt a chill as she recalled her disturbing discussion with Camberg. Her last comment, though seemingly benign, hit a little too close to home.

Ophelia continued. "A better question is why you believe your test drug is legitimate, despite all evidence that indicates otherwise." Her question hung in the air and Cooper was unable to mask his discomfort. He had no quick comeback.

They were two days into the two-week testing period, and there were no conclusive results at this point. They had run new blood work on each participant, to determine fresh baselines prior to drug administration, and were awaiting the report from the lab. As much as Cooper hated to admit it, he wished Jon was in his corner again; he realized just how much weight his boss's signature carried at Proteus.

He wrestled daily with the exact question Ophelia had posed. He felt desperate to be vindicated with the findings on these kids. The fact that he was holding them hostage for the next two weeks as his personal lab rats was not lost on him. He had spared no expense on their playroom on the seventh floor in an effort to make their downtime as enjoyable as possible. He really felt for them; these kids had been through enough.

He could only imagine how the cold, sterile testing facilities of the Upton wing translated in their young minds. Was it frightening or boring? Were they interested in the results at all or was this just more testing in addition to the two years they had already suffered? It was heartbreaking, but at the same time, he could think of no better way to prove his hypothesis.

He envied Sasaki; her data was solid. His was little more than a hunch, and he was running out of time. No one knew better than Cooper that this was his last chance. Should he fail, he would have nowhere to turn. There are moments in life that one finds themselves in the wrong place at the wrong time. In Cooper's case, it was ironic that, while he was busy lamenting the testing, he should have been back at the lab overseeing it.

Maggie's "assistants," Marcus and Rosemary, had graduated top of their class and were the latest acquisitions at Proteus. Cooper had the utmost faith in their attention to detail and knew from experience that they would be competing for not only his approval but that of Jon's. At their initial meeting, as they inspected the state-of-the-art facilities, they seemed like kids in the candy store. Rosemary was intense and super smart, but it was Marcus who stood out to him. He reminded Cooper a bit of himself, eager to win, and Cooper recalled falling into an easy banter with him the first time they'd met.

Taking blood from the kids had not been well received, by either the patients or the parents. Despite attempts to explain the absolute necessity for the blood work, it was a tough way to start on yet another round of testing with this group. Some made out better with the needle than others, but in the end, baseline samples were collected from all thirty participants. Rosemary and Marcus had insisted on logging the results personally. They both felt it imperative to oversee every aspect of the testing to ensure nothing was overlooked or compromised.

The necessity for the fresh baseline was twofold: to update the samples in order to identify any changes; and secondly, to increase the breadth of the testing. Cooper had wanted full genetic information on each participant. He believed the answer to the drug's failure would be uncovered with these kids, and he didn't want to leave any stone unturned.

The ladies continued their discussion as Cooper reflected on how things had been proceeding back at the lab. He didn't even notice Mandolin's disapproving looks at his inattention until after he disconnected from a phone call that he should have known better than to have made and returned to the table.

As he sat and stared off into the distance, sporting a satisfied smile on his face as he thought about everything he had just learned from Marcus at the lab, he was quickly brought back to reality.

"Cooper, did you hear me? We have to go."

Mandolin was annoyed that Cooper would return a call in the middle of their meeting, but it was beyond rude that he now sat staring into space. She chastised herself for being curious as to who it was that he had just ended a conversation with.

"So sorry, ladies, please accept my apologies. No rest for the wicked, I fear." This was the best Cooper could come up with in response to her attack.

"In my experience," Ophelia said, "the wicked have no need for it."

With this observation, or perhaps self-reflection, they all decided to end the meeting.

"Oh, I almost forgot," Ophelia added, in a voice dripping with sarcasm, "my good friend Malcolm asked me to discern if your accident had rendered you completely incapacitated, because he could think of no other reason that he would still be waiting on his sleep-test results."

Cooper figured the question was probably being quoted word for word, directly from the lips of Malcolm Schwartz. "Please tell Malcolm I will call him tomorrow."

Cooper rolled his eyes as he hugged the duo goodbye. He had no idea what to tell Malcolm, but now that he knew Sasaki and he were buddies, he would have to come up with something. He would have to come up with something fast.

CHAPTER 24

COOPER DELANEY
3:25 p.m. Clock Tower Condo, NYC

COOPER LOVED—GENUINELY LOVED—VERY FEW THINGS IN LIFE. He counted friends and family on one hand, and there was still a digit to spare for his coveted loft. It had come at a price, which quite literally included a war with the previous owners—a war he had refused to lose. Despite the victory, he always wondered if he actually loved the space on its own merit, or if the cost had been so dear that love was the only acceptable justification.

He leapt into his favorite Sunday spot, his black Eames lounge chair, and winced as his left leg met the ottoman. A few months had passed since his accident, but old habits were difficult to abandon and Cooper continued to jump in. He had opted for the classic/modern piece at the suggestion of Anna, the attractive sales rep at the modern SoHo boutique his buddy had recommended. Almost every time he sat in it, he recalled that she had helped him break in most of the furniture that graced his surroundings, pretty much all of which she had sold him. It seemed the perfect way to celebrate his purchase of the place. They had dated for a month or two after, which was long term for Cooper even now.

The thirty-foot ceilings and penthouse view ensured that he literally felt on top of the world most of the time. Unfortunately, he needed to come up with a story for Malcolm, and he debated telling him the truth. He wondered if Jon had already beaten him to it. It was unlikely though. Jon would protect himself; his reputation meant everything to him.

Cooper tried to envision enlisting the help of the scientist, but couldn't imagine holding onto the project once Malcolm was involved, especially when he discovered that his own test results proved the drug was ineffective. Convincing Malcolm that further testing on thirty minors was necessary bordered on ridiculous. Malcolm would never involve himself in something like this. Cooper could scarcely believe he was actually leading the project; it was absolutely surreal, and no legitimate researcher would ever participate. To be honest, he wouldn't blame them.

Why would Malcolm invest? How could he gain his trust and convince Malcolm to leave Jon in the dark? How could he involve him without sharing all the details? That was impossible. Malcolm was too smart and would ask too many questions, so what did he need to seduce him? What was his currency? What did the man who knew everything have to gain?

As if he'd answered his own question, it became obvious. Malcolm needed to know that there was something he didn't know. Cooper would lure him to the dark side one secret, one question at a time. Selfishly, he knew that having his help would be a great relief. Malcolm would lessen his burden.

The question of why the drug was inconsistent crippled Cooper. He had to admit that it was eating him up, day and night. If nothing else, with Malcolm involved, he would have company to go along with his self-inflicted misery. He just needed to play the man the right way, because if he fucked it up, he would never get a second chance, not like this.

It was well after noon, so he decided to pour himself three fingers of twenty-one-year-old Glenfiddich—his "go to" liquid courage. It would do the trick. Just one glass was all he needed. He had to stay sharp but be on the verge of not giving a shit. He rolled the scotch across his palate, respecting its complex flavor. The truth was that he did give a shit.

This was everything: his career, his reputation, his self-worth. His personal success or failure hinged on this gamble, on this drug, but he couldn't give that away. He had to be aloof, full of hubris, basically the Cooper that Malcolm would expect—the Cooper Malcolm had first met—even though that guy no longer existed. He was just a lie Cooper clung to.

Although he refused to let anyone know the truth, the accident had altered him from underneath, so much so that he salvaged his old skin only as camouflage to continue with research that was technically criminal.

He would lay the bricks carefully, one at a time. He would cut the conversation short and leave as much as he could undisclosed. He had to take care not to scare Malcolm away or send him running to Jon. That was the biggest issue: how to get him on board without Jon's support.

Cooper knew Jon wanted him gone and was already an unwilling participant at best. He knew that, at some point, he needed to free himself of Jon, but he wouldn't be able to do that without Malcolm. Cooper needed him on the inside when that day came.

When the cubes of ice sat on a paper-thin pool of amber at the bottom of his glass, Cooper knew it was time to make the call. He hadn't gotten to where he was today by hesitating, and he had to accept that he had very little to lose at this point. With Sasaki in the picture, it would only be a matter of time. She had basically called him out at the Plaza and, worse yet, he personally felt he owed Malcolm the results of his test.

"Yes?" Not much of a greeting from Malcolm. Cooper wasn't surprised and thought it could have been worse, given that his name would surely come up on Malcolm's display.

"Hello, Malcolm. It's Cooper. Let me apologize. I realize this call is long overdue." Cooper's palms were wet, and his heartrate accelerated, but he could feel the scotch warm in his chest and knew he had timed the call just right.

"Indeed, overdue is an understatement. However, I heard word of your misadventure, and given my continued loss of sleep and your calamity, I have had no choice but to exercise patience. God knows Jon is a vault when it comes to your wonder drug."

Cooper could see through Malcolm's sarcasm, and his resentment at being made to wait bled through the phone.

Cooper sank back in the chair and longed for another drink, letting dead air hang between them and trying to formulate a path forward, knowing that all cards were stacked against him.

"I'm waiting, Cooper. You do realize exactly how old I am, don't you? How little time I have for this red herring? How little time I have for you?" Malcolm's impatience grew. He was frustrated at being forced to fill in Cooper's deliberate silence.

"That is exactly what I am relying upon, Malcolm, your Pyrrhonism." Cooper became a diplomat. From abductor to diplomat in a three-day span. He had to say enough to pique the old man's interest while leaving out as much as possible.

"Let's get to the point here, Dr. Delaney. I want to know the results of my test, and beyond that, I have no time or inclination." Malcolm was beyond indignant. How difficult could this possibly be? There were two possible outcomes: the drug either worked or it didn't.

"Yes, Malcolm, I received your test results, and as you know, I expected them to be straightforward. However, an incongruity was identified, and I have initiated further testing."

"How is that possible without my involvement? What incongruity?"

Cooper smiled to himself. Perhaps this would be easier than he'd thought. "To be honest, Malcolm, I am all but convinced that you would not want to involve yourself in the second round. Besides, with all due respect, you are no longer an eligible candidate."

"What are you talking about? What are you hiding, son? Are you so arrogant that you won't accept that this one just doesn't work? Jon hired you, so you must have a basic grip on the science behind this drug. The absence of effectiveness does not constitute further testing at this point. I don't understand your insubordination, but from what Jon didn't say, I have deduced your days at Proteus are already numbered. That is what doesn't make sense to me. Someone like you will toe the company line no matter what, and yet here you are, against all better judgment and authority, committing career suicide. That is the real question, Cooper. Not why this drug is not working, but why you won't let it go."

Malcolm was genuinely bewildered as to why someone like Cooper, so self-absorbed, Jon's bright new star, would go to this extreme. Sasaki had been quick to inform him that she thought the drug was a bust based on her brief discussion with Cooper and his quick departure to call the lab even during their meeting. But to have Cooper of all people meeting with Sasaki in the first place didn't make any sense to Malcolm.

What was the connection there? She was too smart and knew too many people to agree to meet with him without some personal benefit, which was Malcolm's first question. The second was just as baffling: What did a pharma drug lord want with a scientist who had devoted her existence to the study of evolutionary mismatch? These were the real questions that kept Malcolm from hanging up the phone. It wasn't his first time at the rodeo and now, almost against his will, he and Cooper shared their first sentiment: Both had a hunch that there was something more to this.

While Malcolm continued to convince himself that he should stay involved, Ophelia was busy on her own, convincing her benefactor that time was running short, and they needed to ramp up the testing. Big pharma was now on their tail, potentially by coincidence, and as a result, they needed to complete the experiments that had been in the works for over twenty years, as quickly as possible.

CHAPTER 25

MANDOLIN GRACE
5:00 a.m. Central Park, NYC

A VEIL HUNG OVER CENTRAL PARK AT 5 A.M. THE FOG THAT accompanied Mandolin on her early morning run mirrored her unease with the investigation. She quickened her pace, deeply breathing in the scent of the damp leaves that clung to the branches. As she entered the tunnel, as always, there was a brief moment of panic before her eyes adjusted to the dark. She realized that running through the park in the early hours was a risk, but she loved the fresh chill and the stillness too much to give it up. Relieved to be alone, her mind drifted to the cello/violin duet that often played in the space during the day to take advantage of the acoustics. The echo was perfect, and it left goosebumps on her forearms every time.

As she exited the stone-lined passage, the fog enveloped her again. The embrace from her ghostly running partner reminded her that, if she wasn't careful, she would lose direction on this story. As a result, her mind turned to Jack.

Cooper was a poor substitute for her long-time friend and mentor. The meeting with Sasaki was a bust, in her opinion, and Cooper was to blame. Jack would have had Ophelia eating out of his palm, and at the same time, collected all the information they required to figure out exactly what role she played. As it stood, Mandolin had not even come away with the specifics of her knowledge of Irwin's work, or if she had even attended the press release, for that matter.

Perhaps it was foolish to expect that Cooper would know what to ask her from a reporting standpoint, but he actually got up and left the meeting to go make a call regarding his own testing, that was unforgiveable. It was now painfully obvious to Mandolin that she needed Jack more than ever. She needed him here with her.

Finishing the last fifty yards of her six-mile run, she took the front steps two at a time. She entered the brownstone, tossed her keys on the petrified wood that served as an entry table, unplugged her earphones, and almost said, *"Call Jack,"* before she realized he would be fast asleep on the West Coast.

She fought with herself. This wouldn't be the first time she'd called him in the middle of the night. He never seemed to mind the interruption, and on some level, it would punctuate the importance of the matter. As she stretched on the floor, she decided it was worth it and pressed her index finger purposefully into his name.

"Hello?" A bewildered, childlike greeting was the best he could muster. The fact that it was devoid of any irritation was all the encouragement Mandolin needed to fully extinguish his slumber.

"Jack, so sorry to wake you. You know I wouldn't do it if it wasn't important." Mandolin's velvety voice dripped across the continent.

"Of course, of course," Jack replied, barely above a whisper. He wasn't entirely sure if he was actually awake or dreaming.

"You know, I have to say, I wasn't sure I believed you, but now I owe you an apology. You were right about your buddy Cooper. He is an ass."

Jack was awake now, laughing out loud. A chance to bash Cooper was definitely worth getting out of bed for. What stunt had he pulled now? For a moment, he hesitated. If he had hurt Mandolin in any way, Jack would never forgive him.

As if she sensed his distress, Mandolin immediately set out to calm him, and laughed. "Now I understand why you never spoke to him for years, my friend. I am ready to do so myself."

"I take it the meeting with Sasaki did not go as planned?" Jack was now standing barefoot in the kitchen. making himself a coffee so he could continue with a more coherent conversation.

"I am afraid Cooper is too wrapped up in his own problems to help with mine." Mandolin heard herself and thought she had overdone it. She winced at the sound of the whine in her own voice.

"I see." He wondered what was really going on with his new/old best friend. He had been busy with his own research of Sasaki, and had almost asked Mandolin to call off the meeting. It was too early to tell, but now more than ever, he was convinced that she was key to their story. He just hadn't decided if she was friend or foe.

"Jack, would it be a terrible imposition to ask you to—"

"Yes, of course, no problem at all," Jack said, reading her mind. "I will make arrangements."

"You will stay with me, of course." She knew Jack's financial situation was tenuous and didn't want to put him out.

"If you insist, my dear," he replied. If nothing else, staying with Mandolin would put Cooper off his game. He had no desire to see him become Mandolin's plus one.

Jack hung up the phone after promising to forward his flight details so that she could pick him up from the airport.

Now his biggest concern was determining how to hide the truth from them both. Mandolin would never forgive him if she knew the jeopardy he had placed her in. It had been innocent at first, but now he had no excuse.

He wasn't sure how it had all started. Perhaps it was a slippery slope. Perhaps drinking and gambling are inevitable bedpartners. It seemed that the more Jack ran away from life, the more the worst parts of it followed him home. No one knew about his gambling addiction.

He shook his head as he closed his laptop, which displayed the results of his latest on-line binge. As if things weren't bad enough, he was now forced to take on the kind of work that would make him lose his career a second time.

Jack had stretched the elastic band from reporting to espionage until it was about to snap. He used his contacts and press authority to collect confidential information from underground sources that was then sold to individuals he knew little or nothing about. He had accepted the shady reality of his work; however, Mandolin's visit and his reunion with Cooper had breathed new life into him.

He was on the good guys' team. Jack believed he was critical to the story and was doing his best to be part of something bigger than himself, if for no other reason than Mandolin's safety. He just hadn't realized how far he had fallen and shuddered to think that he was now officially a criminal—shuddered to think of Mandolin's response if she found out. He considered turning himself in, but at the end of the day, he remained a coward and decided he would hide as long as he could. It was his way.

Heading off to New York would be timely. He could better manage damage control from there. If Jack had correctly anticipated his biggest client's true plans, it wouldn't be long until they suspected it. His boss was not to be underestimated. Jack had known that the first time they'd met. It had not been difficult to recognize a fellow genius, and on some level, Jack had welcomed the challenge, reassuring himself that what he didn't know couldn't hurt him.

He had come to terms with the fact that he could easily be in danger himself. Failing at a second career after he had already been forced to return home was too much for him. If his miserable life was on the line, so be it. The only thing he could not live with was if something happened to Mandolin. He had to do everything in his power to protect her, to get her a win with this story without putting her in harm's way, no matter the risk to himself.

CHAPTER 26

KHALID AL GAMDI

11:23 p.m. Madison Square Park Tower, NYC

THE ELEVATOR TO THE UNOFFICIAL PENTHOUSE COULD BE accessed by invitation only, via a password expiring in thirty-minute intervals. The prince's arrival back in NYC left his personal security with a steady stream of "guests," with the ratio of women to men at 4:1. His entourage would arrive much later, in the wee hours, to enjoy the after party. It was an orgy of sorts, or as close as the prince could come away from his Saudi home. He joked that it was his "American harem" and took great pride in how quickly it could all be organized, for just one night.

Khalid was deceptive. It was all in the eyes. His gaze was pensive and demure, devoid of the sinister thoughts in his head. His eyes alone generated irrefutable trust. Dismally, it was always misplaced. Khalid was personally capable of merciless torture, and prided himself on keeping abreast of the latest methodology.

Due to his station and endless funds, he frequently and literally got away with murder. All things being equal, the stars always seemed to align in his favor, and despite his advantages, he left one with the impression that he would have gotten away with his trespasses anyway.

He wore too much bling to be American and not enough calories or cologne; although no one around him was stupid enough to mention his gaucherie, however well intended. What he lacked in elegance, height, and charm, he made up for in looks. Khalid was a beautiful man; his looks transcended gender, as did his sexual preferences.

Khalid's existence revolved around the placation of his every whim, unless his desires were superseded by the demands of his father. His education, position, and fortune were all essentially out of his hands. The only thing he brought to the table independent of his family was his own ambition. Khalid had his own plans and was determined to make his mark on the future.

His father's legacy was tied to oil, and Khalid vowed he would propel the kingdom forward as a leader in alternative energy, now that fossil fuels posed nothing but financial risk as the world progressed to a low-carbon economy— or at least this was Khalid's point of view.

Over the past decade, he had personally raised a task force to uncover the most powerful alternative resources on the planet, and beyond. Khalid had successfully recruited some of the brightest minds in the field, and considered himself lucky that everything and everyone seemed to have their price. Working for him meant that you knew only what was required, no questions asked. Your paycheck reflected this expectation. Contributors signed off on all research and findings to be used at the prince's discretion, and only three individuals excluding himself had full access to the project. None were outside his family.

Khalid had been introduced to Jack through a mutual acquaintance from Jack's former life. Prior to the crash, they had partied together. Jack had impressed Khalid not only with his wit and long list of contacts but his capacity for drink. No one could keep up with him. Even now, it brought a smile to his face. Those were the good old days.

Khalid would never forget their first exchange. Even then, Jack was a portly fellow who reminded Khalid of an English professor as he delivered one humblebrag after another. Jack was an individual most people would have overlooked, if they did not closely follow the high-level conversations in which Jack would quietly correct even the most sapient among them.

He'd earned Khalid's respect and admiration since that first meeting, and Khalid had remained friendly with Jack despite his misfortune at being made scapegoat. He felt Jack was an easy target due to all the drinking and late nights. He also knew Jack's boss was afraid of him. They all were. Jack was just too damn smart.

Khalid knew he was getting close to something big, and it had been Jack's intel and advice that bolstered his position in the energy field. Khalid knew his endeavor was cutting edge; he just didn't know who the other players were going to be quite yet. He relied on Jack to make sure he was kept abreast of any new developments or competitors. Khalid was ruthless when it came to this venture, and he would remain on top at all cost—whatever it took to be first.

The night was young, and Khalid was in the mood to party. He wasn't ready to head back to his place quite yet, and wanted an update to put his mind at ease before committing himself to the evening. As he called Jack's cell, his monitoring app indicated that Jack was here in the city as well. Khalid didn't like surprises. He wanted to know where his employees were at any given moment and insisted that they use the cell provided to them exclusively, so that he was able to monitor every conversation: personal, professional, and everything in between.

"Jack, my friend," he said, when his call was answered, "you are here in the city with me! You should have let me know. No matter, you will join me tonight at my place. Will be like old times." Khalid could hear Jack coughing on the line; he had obviously been caught off guard. Khalid liked it this way. He always kept a step ahead, because he held all the cards.

"Yes, of course. I apologize. I received a tip last night that I felt I needed to investigate myself. No sense in harassing a prince without good reason. I am sure you agree?" Jack was back on his feet, despite the fact that all the hairs on his arms were standing on end.

"Good, good! We can catch up later then!" As Khalid hung up, his smile lingered on his lips. Jack always made Khalid laugh. He knew his place and had never let him down, although he had to wonder what had made Jack come all the way back to the Apple. Khalid knew Jack hated this place after everything that had gone down. What was important enough to get Jack on a plane last minute?

Khalid was intrigued. He'd thought he was the only one who could have convinced—nay, demanded—Jack fly back to Manhattan at a moment's notice. It had to be big. Khalid decided he would need to stay sober at least until this meeting with Jack was over, and he passed on the cocaine that had made its way to his lap—the limo was headed west toward his private club, his inner circle was anxious to start the night early.

Instead, Khalid reached for his laptop. He wanted to read through the latest report Jack had sent earlier in the week. It was a challenge to stay on top of someone like Jack—a challenge Khalid was always up for.

As Jack rode the elevator up to the penthouse, his heartrate accelerated. He knew Khalid was praetorian, but lately, he suspected much worse. He couldn't help but wonder (and worry) what employment by Khalid might mean for him.

The elevator opened to a scene only rivaled by Cirque du Soleil, albeit an X-rated version of the show. The penthouse stank of drugs, sex, and scandal. Khalid was notorious for his parties, and this one seemed to be in the running for first place.

He felt old as he made his way to the closest bar; it was difficult to take it all in. The variation in exposure, color, gender, and sexuality made sure Khalid adhered to equal opportunity guidelines; it was like the UN. Jack doubted any supermodel or superhero was absent tonight. There were no boundaries in Khalid's playpen.

As Jack stood at the bar waiting for his double martini, the nude trapeze artist caught his eye from above. Until she swung herself into a hands-only position, he hadn't been sure if she was male or female. He smiled to himself—only Khalid could get away with this.

"Jack! I have missed you, my friend." Obviously, Khalid had been watching him from the moment he stepped off the elevator. It unnerved Jack. He had dismissed it before, and only now did he truly acknowledge the extent of Khalid's surveillance.

Jack followed Khalid to his private quarters, which were anything but that. Khalid surrounded himself with an entourage at all times, as much for protection as for pleasure. An unimpeded demographic in various stages of undress massaged each other at numerous stations throughout the palatial master suite, while Khalid's security only had eyes for Jack. It was a like a sampler of live porn with an open invitation to all that passed by. In an attempt to stay focused, Jack kept talking until they reached their destination at the large banquet table in the back of the suite. He was surprised the table hadn't been claimed already, but it likely wouldn't be long once Khalid and Jack finished their meeting.

"I looked through your report from Monday, and I have to wonder what brought you to New York so quickly. Nothing you provided hinted at anything urgent." Khalid was not one to mince words or waste time. He liked to get to the point, and if he was honest with himself, he was ready to put this business behind him for the evening. The party had already begun.

"I heard it myself just last night, Khalid." Jack was grateful he'd kept a cell for private calls in addition to the phone Khalid required. A bead of sweat ran down Jack's cheek as he perused the room from the back table. The spectacle confirmed that he needed to protect Mandolin from this underworld. Protect her at all costs.

"You like what you see, my friend." Khalid laughed as he observed Jack taking in the show. "We will have fun tonight, Jack. I have something special for you." Khalid loved this game. Cat and mouse was good fun when you were cast as the feline in perpetuity.

Jack smiled. Khalid's parties were epic, and he would definitely stay, as much for his own protection as for the party. He needed to keep Khalid on-side. Never had he been more aware of the risk he was taking, or how he had inevitably become Khalid's spy.

"Let's put all this business behind us, Jack. What have you got for me?" Khalid was worried about Jack. Every time he saw him again, he seemed to have aged ten years and gained ten pounds.

"The murder of Camberg I reported on in Paris last week did not go unnoticed. The Feds discovered the body and participated in a car chase with a potential suspect. They are actively investigating the murder." As soon as the words left his lips, Jack was relieved. It was Khalid's turn to sweat.

"You are sure about this? One hundred percent?" Khalid was calm as he steadied himself; he wasn't about to give away anything to Jack.

"Khalid, it's my job to find out if it's true and make sure you are informed. As much as I hate to, I came down here in person. I needed to be positive." The look on Khalid's face let Jack know he agreed with his last-minute plans, and appreciated the heads up on this one. Jack also sensed something else there— something he would rather not know.

As Khalid sat back in the dining-room armchair, he stared deeply at Jack with a dark look Jack had never witnessed before. Jack could feel another bead of sweat escape his forehead and bleed a trail down his right cheek. Khalid leaned forward, pulling a tissue from his jacket and pressing it into Jack's damp palm.

"Thank you, my friend. That will be all. Please enjoy yourself. You have earned it. As I mentioned, I have a surprise for you."

As he dismissed Jack, Khalid made his way to the adjacent office with two guards, and a tall brunette immediately took his place.

If Jack had been less traumatized by the conversation, or less intoxicated by the double martinis, the fact that he was being sent a message may have crossed his mind. Instead, he just appreciated that the woman Khalid had arranged for him bore an uncanny resemblance to Mandolin.

True to his character, Jack decided at this moment that he would rather not think about it. He followed her to the penthouse dance floor. If he lowered his eyes and finished his fourth double martini, he could almost fool himself that it was Mandolin. Almost.

CHAPTER 27

MANDOLIN GRACE
3:45 p.m.   BG Restaurant, NYC

HE SMELLED HER FIRST. IT WAS ONLY FOR A MOMENT, BUT HER perfume was unmistakable, and he went weak just before her elbow locked with his. A hug from the side was all that was allowed, sandwiched between the mid-summer tourists on 5th Ave. Jack was disappointed. He felt robbed of her signature embrace, which was a ritual Mandolin seldom skipped.

The pair exchanged no words; he just smiled back at her as she led him to Bergdorf's for a drink and undoubtedly some sale she was dying to hit. They had shared many cocktails overlooking the park, and this trip back reminded him of better, safer days.

"I am so glad you came down, Jack." Mandolin broke his fixation on Khalid and the unsettling meeting at his party. Staying with Mandolin had been a wise decision. He'd forgotten the advantages of the time difference. Jack had been keeping up with existing work, starting new projects, and leading Mandolin through the maze that Human Pinnacle Theory had presented them. It seemed easy somehow. Everything seemed easier with her by his side.

Their drinks arrived, her Red Russian in true Canadian contrast to the white tablecloth. He smiled to himself; she was as far from Canadian as one could be. Jack tried to make himself comfortable in the gold French Canopy chair. He could not deny that it was definitely a tighter fit than last time, and the smile slowly left his face.

"During the interview," she said, "Sasaki brought up a mutual acquaintance with Cooper: Malcolm Schwartz. Have you heard of him?" With Jack here, she finally felt confident about the story, the direction she would take, and even her next steps with Cooper. All thanks to him.

"'Schwartz is the head of research at Genetech. Old fellow. I can only imagine they would be looking for a successor soon. It will be difficult for them though. He's an icon over there. Some people are irreplaceable, regardless of common sentiment." Jack's mind was racing behind his words, churning through everything he had ever heard or read about the man.

"What would the connection with Cooper be?" she asked. "It sounded like he was involved with the testing for your best friend's new drug. Is that typical? Why would genetic testing be required for a sleep aid?" Mandolin had overlooked this piece of information until she'd reviewed her dictation from the meeting. She'd made note of his name and then had forgotten to mention it to Jack until now.

"No idea," Jack replied, curious as well. "Did you ask Cooper?"

"No, I never got the chance. He and Ophelia were so wrapped up in outshining one another that, when it came time to leave, they were literally in a debate about the best way to hail a cab." It was obvious to Jack that Mandolin had presumably had enough of them both following the meeting.

Jack nodded, anxious to move the discussion away from his nemesis, Dr. Delaney. "So, how did you make out with Irwin? How did your meeting with Sean go?"

"Very well, actually." Mandolin smiled, remembering the exclusive she'd been granted by Sean. He had new research findings to divulge that had not been shared during his presentation, and had agreed to meet prior to its release so that she could break the story. Everything seemed to be falling into place.

"What did he have to say?" Jack was anxious to learn about Sean's update. Irwin had agreed to meet with her via Jack's connection to Barnett. Jack's drinking days still served him well.

"His latest discovery revolves around the evolution of the human brain. According to his findings, for the first two thirds of our human history, our brains were similar to apes', between 400 and 550 milliliters. During the final third, Homo erectus, 1.8 million years ago, had brains approximately 600 milliliters in size. The size of our brains continued to increase, reaching more than

1,000 milliliters by 500,000 years ago. In fact, early Homo sapiens' brains averaged 1,200 milliliters or more, the same as people today.

"Then, surprisingly, the past 10,000 years of human existence actually shrank our brains, potentially due to poor nutrition in newly developing agricultural populations. However, over the past hundred years, we have witnessed brain size rebound in industrial societies, as childhood nutrition has improved and disease has declined. But when we look closely at the last hundred years of the rebound, and once they are charted, we can witness a dramatic plateau, especially over the last twenty-five years, despite the fact that the majority of modern society has moved to better nutrition, even organic foods and more advanced disease prevention and regulation."

"Psychological research has also demonstrated that our reliance on smart phones and smart technology has dramatically decreased our interpersonal communication. Twenty years ago, an eighteen-year-old would have the same social insight and maturity as today's twenty-eight-year-old. Our dependency on technology has stunted our development by at least ten years."

Jack looked at her, intrigued at the direction the research was taking. "So, in essence, when you consider the environmental factors, it makes no sense that we should be experiencing a plateau."

"That's right," she said. "In fact, Irwin charts a dramatic jump in the last hundred years back to our early ancestral levels, and then a stagnant plateau, echoing the rest of his previously released findings."

Mandolin had never expected to hear herself reciting scientific facts regarding the evolution of the species. She could hardly believe that she was now recognized as *the* expert when it came to reporting on the subject. It was surreal to her, especially when she considered the implications of what Sean was potentially uncovering.

"His theory seems to be gaining momentum," Jack said. "He is definitely on the radar with all relevant players, from my sources." His mind uncomfortably drifted back to Khalid. He wondered if Irwin and the prince were acquainted.

"Indeed, I just question if we have reached out to *all* the relevant players?" Mandolin tried to keep her footing as this story gained momentum with every passing second.

"Trust me, love, we have covered all the bases. All the bases it would seem except one." Jack's eyes grew dark as he contemplated their next move.

"Who have we forgotten?" Mandolin asked.

"We haven't forgotten him exactly, we just haven't reached out to him yet. In fact, you were the one who mentioned him earlier." Jack hoped to bolster Mandolin's confidence. She would need it when he considered the list of experts they had collected to cover the story.

Mandolin was quick to pick up on his hint. "You think Malcolm Schwartz should be on our list?"

"Considering his connection to both Ophelia and Cooper, I think he should move to the top of the list. In fact, I don't think we should waste any time in reaching out to him." Jack smiled as a look of disbelief touched her features. He reached for the bill and waved the waitress over.

"Well, it's after five now, Jack. It will have to wait at least until tomorrow." Mandolin was reluctant to follow as Jack stood up to leave. She had ignored her drink almost entirely, too caught up in the story.

"Oh, I don't think a character like Dr. Schwartz keeps office hours. Shall we?" Jack held out an elbow to Mandolin, and they left, arm in arm, the same as they'd arrived.

CHAPTER 28

OPHELIA SASAKI
10:35 a.m.   The Essex, Lower East Side, NYC

ONE WAVE FELL INTO THE NEXT, BREAKING OVER THE FRAG-
ments of light the sun produced between each crest. A lone frigate
hovered overhead, creating a solid black puzzle piece that exposed the universe
against the milky blue haze of the evening sky. Its forked tail acted as a rudder,
a steering wheel perfected over 50 million years, equally as effective in air as in
water. Its bat-like presence was unsettling at fifteen feet above the ship deck.

From the starboard side, an orange-pink glow fused with blue, nature's
reminder of what male and female could be together but rarely are. All shades
of pink, all shades of blue, in a perfect harmony, creating an applause that lingered on the rippling waters as the sun took its final bow.

Ophelia's happy place was the Galapagos Islands. She went back in her head
to her many trips whenever time allowed, or on the rare occasion that the events
of the day required. She loved her job, and as a result, truly believed she had
never worked a day in her life. She had been lucky enough to follow her passion,
and life had finally rewarded her for being true to her heart.

So many years of gender dysphoria as a child and adolescent had left her with
forced introversion. Following through with gender-reassignment surgery, she
truly became who she'd always been meant to be, inside and out. And now she was
part of the most significant evolutionary research the planet might ever know.

Since meeting with Mandolin and Cooper, she had been drifting back and forth from her time on research vessels in the islands, and the reality of what she had uncovered, trying to weigh the implications of what Cooper had literally blundered into. She'd always known the day may potentially come, but now that it had, she found herself increasingly sensitive and secretive.

She wasn't ready to give up yet. They were so close. She found herself torn though, because for so long she had erected multiple layers to protect herself and the research, and now those layers could be allowed to gradually fall away. It was a relief, or at least it would be, provided her team agreed that they needed to go public. Advising them on the issues with Cooper's sleep aid had triggered an emergency within her group, and they were scheduled to meet this afternoon to determine the best path forward.

Coming clean with Malcolm had been a huge relief. She'd spent the better part of the day before locked in his office as he threw every question and argument that entered his magnificent mind at her. He refused to believe that what she told him could be true—refused to believe that everything he had ever learned about the origins of human existence was wrong.

The end of the day had left them both spent, him in disbelief and her defending what couldn't possibly be true but was. He reviewed her data multiple times, and spent nearly two hours at his Dino-Lite digital microscope, attempting to prove her sample a fraud, only to step back in awe that he was witnessing the genetic code of our hominid cousins, left behind millions of years ago. It was so beautifully perfect, the single strand of Z chromosome.

As she'd left for home, they had little to say. He'd looked as if his life had been stolen from him, literally wasted on work that had no significance by comparison. Ophelia had never witnessed that deep sadness on another person's face and instantly apologized. In response, he'd shaken his head and thanked her, despite the tears in his eyes. She had changed his life in one day, and was now on the verge of changing the lives of the rest of the planet's population.

She was not looking forward to the meeting. Ophelia had spent nearly twenty years working within Beagle, and now to see all they had built prematurely come to a close devastated her. She had protected the existence of the group, and the identity of its members, to her own detriment. She had turned down more offers from Malcolm than she could remember, for more money than she could possibly spend.

They were so close to cloning an original XYZ. Beagle had identified individuals that carried an evolved XYZ genetic makeup through a security measure implemented in 2016. It was quickly covered up, save the few individuals that had discovered the XYZ mutation. These scientists now made up Beagle, and its benefactors including representation at the highest levels of the FBI and CIA.

Tests on the XYZ population (which included only three subjects within the US) had been kept strictly confidential, and the breadth and depth of the testing had been controversial at best. However, even in her darkest moments, Ophelia still felt it was justified; after all, they were now on the verge of cloning one of our ancestors. The DNA provided all the required information to recreate the original hominid species on earth, instead of the mutation that current-day XYZ had become.

It was ironic and unkind that someone like Cooper would be able to unravel their carefully laid plans. Especially when the human race was positioned to gain so much from Beagle's progress.

Although limited compared to our super-race cousins, the XYZ mutations identified had the ability to organically capture energy, although they were all reluctant to exercise it and did so only under duress or perceived duress. They used what was identified as an "advanced environmental biology sequence," which is, in essence, how energy travels through an ecosystem. Their ability was not unlike how plants capture energy from sunlight (a star some 150 million kilometers away) and use it to convert carbon dioxide into glucose.

However, as may be expected by more intelligent species, and like our ancestors, XYZs were capable of converting, sharing, and controlling the waves of electrical activity produced in the brain. Millions of years of evolution allowed them to exploit the otherwise wasted energy in brain waves inherent in advanced biological organisms and maximize their collective society. No brain power was wasted.

It was standard, the way they responded. All XYZs were capable of capturing energy, and each identified potential sources identically, preferring subjects that were sleeping, as energy collection was easier and much faster for them. The collection process left no visible damage to the contributor; however, a mild level of fatigue could be observed, and over time, a consistent contributor's fatigue grew in correlation.

Prior to identifying the XYZs, the most relevant research at MIT had just begun to identify the cusp of this mass energy source, through brain-wave pattern research and theories on burst suppression. Our ancestors not only discovered the greatest source of biological energy; they harnessed it on a mass scale. However, when they found themselves fighting for survival, harvesting energy was not the foremost concern. They used their intelligence to predict the pending ELE and then devise a way to leave the planet before they were destroyed. Leaving behind the capsule was the only proof of their existence. Not unlike Darwin's belief that nature will find a way, these hominids became a small part of the few XYZ individuals that have been identified today.

It was literally a miracle that the capsule DNA made its way into our genetic code at all; and so it made sense that it was discovered to be more prevalent in the populations that greeted its entry to the surface, be they plants, sea life, or other mammals.

The identified XYZ subjects were also able to share information through thought, without the detection of any verbal cues, over thousands of kilometers. They were able to identify each other and communicate through the same advanced cognition, an elevated realization of brain-wave potential. The closest we had come to recreating this Vulcan mind meld were studies with one set of subjects in India, hooked up to impulse readings from an EEG used in conjunction with TMS (Transcranial Magnetic Stimulation) communication with subjects in France.

The mutated XYZ communication made these technological attempts appear childish, as they were able to share vast amounts of knowledge and achieve fluid communication, regardless of the distance between them. Ophelia believed that this type of advancement only scratched the surface, and that once Beagle was able to clone a true ancestor, they would witness advanced function of the species that could not be imagined.

She had been convinced when she witnessed the organic progression of the XYZs' abilities in the past two years, since testing began, and they had been introduced to each other. If it hadn't been the most exhilarating discovery of her career, it might have scared her.

CHAPTER 29

MJM (MANDOLIN/JACK/MALCOLM)
6:16 p.m. Genetech, NYC

THE ANTISEPTIC WHITE CORRIDORS THAT LED TO MALCOLM'S private lab stretched on forever, especially at Jack's overweight canter, his speedometer permanently set on zombie. A hint of an old-fashioned filled the air—the whiff of orange from the cleaning solution perhaps—and from Jack's perspective, all that was missing was the bourbon.

"I'm not sure this was a good idea, Jack. What if he's not even here?" Mandolin was losing her nerve. Getting past security had been an ordeal neither Jack nor Mandolin had anticipated, and they had handled it gracelessly thanks to their afternoon cocktails.

"We still carry the surprise advantage," Jack responded. "Fortunately, they couldn't reach the old man, but that doesn't mean he isn't rattling around in here somewhere."

"What if he refuses to talk to us?" Mandolin's faith in their plan dissipated more by the second.

"Oh, he will, love, not to worry about that." Jack had formulated a strategy to lure in Malcolm within the first fifteen minutes of their cab ride exiting Manhattan. Having Mandolin by his side allowed him to kill two birds with one stone. Besides the investigation, he could also advocate for himself as the hero in her mind, as long as all went as planned.

In Jack's experience, success was all in the posturing. More power lived in deliberate silence than the negotiation itself. Presence was everything, and if you could follow it up with smarts to match, you were almost always guaranteed the victor.

"I bet he's hiding, ensconced within his lair of evil genetic experiments. . . ."

Mandolin's laugh cut through the silence as they reached the end of the corridor, but was interrupted suddenly as the steel security latch on the door to Malcolm's private labs gave way to his disapproving glare.

Determined not to squander the opportunity, Jack held his ground, toe to toe with Malcolm's six-foot frame. They were well matched indeed. It was interesting to observe the recognition of an equal, through the eyes alone, even before one word was uttered by either side.

"Timing is everything, Malcolm, is it not? I apologize as ours could not be worse I am afraid. It is by chance that we still find you here." Jack bravely held out his hand to Malcolm, formalizing the introduction. Playing the intruder, Jack felt it was up to him to make amends. "Jack Christie, and this is my colleague, Mandolin Grace."

Malcolm shook their outstretched hands in turn, scowling through the ceremony of expected pleasantries, which as time passed, he had come to detest more and more. Malcolm had not left the lab since Ophelia's visit. Truth be told, he had sequestered himself, prostrating over the sample of XYZ she had deliberately left behind.

"I feel as if I am experiencing déjà vu. Once again cornered by a youngster with more cock than brains. Please accept my apologies, young lady. It is your misfortune to be caught up with the likes of this one, surely through no fault of your own."

Jack didn't miss a beat, "Yes, but the only difference is that Cooper Delaney, despite his credentials, has no concept of Methylation Analysis, the field you, sir, have essentially pioneered. Whereas, I've read everything you've published. Quite sincerely, it is truly an honor."

"Can you believe, they grew up together?" Mandolin felt compelled to contribute, hoping to eventually erase the look of dismay that would not leave the old man's face. At that moment, Malcolm looked very old, very old, and tired.

"Why don't the two of you get to the point? As you can see, I have very little time to waste." The words left Malcolm's lips as he comically gestured toward the sagging skin beneath his own eyes. XYZ coupled with insomnia had created two oversized purses beneath his bottom lids.

"Are you familiar with Sean Irwin's research and his introduction of Human Pinnacle Theory?" Jack was all too happy to propel the conversation forward. So far, so good.

"I have no time for random theories from a 'scientist' incapable of conducting his own research. It is modern-day philosophy, unsupported by primary research, and from my perspective, not worth a second thought."

"Ophelia Sasaki found it interesting enough to attend his recent conference," Mandolin said, putting him on the spot. "I understand you are close friends with Dr. Sasaki, and therefore your dismissal of the relevance surprises me." The Red Russian she had downed before leaving BGs had not quite worn off.

Jack could not suppress a smile; it made him proud that "hero of the day" was quickly morphing to "heroine."

Malcolm was not about to discuss Ophelia with the likes of these two, especially given their allegiance with the rogue Dr. Cooper Delaney. They would circle back to that one. However, he did have to admit he was curious as to how they were connected to Ophelia. As it turned out, he would not have to be curious for long.

The tapping of Ophelia's heels, as she raced toward them echoed like an AK-47 on the marble floor, turning their heads.

"Judging by the looks on your faces," Jack said, "I am left to assume that this is the esteemed Dr. Ophelia Sasaki." As the name left his lips, Ophelia gave him a firm handshake and an unwavering smile.

"Ophelia, this is my colleague Jack Christie," Mandolin offered.

Malcolm was not impressed with the company Ophelia was keeping. "So, the gang's all here. Dr. Sasaki, tell me you have something of greater importance to discuss than Human Pinnacle Theory."

"No, but I am tempted to speak to the media, so I will take this as a sign." Ophelia gestured toward Malcolm, indicating that he should lead them back to his office, and when he didn't move fast enough for her, she pushed past him to lead the way herself as soon as the security door opened.

Malcolm was privy to Beagle, not due to his direct involvement but thanks to Ophelia's full confession two days prior.

"They are shutting us down, Malcolm."

"Who is?"

"The FBI."

Jack and Mandolin's eyes widened in synchronicity.

"What does the FBI have to do with Beagle?" Malcolm wasn't quite following, and her outrage made it all the more trying.

"They were the ones who identified the first XYZs, as a security measure. They're our founders essentially, if you can believe it." Ophelia visibly shook as she answered Malcolm with contempt, as if the situation was somehow his fault.

Malcolm frowned. "But Beagle is funded autonomously and comprised solely of members of the scientific community. I am sure this is beyond the scope or interest of the FBI. It makes no—"

"The FBI classifies us as a security risk. They are treating this like the fucking *X-Files!* Like we are dealing with aliens here. It is absolutely ridiculous. The world has a right to know."

"A right to know what?" Mandolin could no longer hold her tongue.

Ophelia and Malcolm shared a silent moment while they tried to determine what to reveal and what to leave out without a word between them. In that moment, both wished they were capable of the telepathic abilities of their XYZ cousins.

Jack, on the other hand, knew exactly what they were talking about, and tried his best to prevent fear from taking over his face.

CHAPTER 30

JON CAMERON
5:18 p.m.   Proteus, NYC

HE HATED THE RIDICULOUS MOTIVATIONAL QUOTES PEOPLE PUT at the bottom of their email signatures. Worse were the ones he received as unsolicited attachments from acquaintances he was unable to avoid. Board of directors' wives, their children, or, worst of all, their personal trainers. They were like that poster with the kitten clinging from a wire with the caption "Hang in there!" Useless fodder designed to help people who were beyond help. He had yet to find an algorithm capable of filtering them directly to junk mail. Whenever he didn't respond, they all seemed to invent an alternate address to deploy them from. Today was no exception:

"We shall not cease from exploration. And the end of all our exploring will be to arrive where we started and know the place for the first time."

T.S. Eliot

Despite his contempt for the onslaught of inspiration, he was not immune to the irony of this quote, especially with the lab results from the blood sample of XYZ resting on his desk.

"He's here, boss!" Daphne interrupted Jon's thoughts to alert him that Khalid had just arrived.

"Give me ten minutes. I need a drink." Jon could avoid Khalid no more than he could the infuriating quotations. When it came to Khalid, the status quo was never an option. He decided upon liquid courage in lieu of a clear head. What did it matter at this point anyway?

With Cooper having gone rogue, Jon had been forced to keep tabs on him through his network of internal spies. He was averse to conducting business this way, but after all, that's exactly what it was: business. Cooper put far too much faith in the new hot shots he had recruited. His inexperience and arrogance allowed him to place more weight on their credentials than their egos. The error on the bloodwork was no error at all, as it turned out. Cooper was just too caught up personally conducting the research to be running through the results himself, and had missed out on the most important finding—something vastly more significant than Noctural.

Jon had met Khalid years ago. Proteus had been in need of a cash injection from alternative investors due to the Wall Street crash. The funding for drug companies never dried up, but at the time, Jon had a number of cutting-edge projects nearing market entry that he could not afford to put on hold until the banks were clear. Khalid had ultimately come to his rescue, but not without a price. A "long range" plan was how Khalid referred to their partnership. Now looking back, Jon regretted both the decision and their alliance. Few people scared Jon, but Khalid was one of them.

There was not a pie Khalid did not have his fingers in. He bought his way into the highest circles of global influence. Pharmaceuticals was just one of his many "passions," or so he called his numerous ventures. What Jon had failed to delve into at the time was that these investments were not random; they were all deliberate, one tied strategically to the next. It was a web of sorts that Jon was now tied up in—a struggle to escape the proverbial spider only made it worse.

Khalid was not concerned about legalities and always seemed able to bypass regulations, one way or another. His army of contacts was able to push through his projects at a staggering pace, which frequently left Jon at his mercy. It was impossible for Jon to deny him. There was no FDA to blame or red tape to hide behind.

Their latest project kept Jon up at night. Until now, they had been testing the drug on animals only, but due to their success with PirB suppression, Khalid was undoubtedly here to push for human subjects in the next round of trials.

They had gone as far as to identify that the suppression of LilB3-5 proteins could create the required neuroplasticity in the human brain needed to reorganize the neuropathways responsible for learning a new function. In this case, communication from one mind to another.

In addition to the inevitable pressure Khalid was about to invoke, Jon now sat with a test proving the existence of the genetic mutation that may have inspired Khalid's insistence on this project in the first place. Jon was 100 percent positive that, if he asked Khalid about XYZ, he would push back in his chair as he had done many, many times before (with a knowing grin on his face) and indicate Jon fill him in.

Khalid's intention was not for Jon to educate him but for him to confess just how much he knew on the subject in order to determine if Jon's knowledge was an asset or a threat. Jon had learned to wait in anticipation until the die was cast whenever having acquired some threatening intel by accident. Oftentimes, it altered not only the projects themselves but the very foundation of his alliance with Khalid. He had tried withholding information to avoid this scenario in the past only once, and the result was adverse enough for Jon to discard it as a future option.

The time had come. Jon's glass sat almost empty, his massive pivot door unable to shield him from what waited on the other side. One last sip and the music would start to play.

They both processed at Coltrane pace and quickly fell in line, thrashing at their own version of Giant Steps. Khalid gave Jon the lead on sax, and Jon, by nature, was only too happy to oblige. When in reality, Khalid on the bass line was in the driver's seat, and when he picked up tempo, Jon had no choice but to follow his lead. So was their relationship: a balance so fragile that one missed note at breakneck speed would overturn the ride—a ride Jon was unable (and Khalid unwilling) to get off.

Daphne led the prince in, and the room did little to absorb his presence. Kahlid filled the space, and in spite of Jon's height and stature, he had no choice but to acknowledge his ubiquity. Only the three sheep seemed unperturbed by Kahlid's presence, as they stood ominously beside the office door.

"So, what do you have for me, my friend?" Khalid led the conversation, as he always did, his own glass of scotch in hand thanks to Daphne's suggestion and her endless legs. "It has been too long."

Jon could feel the sweat run down his ribs from his right armpit as Khalid slammed his now-empty glass on the XYZ results folder, which was luckily closed. Thank God he had kept his suit jacket on. It was Jon's only armor against Khalid, and he prayed it would not let him down.

He decided at the last minute to cover Khalid's favorite riff and slowly sat down in his chair, allowing silence to envelop them both.

Khalid immediately recognized the maneuver and chuckled as he raised his eyebrows and took his seat. Always the guest chair on the right, the one closest to the door. Khalid was always ready for a hasty exit, should the occasion demand it.

"It's never been about what I have for you, my friend," Jon said. "Tell me 'our' next move. You've seen the results. The balls in your court, as usual."

Jon had made a gutsy decision against his better judgement. He had no choice but to try to protect Cooper, as much as he hated the little fuck right now.

After Khalid had revealed years ago that he, or rather his father, had attempted to lure Malcolm to the dark side, Jon had no choice but to protect both Cooper and (more importantly) Malcolm as best he could. Khalid's father had run the show back in the day. If Khalid had been at the helm, he would have found his own way to convince the old man. Jon had no doubt.

Jon could only imagine the lengths to which Khalid would go once he found out what Jon was hiding. He needed more time. His mind raced through the potential scenarios, the players involved, and the impact on science, society . . . everything the world believed about our existence and how we came to be.

Jon was admittedly no saint, but instinctively he knew that, if the XYZ test subject fell into Khalid's hands, they would be exploited in the worst possible way. His thoughts turned to Will, and his instinct was to shelter the closest thing he had to a brother from this as well. After all, these were Will's kids. This Noctural testing fiasco could not have been worse.

Jon had no choice but to buy some more time. Hopefully, Khalid would not uncover the truth for the time being. It was a gutsy move, and not one for amateurs, but Jon was no rookie and a gambler by nature. His head told him to run, but his heart was doing the bidding this time, so he picked up his sax and started to blow a diversion so sweet it would satisfy even Khalid.

CHAPTER 31

COOPER DELANEY
10:14 a.m.   Upton Wing, Proteus, NYC

"WHAT IS WRONG WITH YOU?" FIONA XAVIER BERATED HER only son, Albert, for the fourth time in the last twenty minutes. Her shrill voice pierced the crowded room. She made no effort to disguise her lack of etiquette or equanimity. She was oblivious to her impact on the child, even though it was painful for everyone else to endure.

Cooper turned toward the boy in disbelief and shook his head. A few parents who noticed his expression were caught off-guard, surprised at his candid disapproval, when in fact what they had witnessed was Cooper's reaction to the discovery that little Albie was XYZ.

He oscillated between being furious with his own careless behavior and his temptation to have Marcus fired for incompetence for how the child's gene coding had been handled; he should have trusted no one.

During his meeting with Ophelia and Mandolin at the Plaza, when he'd stepped away to call the lab, he'd learned that no gene coding had been done for "Subject 17," Albert Xavier. That had since been corrected . . . and Cooper found himself in shock.

He tried to wrap his head around all the implications of their findings, and didn't even know where to start. *He's XYZ? How is that even . . .* Cooper's next thought made his blood run cold: *What if someone else knows? Does Will know? Does Jon?*

This was well beyond his area of expertise; he was testing a sleep aid, for Christ's sake! Testing a sleep aid on on a child that should not exist. It was maddening and mind-blowing all at the same time. His pulse raced as he tried to determine his next move. Who could he trust with this? Who could he turn to? The only relevant individual he could come up with was Mandolin's source: Ophelia Sasaki. This was her world, but he couldn't go to her without revealing their illegal testing on minors.

He shook his head and laughed. The only other choice was Malcolm Schwartz. Malcolm knew everything. Cooper ran his hands through his hair. This just got better and better. He had come full circle. Malcolm, who'd gotten him into this whole mess with his incurable insomnia, would be the best choice to help him out.

Cooper failed to take in the incredulous expressions of the parents who had drawn their own conclusions regarding his seemingly exaggerated response to Fiona's parenting. He walked straight past her as he fled the room, unaffected by her murderous look.

He made the drive over to Genetech in forty-four minutes, at 165 mph, a new record. It felt good to push the Porsche. The car had been built for speed, after all. The classic turbo's spartan controls had no option for self-drive. Cooper felt in control—at least of his ride.

It seemed like déjà vu as he marched down the corridor to Malcolm's office, much as he had done prior to the accident. The difference was that he had been confident at that time, convinced the sleep aid was not the problem. Now he walked on with the realization that he was only at the precipice. Noctural was an adumbration of what he was truly meant to discover.

When releasing a new drug to market, above all other considerations reigns the simple truth that timing is everything. Cooper had learned to navigate the waters not with a schedule but with intuition. He could sense when he should deliver relevant information regarding his latest drug and when to hold back. Often the decision would be made without any forethought, because he was forced to protect a new release from more and more advanced and unforeseen maneuvers from the competition.

Cooper had this same feeling as he rounded the corner after crossing through Malcolm's private-wing security doors, only to find that the old man was not alone. He had the advantage of seeing them first, huddled over some test results—results that were apparently of great importance judging by the animation of their discussion. Cooper knew he had but a moment to decide on his play.

Since his entrance had gone unnoticed, he took full advantage of the element of surprise. "This is a first for me. I don't remember ever having to crash a party. Here I find the A-team, already assembled." What surprised him was not the scared look on Mandolin and Malcolm's faces but the flicker of it on Jack's.

"Cooper!" started Ophelia. "So great to see you again. What brings you to us?" She had the most to lose, and the consequence of her leaking this information, or it getting into the wrong hands, was just beginning to take hold of her despite her initial bravado.

"Malcolm is my patient, as you know, and I am particularly good at making house calls when required." Cooper allowed his glance to travel over her midriff all the way to the length of her toes.

Ophelia's stoic expression in response to his flirtation surprised him. It was unlike her not to play along.

Malcolm grimaced. "Really, boy, leaving pill tower must be difficult for you, but there really was no need." He hoped to deflect Cooper's obvious annoyance at being left out.

He had to give the old man kudos, but the weariness behind his eyes was not lost on Cooper, despite Malcolm's attempt at sarcasm.

Cooper glanced over at Mandolin and shook his head. ". . . and I thought we had something special, but here you are secretly meeting up with my old pal behind my back. Just like old times, Jack."

The history they shared resurfaced. It was near impossible to keep secrets from someone who was in large part the reason Cooper had become what he was. Someone who, during his formative years, had more influence over him than his own parents. Someone who, at the time, knew him better than he knew himself.

With that, Cooper assumed the conspirators were all on defense. He came by his monikers honestly, and was pleased with the overall success of his entrance. Now the real fun could begin.

Turning to Sasaki with his most heartfelt smile, he pressed on. "Now how about you tell me a bit more about your work, doctor. I feel that I have let my good friends here down, as I have obviously done a very poor job of vetting you on their behalf. You are assumedly on the brink of something of great importance to involve Malcolm the Great and the press, to boot."

Ophelia took a step back and glanced toward the table the four had been huddled over. Her voice was calm and convincing, as she strung together a plausible excuse as to why she'd required Malcolm's assistance, but her story started to unravel as soon as it came time to explain Mandolin and Jack.

As her voice trailed off under Cooper's intense glare, it was Jack who put an end to her torment, "Ophelia, there really is no point. He already knows . . ."

CHAPTER 32

JACK CHRISTIE

5:18 p.m. Belle Southern BBQ, NYC

SWEET REBA WAS HIS FAVORITE BBQ SAUCE, EXCLUSIVE TO HIS favorite southern restaurant. She had seen him through many a bad day, and this one was no exception. He licked his fingers one by one, a methodical practice, one that briefly soothed the turmoil of his troubled thoughts. If Jack was going to keep this from Khalid, he would have to be strategic and plan every move step by step. Staying ahead of Khalid was admittedly an impossible task.

Unfortunately, it was one he had no choice not only to entertain but also to carry out—especially now that Mandolin was involved.

"It looks as if you are in need of a salubrious distraction, my friend." Cooper's teasing words came from behind Jack's chair as he entered the restaurant.

"If it is salubrious, how on earth could it be distracting?" Jack smiled widely to his childhood friend, but it did not reach his eyes, which did not go unnoticed by Cooper. Cooper had adopted a heightened sense of awareness since his visit to Malcolm's lab the night before. Discovering that he was the odd man out, and that XYZ had already been discovered, was enough to catapult him into survival mode. He took nothing for granted now, but desperately tried to maintain his signature swagger in order to disguise his mistrust.

"So, what is our next move, Jack? Apparently, you hold all the cards." Cooper's scathing tone was softened with a smirk.

"Yes, yes, all the cards and all the chicken, as it would seem. Help me out with this?" Jack hoped to win an accomplice to his feast and dampen his own guilt at attempting to digest away his woes.

Cooper helped himself to a leg, and the two ended the meal both licking their fingers, just as they had so many times, so many years before.

"Now, with a full belly, perhaps you can fill me in on the details surrounding your big story." Cooper wasn't keen to waste any more time.

"No, no, how about you go first, Coop? Our beans were spilled last night." Jack was also reluctant to waste time. He needed to get out of NYC. He felt safer on his own island.

"A highbrow description of an alternative to man showing up in today's DNA is hardly a full confession, my friend. What you four revealed was comparable to discovering Neanderthal procreated with us humans today. You and I both know that there is a lot more to this, and I'm not leaving until you spill it all." Cooper was not about to relinquish his advantage at discovering their conspiracy.

Jack on the other hand longed for a drink. Hiding information from Cooper was proving to be even more difficult than hiding it from Khalid.

"You remember our discussion on the island, regarding Dr. Irwin's address? His introduction of Human Pinnacle Theory?" Jack was reluctant to fill Cooper in entirely, but it had nothing to do with keeping him in the dark, and everything to do with protecting him.

"Vaguely." Cooper wanted to get through this quickly. He needed to find out all he could in order to redirect his research back at the lab, specifically his testing on Albert.

"Essentially, Irwin revealed a stagnation in our evolution: physical, mental, studies on birth rate, cell count, etc. He offers the facts but no leads on cause. Chances are he's onto something, because the room is packed full of every field and representation from most countries, including the FBI. Mandolin steps into the spotlight, something I regret to this day, and I am left no choice but to assist behind the scenes, given the circumstances. Thanks to her being the front runner on the story, she receives an invitation to meet with a source immediately following the conference.

"A physicist by the name of Dr. Armand Price contacts her directly. The guy is a leader in his field, studies alternative energy. Only it's not Armand Price.

His colleague, Peter Camberg, using Armand's identity, shows up instead. He is hell bent on meeting with Mandolin, convinced he has discovered the reason we are all doomed. Now the guy's credentials check out. He did work with Price but was forced out due to his heretic notions." Jack needed to stop for a breath. He took a sip of his water, wishing it was anything but.

"Go on. You have my attention. I can't imagine that physicists would be capable of inventing heretic notions." Cooper was intrigued but didn't trust Jack; he didn't trust anyone now.

"Fair enough, but Price doesn't focus on the typical alternative energy sources. He has discovered, and is beginning to harvest, what is referred to as intelligent energy. In a nut-shell, according to Camberg, given the appropriate advanced technology, one can harvest the caloric output of our brains while we sleep and convert it into usable, bankable energy—energy that would otherwise remain with the host."

Jack's voice continued its crescendo as his speech became more and more pressured without his even realizing it. "You see, Coop? This *is* the answer to Irwin's observations; we have stopped evolving or stopped getting 'better' as a species because each and every one of us is chronically losing varying degrees of energy!" Jack was on a roll, and his boyhood friend had not missed a word.

"OK, cutting edge, I agree. But hardly crazy." Cooper wasn't letting Jack off the hook without a fight.

"That is where Camberg takes a leap. He believes that we are not the first to discover intelligent energy. According to Camberg, not only has it already been discovered but it is already being put to use." Jack waved the waitress over. The water was just not going to cut it.

"I'll have one myself." Cooper was not typically a scotch man at midday, but if Jack needed one, he assumed he could benefit from the same.

They took a break to check their phones. Then the waitress returned with their drinks.

Scotch in hand, Jack continued, "What I am about to tell you is in no way an opinion I share. I describe it as heretic, because in all likelihood, it is just that. It seemed very important to Peter Camberg that Mandolin should be aware of his theory: that intelligent energy was being used on a mass scale outside any jurisdiction."

"So, what does that mean? The Russians?" Cooper's impatience was growing.

"Outside *all* jurisdictions. In other words, from beyond the planet." After the words left his mouth, Jack immediately finished the last of his drink.

Cooper barely swallowed his sip of the scotch. "So . . . . aliens? Or perhaps the Avengers? Cartoon characters? Are you hearing yourself? Why are you even telling me this?" Cooper was furious; his reaction mirrored Mandolin's during her meeting with Camberg.

"Camberg was murdered in Paris a week ago, despite the FBI following hot on his tail. Price is under their protective custody, and the IP address of any Google search related to intelligent energy goes directly to their watch list. I don't subscribe to this any more than you do, my friend, but I have beat this path long enough to know that something is up. Where there is this much smoke, there is undoubtedly fire."

Jack felt a surge of relief at having gotten this out of the way. It was a comfort to share this burden with Cooper, who ultimately had ended up being the stronger (if not the smarter) of the pair.

Cooper had a million questions running through his head. "I don't understand. I—"

"Now you know everything I do, my friend," Jack interrupted. "Draw your own conclusions. Grapple with your own existence. Fancy yourself the star of a sci-fi flick. It's up to you. The one thing I will say is that looking at Ophelia's work last night makes me wonder. It makes me think twice. Now, how about you tell me why you of all people are already versed on the existence of XYZ?"

It was Cooper's turn to finish his drink. "I wouldn't have believed it, but I discovered one in my test group. I thought it was a lab error, but I retested it myself. I retested so many times I was creating suspicion. One of my participants—a child, for God's sake—doesn't have 'normal' human DNA. One of them is XYZ."

Cooper's eyes met Jack's. Not even the scotch could dampen the blow. They had laid it all on the table, and the whole situation was much more than either of them could have ever imagined. Maybe as a movie or a game they would have invented as kids, but not some prophecy delivered by a crazy man that was slowly becoming reality. Cooper's one comfort was that he believed he had Jack back onside. They would face this together, whatever that meant. No longer would he be the one left out.

However, it was a false sense of security. Perhaps it was too much to take in all at once. It was not Cooper's nature to stay on defense. He needed to take the lead. It was his need for control, or order, or the desire for things to be as they had always been between him and Jack that allowed him to accept Jack's omission of the full truth. Jack would never tell him everything. Cooper could never know everything Jack knew. Cooper's life depended on it.

CHAPTER 33

THE A TEAM

10:14 a.m.   Upton Wing, Proteus, NYC

"CATHERINE, THIS IS NOT AN OPTION. IT'S AN ORDER." Cooper had no idea how Will could have worked with this woman for so many years. She was like a bull in a china shop, completely unmanageable when it came to these kids. He applauded her commitment but was ultimately annoyed. It went beyond reason.

"I don't believe these results at all. What you have provided us here is impossible, and you know it. This is absurd, Cooper! How in the world did you come up with something so ridiculous? As if we are going to allow you to embark on some mad-scientist experimentation with Albert! You know I was against this from the start, but now it has gone from illegal to dangerous, and there is no way I am going to stand by—"

"Catherine!" It was Will's turn to interrupt her. "I ran through the results myself! I took more blood. They are accurate. Cooper is not making this up."

Cooper nodded at Will, thanking him in silence before continuing. "As I mentioned, the previous test parameters will terminate immediately, and we will refocus our study on Albert exclusively. In order not to draw suspicion, we will retain all participants but will reframe our testing to show the impact of the sleep aid as a long-term study on all other participants. With any luck, this will buy us time to learn as much as we can about XYZ. Ophelia Sasaki will be joining our team and will oversee all tests administered to Albert."

"Why are you doing this? You don't care about this child, Cooper! We need to report this to the authorities. Withholding information? Performing our own tests? We will all end up in prison!" Catherine felt that she was the only sane individual in the room.

Ophelia interjected abruptly, "Catherine, I am the most qualified to take this forward. If we did go to the appropriate authorities, I would undoubtedly be contacted. What we are all trying to avoid is this information getting into the wrong hands. Especially now that a child is involved. My research is being shut down and taken over by the FBI as we speak. We have no idea why or what they plan to do with the results, but I am sure you agree that it is no place for a child. Please believe me when I say that I am your best and only option at the moment."

"You are as crazy as Delaney. You just want to get your hands on poor Albie to keep your Frankenstein research going! You are here because they are shutting you down. Have you known about this the entire time, Cooper? Is this why you did this to us in the first place? There must be a lot of money in this for Proteus, I'm guessing." Catherine would no longer be silenced and continued with her rant on Cooper and Ophelia in equal parts.

"Catherine, really? Why would I want anything to do with this? Please tell me how in the world shutting down testing on a drug that has been three years in the making is lucrative to me? How could this discovery possibly be lucrative to a pharmaceutical company? The only reason I am involved is because there was no logical explanation why the sleep aid wasn't working. As it turns out, and trust me when I say this, because no one wants to believe this less than I do, perhaps, just maybe, it is not working for a reason completely outside our existing framework."

Cooper was at his wit's end. He was just about to tell her to pack her things when she slowly reached for the arms of her chair and slid carefully to her seat. Hands covered her eyes, she started weeping. She had finally started to accept what all of them had been trying to digest in the past twenty-four hours.

"I am sorry, Catherine," Cooper said gently. "This is a lot for all of us to take in. I need you to keep in mind that strict confidentiality is paramount, as it always has been, given the involvement with minors and now the sensitive nature of our findings." Cooper knelt down at her chair and took her hand. He had to try to keep her with him, especially witnessing her display of instability regarding these kids. He could not risk her turning on him.

She nodded in agreement, finally coming to the realization that she could do more to protect Albert by remaining part of this craziness than by bolting.

Ophelia looked over at Catherine. She needed her onside. It was clear these children trusted, and in some cases probably even loved, her. "You need to imagine what life has been like for Albie," she told her. "How alone he must feel. We have also tested his mother and know that she is not XYZ. It is impossible for her to fully support his development. As you know, the identity of his father is unknown. How frightened Albert must be, developing abilities that no one can understand, let alone believe. Catherine, it is a gift that this has happened. I can help him. I am the only one who can. I have an understanding of his capabilities, albeit only a small one, from years of research with other XYZs. At the very least, I can help him feel normal. Not so alone."

Catherine hid her dislike for Ophelia. They'd met for the first time yesterday, and her opinion only seemed to get worse with every passing minute in her presence.

"Thank you, Ophelia," Cooper said, taking a deep breath before continuing. "I think we can all agree that Albert will benefit from your involvement. As discussed and agreed, we will not make any unilateral decisions regarding Albert's testing. We will take it day by day and will make adjustments when required. We also need to remain cognizant that the FBI is not only aware of XYZs but have also shut down Ophelia's testing for their own reasons. It is vitally important to find out as much as possible about the scope of Albert's abilities and how they reflect the research Ophelia has already conducted.

"It is paramount that our research goes undiscovered, not only for the child's benefit and safety but for our own." Cooper felt more at ease now that it appeared everyone was onside. If anyone would have suggested a week ago that he would essentially abandon his research on Noctural, he would have laughed in their face. Everything was upended and surreal. He loathed this feeling of having no control.

"So, there is only one last unanswered question, Cooper." Will's interruption was unexpected and all heads turned in his direction simultaneously. "How long do you think we can keep this from Jon?"

CHAPTER 34

RAY GARLAND
Saratoga Avenue, Brooklyn, NY

KHALID AL GAMDI
Madison Square Park Tower, NYC

6:20 a.m.

Ray hit the snooze button one last time. It was going to be a three-snooze Monday.

6:20 a.m.

Pigeons scavenged the edible remains of last night's debauchery on Khalid's penthouse patio.

8:53 a.m.

He was going to have to respond to the kid at some point. Since Paris, he had been bombarded with emails from jaxxsonc2030@hero.com

Ray had to admit he would have been fucked without him that day, but Carl had yet to decide how to proceed. Carl knew Ray preferred to work alone, but if he thought Ray was in danger, he wouldn't budge. Sometimes Ray wondered if he was as important to Carl as Carl was to him.

8:53 a.m.

The only downside of a weekend-long party were the randoms that didn't know when to leave. Khalid hated waking up to lurking strangers. Especially the bitches.

He tossed a rainbow-colored thong across the room. It had been resting on the pillow beside him and was consequently the first thing he'd seen that morning. He needed to find his phone. This was a crazy week, and he was now regretting the night/nights before.

10:11 a.m.

"We have a new lead." Carl wasn't one to waste time.

"You mean in addition to the XYZ patients we have identified and placed in protective custody?" Ray asked, looking at Carl in disbelief.

The case seemed to be moving at hyper-speed. Ray would have never believed this folklore would become reality and completely monopolize his time.

Carl nodded. "Yep, well, leads, actually. We have identified a coalition, so to speak. It's a mixed bag that seems to have stumbled onto this."

He started flipping through pictures on his desk. "You may remember Mandolin Grace, from the Irwin's presentation." Carl slid the enlarged photos across the table for Ray to peruse.

This was not common practice; everything was digital now. The bureau had done away with hard-copy photos years ago, but Carl and Ray kept what they could alive; It gave them a sliver of the old ways—a time when things were less complicated.

"Who are the others?" Carl took in the surveillance photos Ray slid across the table to him in turn.

"The other female is Dr. Ophelia Sasaki. We currently have her under twenty-four-hour surveillance. She

10:11 a.m.

"WHAT DO YOU MEAN YOU DIDN'T GET TO THEM?"

Khalid screamed into the phone at Omar. It seemed that he was being punished for his weekend of overindulgence in more ways than one. Just when the painkillers began to numb his hangover, the pain of incompetence was there to take its place.

"I can't believe you let the Feds get to the XYZ patients and shut down the research, and you still haven't brought me Sasaki. Now it's probably too late, and she is right in this very city, is she not?"

Khalid was furious. He'd had full understanding that this was all a go. Had he thought otherwise for a second, he would have put everything else aside. He made a mental note that Salim would take over immediately.

"I tried to meet with you last night, Khalid. I really tried," Omar pleaded with him.

Khalid had to give him that. He had been pestering him for hours, but somehow the festivities had taken hold of him, or maybe it was the drugs or that rainbow thong.

"It is more complicated than we originally thought, and you need to know that it's not just Sasaki and has been studying the XYZ patients for years. She likely knows more about our XYZ group than anyone else on the planet."

Carl sat back in his chair, and Ray followed suit. This case just kept escalating.

"I guess I have my work cut out for me" Ray was still in disbelief.

"Not just you, my friend," was Carl's pointed reply.

So much for ignoring Jaxxson's emails. This day was just getting better and better.

1:36 p.m.

Ray hated the afternoons. He would get a second wind in the evening, but afternoons sucked. He felt like a nap, especially after the Philly cheesesteaks he and Carl had just consumed.

Jaxxson, eager as ever, was on his way down so that they could formulate a plan together.

In the meantime, Ray argued with Carl, unable to believe that a couple of scientists and reporters could possibly be a threat.

Ray had to believe that their time could be better spent doing anything other than focusing on a few talking heads and bookworms.

They agreed to disagree, and Ray had to admit that it was all moving

Malcolm now." He just did not get paid enough for this.

"What do you mean it's more complicated now? I thought we had everything we needed with Sasaki, that she was the key. You said it would be easy to get her onside, especially now that they shut down her research, despite old-man Schwartz." Khalid's head started to throb again.

"It may still be, Khalid. There are just more people involved now. I knew you would want to make the call." He sent the pics on his phone to Khalid.

1:36 p.m.

Khalid needed to eat. On Mondays, he favored tradition, and as such, Bamonte's. He loved Italian and would pretend he was a Soprano for a few hours.

Khalid made his way to the master closet, followed closely by his footman. Khalid never really selected anything but was always presented two outfit options. It always left him slightly insulted, but had been the custom since he could remember. It was the way one treated a child. No matter, he had more important things on his mind than which Stuart Hughes to wear.

Khalid grabbed his case and made his way toward the entry. Upon approaching the penthouse elevator, he noticed faster than either one of them were comfortable with.

It looked like the fat one would be the next target. He was an interesting guy, from what Carl revealed. Ray felt sorry for him.

From what Ray could tell though, trouble just had a way of finding the guy.

3:13 p.m.

"I don't think we should waste any time. Based on what you have told me, and the way this case is moving, we are going to end up with another Paris on our hands," Jaxxson said.

Ray had to admit he agreed with the kid. He even reminded Ray a little bit of himself at that age. He wasn't one to let someone else take the lead. Ray wanted to see what Jaxxson would come up with. To be honest, he couldn't have said it better himself.

Ray looked over at the kid, "So what are you waiting for? Dial the number."

that rainbow-thong's owner was still milling about the foyer, despite the concierge's attempts to encourage a cooperative exit. He almost asked her to leave himself but then reconsidered.

After what he was about to put in play, a temporary diversion might be just the thing he needed. Khalid waved his hand, and instantly a smile spread across her face, both understanding that she would not be leaving anytime soon.

3:13 p.m.

"It was perfect as always," Khalid told the server.

He always sat at the same table. He liked to be able to see the kitchen. It reassured him somehow that he was the one in control.

Khalid picked up his phone and made a quick call, one he hoped would confirm that everything was as it should be.

"Jamal! Hey! Is the flight booked? Good. How about the crew for the seaplane? Excellent. Yes, he will be there. I am about to call him right now."

"UNKNOWN NUMBER" FILLED THE SCREEN ON JACK'S MOBILE. HE knew better than to pick it up. It did pique his curiosity though, given everything that was going on and all the players involved, and he almost answered it on the last ring, but stopped himself.

He wasn't left wondering who the mystery caller might have been for long. The next name to pop up was Khalid's. Unfortunately, it was impossible to ignore that one.

CHAPTER 35

JACK CHRISTIE

2:23 p.m.   Vancouver Harbour Flight Centre, Vancouver, BC

THE SHAKEN SCREECH OF THE PLANE ENGINE MADE HIM DEAF to the discussion between the Saudis. In all his time on the coast, he had never bothered with harbor planes. He really hated to fly.

It was Khalid who had insisted that he share a ride with his Saudi associates on his private jet from NYC, as he had "business" for them to take care of in Vancouver. He had apparently been pursuing an unnamed alliance with the Chinese for years and thought that a visit in person might just be the trick. Or at least that is what he said—one never knew for sure with Khalid.

What Jack found odd was his fleet of aircraft. It wasn't that Khalid wouldn't have a plane or two, of course. He owned a fleet of luxury cars, for sure, and Jack had never witnessed him in the same vehicle more than once. It just surprised him that a seaplane would be in the repertoire. He could not imagine the island would hold any appeal to his boss. The bottle of scotch they had shared on the flight from NYC was still running through his veins. It teased a smile from his lips as he contemplated the possibility that perhaps the seaplane was just for him—perhaps he was the main attraction.

Jack had answered Khalid's call with all the confidence he could muster; he had to stay in the driver's seat if he was going to shelter Mandolin and Cooper until they could figure out their next move. They had agreed with Ophelia's suggestion that all XYZ identified needed to be contacted. She was already reaching out to her remote participants, despite the fact that her group had been dismantled, and in doing so, she would be considered a felon.

The resident grey cloud that followed Jack was slowly turning black. He always seemed to attract trouble, no matter how hard he tried to escape it, but this bordered on ridiculous. If someone had told him a year ago that he would be discovering aliens and running with the Saudis, he would have laughed in their face. What would anyone want with a used-up Wall-Street-bum-cum-small-town journalist?

The scotch was making him sleepy. It was a quick jaunt across the Strait, forty minutes max, but his eyes felt heavy, and he let them close for a moment as he sank back in his seat. They would reach the inner harbor soon. It couldn't be more than ten or fifteen minutes.

The Saudis were arguing about something loud enough to convince Jack that he should open his scotch-heavy lids. At first, he couldn't believe what he was seeing. The pilot was forcing his assumed co-pilot into the driver's seat at gun point. Jack was instantly sober.

His blood ran cold, and he shuddered as he shook his head, unwilling to believe what was happening. He had been grievously correct; this plane had been for him all along. Jack wondered what offense this other guy was guilty of, but it looked like they were both about to pay for it. No one fucked with Khalid.

The poor guy was apparently begging for his life as the tears coursed down his face. Jack could feel the plane start its descent toward the inner harbor and knew he had only minutes to make his move.

He reached to unlatch his seatbelt only to find that it had been disabled. Apparently, it was a disabled seatbelt epidemic in the small plane, as the co-pilot was attempting to crawl out of his own belt, which was cinched tightly across his chest and waist, despite the gun pointed at his head.

Satisfied that the belts would hold their victims in place, the pilot finished putting on his black wingsuit and opened the door of the plane. The wind whipped in through the open door and drowned the screams of the co-pilot—Jack assumed that his screaming continued as he still flailed helplessly in his seat trying to free himself.

Had Jack been sober, he might have found it odd that the seatbelt was a perfect fit for him when he'd taken his assigned seat. He usually struggled with them due to his size, but not this time.

The pilot made one last trip to the controls, ensuring the plane would nose over as planned. Jack couldn't help thinking that this was not the first time the "pilot" had landed this way.

Jack called out to him, yelling above the noise of the open door. His words were his only hope: "I never got a chance to tell Khalid about the trials! There is so much he doesn't know! He needs to be careful—"

"No, my friend, *you* need to be careful." The grin that spread across the pilot's weathered face let Jack know there was no getting out of this one. He tasted the scotch-infused bile at the back of his throat. This would be his last trip home.

The pilot waved to Jack as he made his way toward the side door. He tucked into a ball as he left the craft and extended his suit only once his body had dropped below the side of the plane.

Jack looked over at the co-pilot sitting in the driver's seat, recipient of an undesired promotion. He seemed to have given up now and accepted his fate. Jack had accepted his long ago, even wished for it. Now staring death in the face, it wasn't fear that gripped him but regret. He had played his hand all wrong and now, as the shadows were approaching and the plane came down hard toward the inner harbor, he wished he had a second chance.

He reached into his bag for one last pull from the bottle Khalid had insisted he take. Now he knew why. The last thing he saw was the familiar war memorial that graced the inner harbor: "The Homecoming."

The little girl with outstretched arms running toward her father reminded him of Mandolin. Who would protect her now?

CHAPTER 36

MANDOLIN GRACE
7:07 p.m.   Lenox Hill, NYC

IT CALMED HER TO WATCH THE BLOOD RUN THE LENGTH OF HER arm, deep burgundy against stark white. She had started cutting to deal with the pressures of dance and had been constantly soaking her blood from her garments in her teens—underwear from runaway periods and dance-shrug sweaters from the cuts on her forearms

Today, this ugly act of self-offence, resurrected from days gone by, was a repeat of feeling out of control, of not knowing how to move forward or what would come next. Without Jack, she felt lost, helpless, and scared. The pain gave relief from the dread that welled up against her abdomen, then her rib cage, threatening to snuff out her very breath.

Mandolin had never fully acknowledged how profound Jack's guidance and protection had been. Perhaps that would have been too harrowing to admit, even to herself. In some ways, you are only as strong as the people you surround yourself with; without Jack, she lost her strength.

She had given up on responding to the myriad calls, texts, and emails following the confirmation of Jack's "accident." She didn't want to continue without him, not at all, and she instinctively withdrew from the situation to the only place she felt safe.

She had become intimately acquainted with her en suite bathroom over the past twenty-four hours, especially with the tile floor. It was her room of choice, the room best equipped to accommodate the vomit and blood. She knew every wave in the grey and white Carrara squares. She had even begun to identify faces and figures in the patterns, which seemed to be succumbing to its waves— an apropos reflection of her own footing in this instant nightmare.

She did not consider that her escape would be unacceptable. Mandolin had always been able to hide until the next rehearsal. However, too much was at stake now for the prima ballerina to go missing at all. Had the opportunity presented itself, to willingly accept the demands that had attached themselves to her as a result of her choice to head up this story, she would have opted out.

It was her most significant lifelong regret that Jack was no longer here because of her—that by asking for his help with the story, she was responsible for the death of the person she needed and relied upon most.

Lost in grief and terror, Mandolin gave little thought to the response her colleagues would have to Jack's death. Her self-extrication was in some ways selfish. Entitlement underlying the extent of her reaction to being abandoned by Jack, only to be reminded in the end that it had been her fault, all along, that he was involved in the first place.

It came in waves: guilt, then disbelief mixed with denial, and back to guilt. It was this pattern of cyclical thinking that kept her on the floor, unwilling to make the decision to get up. Going underground was the exact opposite of how Cooper chose to deal with the news.

"What did you do?" The accusation came from the open doorway leading to her en suite. At first, Cooper thought he was witnessing a suicide attempt, only to be relieved by the dried blood outlining the fresh cuts.

The shock Mandolin felt was chased with humiliation. Cooper was the last person she wanted to witness her in this state. It was all happening too fast for her to comprehend. Their relationship was filled with flirtation and sarcasm. She was not prepared to face this true vulnerability with him—now only anger would allow her to cling to what little dignity she felt she had left.

"You can't do this, Mandolin; we need you. You owe it to Jack to stay strong through this. I need you."

She couldn't see his expression through her own tears. If she had, she may have pushed him away. His words spoke to her heart and the guilt she felt in

Jack's death, but his motivation was selfish on multiple levels, and it showed in his eyes.

The sex was little more than a handshake. A new pact formed, an alliance of sorts. Without Jack, they had little choice. Her tears fused with his sweat as they consummated their bond. It was a momentary escape for them both from the horror of losing Jack. Jack's death had robbed them of any romance they might have shared; their love was frantic and demanding.

Lost in the moment, Cooper's pressing grip caused Mandolin's fresh wounds to open anew, and her blood painted the white sheets like a canvas. He looked into her eyes with a combination of pity and desire. In response, she traced the stretch of hair from his stomach down, until desire won. Everything swirled around them, like two feathers in a cyclone. If they didn't hold fast to each other, it threatened to destroy them entirely.

His breath was uneven as he slept beside her. The smell of sweat and blood still lingered in the air. She never predicted things would happen this way. Tears threatened to fall once more, but she fought them back. Cooper made a poor substitute for Jack. She allowed herself to imagine what it would have been like to be lying next to Jack this way instead—something she had never dreamt while it was still possible. She could still hear his voice in her head.

He was telling her not to give up, to take center stage, to perform despite the pain. She looked down at her blood-striped forearm and decided she had to be strong for Jack. He wasn't here to guide her in person, but she knew that if she could get to his place and find out what happened to him, she would have her next lead.

CHAPTER 37

MANDOLIN & OPHELIA
6:49 a.m.   Blue Fox Café, Victoria, BC

THE COLD EGG WHITES RESTED ON A SWEATY PLATE. THEY GLIS-
tened like a plastic chew toy made dirty by the freshly ground pepper.
Mandolin lost her appetite for what seemed like the hundredth time since
Jack's death.

"Love, please eat something," Ophelia scolded her from across the table.
They made an odd couple, herself and Ophelia. Somehow Jack's absence
weighed even more heavily in his hometown.

"You should have stayed in the lab," replied Mandolin. Ophelia had been
able to connect with several of the XYZ patients outside NA from her trials and
was in the process of flying them to NYC via the FBI.

"Until they are with us, there isn't much I can do anyway. To be honest, I
think you need me here more than they do back at the lab." Ophelia was unde-
terred and apparently oblivious to Cooper and Mandolin's affair. She continued to flirt with him at every opportunity. Mandolin was grateful that he had
decided to stay behind and oversee the testing. Having him here with her, when
she should have been with Jack, seemed too much to bear.

Back at home, Cooper had moved Albert to the safety of Malcolm's private
labs undetected. The Noctural testing continued under Will and Catherine.
Marcus, Rosemary, and the rest of the testing staff were none the wiser. All of

them had been told Albert had taken a turn for the worse and that he needed individual attention in order to recover before he could return as a participant. The fewer individuals who knew the truth, the better.

Working with the FBI had been a reluctant partnership. Upon discovery that Jack's apartment had been all but destroyed following his accident, the authorities began investigating his death as a homicide. All his belongings had now been confiscated, and the FBI, working with the local police, controlled access to his place. They were always a step ahead, and they wanted all the information, unwilling to share even the slightest details in return.

Ray had been alerted to Mandolin's arrival in Victoria and made sure that security was tight at Jack's apartment. The only secret they kept from Ray was little Albert, and they were fighting hard to keep it that way. They felt it was best to leave any connection to Proteus out of the equation.

Mandolin rolled her eyes. It was suffocating being "babysat" by Ophelia, and she contemplated confiding to her that she and Cooper were together.

She decided against it. "Let's go back to the hotel. I'm feeling tired." The truth was that she had made arrangements to visit Jack's mom. She wasn't looking forward to it but felt that she had to follow through. The last person she wanted with her was Ophelia.

"Mrs. Christie, I am so sorry."

Tears filled the older women's eyes upon seeing Mandolin. Jack and his mother had been very close, and she knew exactly how much Mandolin meant to him.

In homage to days gone by, they sat down to afternoon tea, both in disbelief that Jack was gone, never mind that his death was now a potential homicide. It was big news to a city the size of Victoria, especially given that Jack was a prominent member of the press himself.

"I just can't believe this is happening. It seems so unfair, especially after all he had been through. I just wish I could have helped him or been more aware of how volatile his life had become. So many times, I wanted to save him from himself." Alicia's grief threatened to overtake her. It was as if Mandolin had opened a floodgate.

"I wish I could have saved him too. I was hoping to find something to give us some answers as to what happened, but as you know, we can't get near his apartment." Mandolin felt her words were hollow, but she wanted Alicia to know that she was trying to help as much as she could.

Alicia curled a shaky hand into a fist, then slowly brought it to rest under her chin and lower lip. She sniffed loudly, making a conscious decision to finish her tears. As she wiped them away, she replied, "You just reminded me of something."

Mandolin followed Alicia down the steep original 1920s stairs to their unfinished basement. She led Mandolin to a makeshift office, complete with antique desk and chair, covered in cobwebs and dust. The only item that had escaped their embrace of neglect was a shoebox placed deliberately in the corner.

"The FBI has been relentless with their questions, firing them at me, one after another. They actually made me feel guilty when here I am the one suffering. In all their visits, frightening me half to death, I completely forgot to mention that Jack had left this here a couple of weeks ago. I fear that even you would have come and gone, but when you mentioned going by his apartment, it reminded me to give this to you.

"I shouldn't have peeked, but inside there is an envelope with your name on it. When Jack brought this down here, he seemed off somehow. I know he was worried I would misplace it, so he brought it down here for safekeeping. I rarely come down here; you can see for yourself how creepy it is." Alicia started to smile, but then it morphed into sobs. The poor woman could barely hold herself together.

"Thank you, Alicia." Mandolin took the box from her failing grasp and removed the lid.

There were a number of invoices, a notebook, and, just as his mother had promised, an envelope resting on top with Mandolin's name written square in the middle, in Jack's familiar cursive. Seeing his writing made Mandolin want to weep as well, but she held back the tears and replaced the lid.

"What do you think it is?" Alicia asked, recovering slightly from her despair.

"I don't feel I can open it now. I hope you understand." Mandolin feigned (sort of) her own set of oncoming tears, knowing that the less this poor woman knew, the better it would be. Hopefully, the FBI would leave her alone with her grief, and hopefully Alicia would forget to mention the box to them again.

"May I use your washroom before I go?" Mandolin was absolutely dying to tear apart the box and find what Jack had left her from beyond the grave.

"Of course. To the left, dear." Alicia gestured toward the washroom.

As soon as Mandolin closed the door, she ripped open the envelope to find a letter outlining bank information, a safety deposit box number, as well as the key, from the First National Bank of New York. What in the world would she find there? She flushed the unused toilet and washed her clean hands whispering under her breath, "Jack, what did you do?"

"Will you be back for the memorial service, dear?" Alicia asked with genuine hope in her eyes.

A hundred thoughts collected at once in Mandolin's head, but the memorial service was the furthest thing from her churning mind.

When she didn't answer right away, Alicia sensed her dismay and filled in the gap. "All in good time, sweetheart! It was so nice to meet you, Mandolin. Oh, and please don't worry, I won't mention a thing about the box to the Feds."

She'd decided to let Mandolin in on her little secret. The apple never falls far from the tree.

CHAPTER 38

ALBERT XAVIER
10:14 a.m. Malcolm's private labs, Genetech NYC

A LONE ON THE PRIMARY-COLORED CARPET, ALBERT BUILT A castle with every woodgrain block he could find. He was methodical, incorporating every piece of the same block family, and appeared to deliberately exclude those from other collections. It was like he was separating Play-Doh after someone else had mixed the colors together—or he was until confronted with Malcolm's attempt to join him, whereby he immediately welcomed the old man's participation, and happily expanded his newly erected castle to include every shape, size, and color.

Malcolm made every attempt to ensure that little Albert did not feel like the prisoner he had become. He spared no expense in transforming the testing space of his sterile private labs into a legitimate daycare. Years of honing a gruff, secretive demeanor had paid off; his success at eluding prying eyes at Genetech had been easier than anticipated. No one was the wiser. It was just Malcolm being Malcolm.

Ophelia had been right. Malcolm now realized how important it was to allow Albert his play time. The progress they had made over the past week had been astounding. Ophelia was shocked herself. Her years of testing adult participants were insignificant to what she had been able to learn from this child.

Devoid of inhibitions and naïve to the adult expectations of what was considered normal, Albert had progressed such that it made a profound impact on

Ophelia's findings in just one short week. The FBI had sequestered all XYZ participants from her previous research; they were now all under FBI protection and brought to the US for further investigation. All save one.

Ophelia's work had steadily spilled into her private life, until the difference had become undetectable. She made herself available to participants 24/7 and had studied every detail of their lives. For the most part, she knew them at least as well as they knew themselves, in some cases more so.

As a result, when it had come time to release her participant list to the FBI, she immediately omitted one name: Jasper Moseley. Jasper was the younger sibling to Aaron Moseley, the twenty-second participant to join the group. Evidence of Jasper being XYZ was still in process; she had not yet received his karyotype when the group had been ordered dismantled by the FBI. However, being suspicious of a positive outcome, she destroyed his file and cancelled further testing to ensure he remain anonymous. Fortunately, for them both, she was correct.

Communication with Jasper had become almost impossible, as the FBI had full access to her phone, apartment, and whereabouts. However, Malcolm's private labs guaranteed privacy and allowed her full access to Jasper, the only other known XYZ outside FBI surveillance.

Over the past week, Albert's testing had revealed astonishing results. Mistaken for ADHD, his lack of attention was not a result of his poor ability to concentrate but instead had been caused by the constant interruption of mind-to-mind transmission put out by his fellow XYZs. Albert had been experiencing a constant stream of incoming messages since birth. Within the last three days, with Ophelia's assistance, he and Jasper were now able to pick up each other's thoughts, devoid the use of language or gestures, from Malcolm's lab to Jasper's flat in the UK, thousands of miles away.

Jasper was relieved to have escaped custody, based on the descriptions from his brother and the rest of the participant group who had become family to him. Jasper and his brother could have been twins. In fact, many of the XYZs had similar features: fair to light brown hair; typically blue or green, wide-set eyes; and sun-shy complexions. Most of them wore ear plugs both day and night, because their hearing was so sensitive.

Jasper was a typical student in second year of university. Popular with his friends, he liked to party, but his grades told another story. Jasper was right at the top of his class. He was considered gifted based on his excellent grades; however, his professors had no idea his "gift" amounted to undetectable access to his classes' notes, whenever he wanted, wherever they may be.

Albert and Jasper were also able to communicate with the rest of Ophelia's group, without any known human sensory or physical interaction. While she and Malcolm had yet to decide if they should encourage the boys to reach out to their counterparts, the fact that they could keep tabs on the FBI's moves through this unique XYZ characteristic was invaluable.

However, eight-year-olds have their limits, and Albert was no exception. Being anchored to an EEG for hours a day and hiding out in Malcolm's lab was not ideal by anyone's standards. Being asked questions and being made to respond to cues correctly, every time, soon became intolerable to the young boy. So he made up a game.

Albert and Jasper soon realized they could send thoughts faster than the EEG could track them. Consequently, in between the sequence of tasks administered by either Malcolm or Ophelia, they would play their own version of "I spy." It was through this game that Albert learned he could see, through Jasper's eyes, the surroundings of his flat, and identify the winning object as if he had been in the very room himself.

Had Malcolm and Ophelia been aware of this fact, it would have had a cataclysmic impact on the two scientists. But Jasper recognized the boy's need for a break from all the testing, and for young Albert, who was just beginning to realize how different he was, it didn't seem particularly strange to play "I spy" using someone else's eyes, thousands of miles away.

CHAPTER 39

PASCALE LAURENT

6:38 a.m.   Auteuil-Neuilly-Passy, Paris

A WHITE ADMIRAL SLOWLY OPENED AND CLOSED ITS WINGS. Fused to the window pane, it was only missing the interlocking double Cs of a Chanel label: black, followed by a strip of white lace, then black again at the tips. Its elegant flutter occurred in slow motion. The butterfly's long tongue tasted the glass, curious about the woman's face just inches away.

Pascale had been lost in thought at her breakfast table. Her raisin fingers gripped her used coffee spoon as an infant would a new toy, while she stared out the window, studying the butterfly who belonged to her beautiful Parisian garden below. Her offensive attention to detail had rewarded her with an oasis featured by many journals and outdoor living blogs. Every moment she could spare, she invested in its ongoing metamorphosis.

She had been appropriately surprised to be contacted by Tomas, the society's current president, who had served on its board for the past twelve years. He had been pivotal in establishing sleep medicine as an acknowledged specialty and was well respected in the field. This had not been an area Pascale had previously encountered. Up until his call, she had not even realized the European Sleep Research Society existed. If there was one thing she had always been good at, it was sleeping. She supposed it would have been anomalous to have previously crossed paths with him professionally. Why would she, as director general of the European Space Agency, have any connection to his society?

Pascale had been groomed in the early days of her career to one day take over her current role, as head of the ESA. She had been meticulously prepared for a deluge of problems to solve across the many disciplines in numerous countries she oversaw. Never once had she encountered or even anticipated a problem for which she had no reference or guidelines to follow. It scared her; she wasn't even sure who she should engage.

Pascale had been a star in what had been, at the time, an unconventional, almost impossible field for women. Had it not been for the recommendations of her vigilant instructors, who literally fought for her entry into the academy, she would have undoubtedly failed. She owed them everything, and felt she had attempted to re-pay this debt by never missing a step, never making a single mistake. Everything she did, the way she dressed, and every word she spoke had been calculated to ensure success at the position she held today.

Her choice in career was like winning the crown. Like a queen's coronation, her title allowed her to survive the test of time. Very few occupations protect women, and consequently hers was worth fighting for despite the many sacrifices. Her position also demanded a wardrobe fit for a queen, albeit the queen of France.

Pascale's wardrobe was as modest as it was expensive. Long ago, she had envied the daring evening wear of her colleagues' wives. It seemed a cruel irony back then, that her sample-size figure remained hidden beneath reams of fabric. Appropriate Victorian-era evening wear was just one more sacrifice she had made to win her position. The risqué lingerie she wore underneath in an effort to placate herself just never seemed to make up for it, no matter how appreciative her covert one-night stands seemed to be.

Pascale had worn her cool blonde mane in the "Anna Wintour sans bangs" style for over forty-three years. She had stopped keeping photos at least fifteen years ago, once the wrinkles on her face defeated the Botox and surgery. Until that time, only the outfits had changed.

Today it mattered little. In the twilight of her career, Pascale—along with all of her colleagues—sported strategic clothing that far surpassed its modest predecessor. Perhaps it came across as prudish, but it had more to do with hiding excess skin, wrinkles, and age spots than cleavage and curves.

As she took a final drag from her contraband Gauloises, Pascale was melancholy. Her success had definitely come at a price. She had literally invented an identity that everyone expected instead of becoming who she was perhaps intended to be. So complete was this subterfuge that she herself did not bother to look past the façade. Not until recently. Not until her meeting with Tomas.

His research chipped away at a lifetime of achievement, and his questions mocked everything she believed to be true about her world, about our world, about the universe. This was not malicious on his part. His intention was only to seek out the most appropriate individual with whom to share his findings.

He was desperately intimidated from the moment they shook hands, and her barrage of accusations and scrutiny caused him to almost lose his nerve. In the end, he handed over his research documents, which he knew she would have to acknowledge. The obviousness of the truth was all there. He had been over it thousands of times and was relieved to finally share it with her. Now that the decision had been made, there would be no turning back.

Pascale was introspective, looking for meaning in her own decisions, reviewing the steps and missteps along her own path. She never stopped to consider that the choice she had made to dedicate her life to her career would one day isolate her. Giving up a family, developing thick skin to the exclusion of competitive colleagues and even close friends, and never allowing for a serious personal relationship just seemed to be part of the price. When life presented these obstacles as choices to her, she avoided them immediately, actually celebrating the forfeiture as being one step closer to her ultimate goal.

A life based on science was surely the most stable, the most secure life imaginable. In her mind, it was the only way to escape her abusive childhood. Not until today, this very moment, when the life in which she'd carefully shrouded herself unraveled around her, did she mourn the soul she might have been.

Today, she realized her choices had been made of fear at the hands of her father, the encouragement of her mentors, and a burning desire to leave her past behind. She'd fought hard to prove to herself and everyone else that it didn't matter what life presented; you created your own destiny, despite where you started.

At sixty-seven, she vowed she would not continue down this path of fear-based responses to life. From this moment forward, she would truly create her own destiny and, quite possibly, the destiny of every soul on the planet. Her path was clear as she reached for her phone and called her long-time friend, Malcolm Schwartz.

CHAPTER 40

KHALID AL GAMDI
12:51 p.m. In-flight somewhere over the Atlantic

KHALID HAD HIS HANDS FULL TRYING TO LAY JACK TO REST. THE investigation following his murder had the FBI on the hunt, and too many fingers had started pointing to his side of the fence. Khalid cursed Jack, who was apparently attempting to have the last laugh from the grave.

Despite Khalid's fortress of intel, Jack had been able to hide the many players with whom he had been working. It enraged Khalid that he had not dug deeper on him, and he vowed to himself that he would never let that happen again. Now he was on a plane to Moscow to meet with some asshole who refused to speak with Khalid's right hand.

Deceit seemed to be the order of the day, but Khalid was no stranger to it. In his line of work, more often than not, people seemed unable to walk the line; it was either ego or money or both. It never ceased to amaze him. They all knew where it would get them, and just how ruthless Khalid was, but for whatever reason, they were unable to stop themselves. Like moths to the flame.

It actually excited him when shit started to go down. It meant something big was about to happen. Something big was just around the corner, and he instinctively sharpened and prepared for the prey. It invigorated him. He lived for the challenge, for the fight, for the win. His was the biggest ego of all.

The beauty of deceiving the deceiver is that they take comfort in their own prowess and typically choose to feel protected, no matter how vulnerable they are. The longer they feel they have gotten away with something, the more they let their guard down. While Khalid was tracking Jon's every move, every correspondence and conversation, Jon became more and more likely to provide Khalid with the information he had been trying to protect.

Khalid found far more success in letting people do his bidding from afar than jumping in to take over the reins. People who were scared did unpredictable things. People who thought they were winning usually did not.

The individual Khalid was most interested in was Cooper. He only had surveillance on him. He needed access to his day to day, and if it hadn't been for this investigation into Jack's murder, he would have reached out to him already.

He wasn't sure what he would do with him; that all depended on Cooper. Kahlid wondered if he would like him as much as Jack. In any case, Cooper was definitely on his radar. If Jon was willing to put himself in the line of fire for him, there must be something to the kid. Hopefully, he would prove to be less troublesome than his boyhood nemesis, who haunted Khalid from the grave. Khalid smiled to himself as he watched live surveillance on his laptop of Jon running through the park.

"Yes, run as fast as you can, little mouse. Too bad for you there will be no escape.

Without realizing it, Khalid had taunted Jon aloud. The flight attendant on his private jet knew better than to raise her eyebrows, but secretly hoped this would be her last flight. She had requested to be transferred, but in her heart, she knew this would be unlikely, as she was one of Khalid's favorites. Once you signed up with Khalid, you sold your soul. He alone decided what to do with it.

CHAPTER 41

WILL & CATHERINE
10:14 a.m.   Upton Wing, Proteus, NYC

THE SILVER AND TURQUOISE BALLOONS SWAYED METHODI-
cally back and forth, evenly caressed by the forced air from the vents above.
They seemed out of place in the Upton wing—as out of place as the tiny participants inhabiting its corridors.

It was almost comical, Will and Catherine's determined observation of the
children's birthdays. It was an attempt to adhere to some type of normalcy as
they continued with the testing.

They took over the facility wholeheartedly and marveled at the progress
they made in comparison to their previous work, with dated technology and
equipment on a shoestring budget. It left Will feeling slightly betrayed by Jon,
his brother of sorts, seeing what was now possible.

"Happy Birthday to you," Will sang wholeheartedly to the two September
births they celebrated. The boys were both elated to have such an extravagant
party—one of the many perks Proteus provided.

It seemed the magic of Proteus extended to the adults, as well. Will and
Catherine had connected in a way Will had never imagined, as he had given up
on the idea of romance entirely. However, late one night in the backseat of the
very Prius Cooper had used to kidnap him, they consummated their relationship in the Proteus underground parkade. It was very unlike Will indeed.

With Cooper now working almost full time in Malcolm's labs, Will and Catherine were left carte blanche with the Noctural testing, which had become somewhat of a decoy for Jon's benefit, or so they all thought. It had Cooper shaking his head. What had once been his obsession had become an after-thought compared to what they currently hid at Genetech.

How easily he left Noctural behind. What had been everything was now almost a distant memory. A past life. Just like his past life with Jack. He still could not believe Jack was gone. He and Mandolin escaped the loss together, one night at a time. More than once, she had reached for her phone when a question arose that Jack could have easily answered. A lost look would take over her fine features, and Cooper would make an attempt to take her hand. They fell into an easy pattern. He couldn't imagine going through this without her. It was like their worlds were turned upside down, and if they just held on to each other, everything would be OK.

Part of Cooper hated it. He hated relying on anything outside of his control. He told himself that it was just a reaction to Jack's death, and once they put all this behind them, they could go their separate ways.

As if Mandolin sensed his withdrawal, she also held back, never sinking into Cooper fully. Perhaps they both felt guilty, knowing how Jack would have responded. It was ironic that his death had been the catalyst for them. Ophelia sensed something was up but wasn't sure what to make of it. And had she and Malcolm not been giddy with what they had learned from Albert's testing, she may have given it more consideration. As it was, Cooper and Mandolin were able to continue undetected (or at least unacknowledged) by the rest of the group.

Life seemed stranger than fiction. Who would have guessed that both Cooper and Will, abductor and abducted, would embark on affairs of the heart? Their fates seemed to mirror each other, at least for the moment. Both were harnessed to their respective testing, and to Jon. The similarities of their situations were ironic, especially considering how different they were.

Will had never been happier, and perhaps if he had been a bit more analytic and a bit less amorous, he would have noticed that a pattern had begun to reveal itself across all sleep tests. Perhaps he would have alerted Catherine, and they could have taken credit for identifying one of the most important scientific discoveries of all time. Perhaps they would have helped identify that the same results were being observed world-wide. But as it happened, fate or his lack of attention to the data, due to his round the clock afterglow, had other plans.

CHAPTER 42

RAY GARLAND

1:23 p.m.   Parked outside Cooper's apartment

I NVESTIGATING SUSPECTS WAS DIFFICULT; INVESTIGATING GENETI-
cally advanced species who could communicate without words was a whole
new level for Ray. It took his best trick right out of his hands. He couldn't play
them against each other. From the beginning, the tables were turned, and he
was the one being played.

Gone was the simplicity of his nine to five, which had never really been nine
to five in the literal sense. It was the predictability of his work that he missed.
Hell, he even longed for those hateful joint CIA meetings. Once a week was far
better than every fucking day now. Day in and day out.

It seemed like his whole world had stopped revolving. The only thing that
mattered was a group of highly evolved hybrids that required all of his focus.
Both day and night. It was the new normal, conceived shortly after his return
from Paris. The folklore File 710 was anything but, as it turned out, and now
it became the new religion to which they all subscribed. Ray would have never
imagined this, not even in his wildest drug-induced dreams. He and Carl joked
that they were Men in Black now, but it was closer to the truth than either one
of them wanted to acknowledge.

The one thing for which Ray was grateful was to be back home. He had spent
the better part of the last month investigating Jack's plane crash. Poor bastard. He

hadn't stood a chance in that modified seatbelt. Ray guessed correctly that Jack probably didn't even realize he was in a five-point harness until it was too late.

Jack Christie was an interesting fellow. It was a name Ray immediately recognized, as he had been on Ray's radar for some time. From what Ray knew, he was too smart for his own good. Too bad he ended up playing for the wrong team. Ray had spent hours with Jack's coworkers, acquaintances, and mother, who was tough as nails behind her waterfall of tears.

The only piece missing was an interview with Cooper. Apparently, they were childhood friends who had recently reconnected. Ray was guessing they had reconnected in a big way, judging by the frequency of their contact found in Jack's phone records in the last few months. He had a hunch that Cooper would be able to shed some light on things that were still in the works. Jack had kept his cards very close. The encryption he used to hide his confidential files was proving very difficult to crack.

Ray could not have been happier to discover Cooper was in NYC. He needed a break from the "aliens" almost as much as he had been itching to get out of that sleepy little prison Jack called home. Small places unnerved Ray. The slow pace of life lulled you into letting your guard down. Small places were good for hiding big things.

Racing to NYC to track down Cooper was a welcomed distraction from the GAS investigation. He was unsure who came up with the "Genetically Advanced Species" moniker, but without exception, he had learned that an acronym was of the utmost importance. It seemed that, by simply applying a label, folks decided they could control a situation. There was nothing like an acronym to put higher ups in the driver's seat, especially if it was the CIA who wanted to drive.

The flight back had given Ray a chance to sift through everything he had uncovered and determine how best to package this for Carl once he returned to Washington. It was proving to be quite the puzzle, with new pieces and people emerging every day. Ray was reluctant to draw any conclusions until all the players had been identified; however, he also knew that no one was better at filling in the blanks than Carl, and so he was willing to share his ingredients in hopes that together they could cook up a plan.

He just had so many unanswered questions: How did Jack become involved with Ophelia and her crew of GAS? What had Jack done that would be worth killing him for? Why had he been at Irwin's presentation six months prior? How did a failed lawyer-cum-journalist find himself a terrorist target? Did Jack's killer also kill Camberg?

The list went on and on. Ray felt that he was going in circles. He was completely chasing his tail when talking to any of the GAS. They sort of drifted off whenever they were communicating among themselves. It was infuriating, but until they found a way to inhibit their communication, Ray had to accept that a response from any one of them would be identical to the rest. They were all for one and one for all. True patriots of whatever it was they thought they were protecting.

It would be a welcome change to meet with Cooper and have a real chance at finding some answers. The only problem was that he was proving hard to track down. He was never at Proteus, and he was never at his apartment, which was the only property he owned. So, the question of the moment was this: Where was a hotshot doctor who formulates sleep aids, whose best friend just got murdered, hiding out at this given moment?

CHAPTER 43

MALCOLM AND ALBERT
12:56 p.m.   Malcolm's private labs, Genetech, NYC

WHAT IS THE MOST SIGNIFICANT THING YOU CAN DO WITH your mind? It was a question that had haunted Malcolm every day of his life. It had become a code by which he lived as he begrudgingly acknowledged his career would soon come to a close. As if he had not a second to waste, he fought hard every minute to focus on the most important items required to make the most significant discovery possible.

Perhaps this explained the popular belief that the elderly were, in fact, wise. Was this decreed through decades of experience from which the youth could only hope to benefit? It was only now that Malcolm suspected that beyond a collected wisdom lay a sense of urgency to achieve as much as possible in the little time one left to achieve goals.

This was his last chance to leave something of significance behind, as the twilight of his career glared obtrusively at him, like the sun just below a car's visor, unable to shield the driver from its penetrating rays despite any amount of futile finagling. Only this state of desperation could project a razor focus on which step to take next.

As such, it was Malcolm who set the pace and direction of Albert's testing, and he would have been the ideal candidate had he not still been suffering from his incurable insomnia. Lack of sleep was a tough one, especially for an old man who'd just found a new purpose.

The testing being steadily (albeit painfully) accelerated left Ophelia scrambling to keep up and second guessing Malcolm on more than one occasion. In response, she had implemented a two-hour reprieve for Albert mid-day. She called it vacation lunch hour, and insisted Albert needed it to rest. He could take a nap, play, watch TV—whatever he chose, as long as it was free from testing. Despite Malcolm's protest, Ophelia would not back down. She needed the time to sort through and document their findings, not to mention review the items Malcolm had conjured up for the next day's onslaught of tests. She wondered if the man ever slept.

While the two of them toiled away at uncovering the boundaries of Albert's mind, Albert was busy making the most significant discoveries all on his own. For two hours a day, Jasper and Albert communicated without detection by the scientists and learned more from their private conversations than either Malcolm or Ophelia could have hoped for.

The age difference between them was overcome by Jasper's ability to play like a child and the significant amount of time Albert had spent with adults due to the ongoing ADHD testing.

What started out as childish games turned to skill development, much like a parent would encourage their little one to speak, eat, and eventually walk. Albert was far beyond discovering his abilities; he was now honing them, able to effectively communicate with the small family of XYZs to whom Jasper had introduced him.

They had welcomed Albert with open arms—or, more appropriately, open minds. From the confines of FBI protection, they gifted something to Albert he never thought he would find: a group of people who truly understood him. What Albert loved most was that the communication with the other XYZs was not confined to language; they were able to transmit feelings of affection and compassion from miles away. Albert experienced a realization that he would never be alone again. His connection with other XYZ transgressed any cruelty this world was capable of inflicting. He simply called upon them, and they would be there.

In front of the TV in his "play room" at Malcolm's labs, he observed the communication of his newfound family, and the incredible speed at which they transferred. There was a growing concern among the confined XYZs regarding the stress the FBI surveillance and interrogation was inflicting on all of them. They were having difficulty sleeping. It was a growing epidemic among the group.

Jasper was about to agree with them, despite the fact that he was miles away; he chalked up his own self-imposed insomnia to too many nights out at the pub with the blokes from campus. When you don't come home 'til four in the morning, it made sense that you would suffer from a lack of sleep.

It was in the midst of the laughter from the group, at Jasper's admission, that Albert made his first tentative attempt at communicating with the other XYZs: "I had a bad dream last night."

Jasper immediately encouraged him to share it with them all, his thoughts echoed by the rest of the XYZs, all reassuring the newest member of their group to feel completely at one with them.

"I am walking alone through a maze in a forest, still in construction, when a figure approaches. I can't make out the face, but he asks me to help him. He says he really needs my help. He says it will be hard work, and it will take a long time, but he promises that no harm will come to me. I nod and tell him I will help, but his instructions are hard to follow, and I keep making mistakes because he is speaking in a quiet voice from far, far away in a language that is familiar but one that I cannot speak and do not understand.

"The figure shows me by example; he wants me to move around carved wooden blocks. I am forced to keep going and move the blocks as fast I can. I am made to do it all night long. He comes to me every night and tells me I must help him, again and again. He wants me to build the maze faster and faster. I tell him I just want to sleep tonight, but he insists, and reminds me how important it is that I help him. I had the same dream every night this week."

Albert's inner voice trailed off, lost in his own account of the dream as he tried to remember, in vain, the first night the recurring dream had begun.

"Is the man wearing a suit with the date and time on his chest?" Emily had been one of the first XYZs to reach out to Albert, the first day the group had welcomed him last week. Her never-ending blonde waves and green-grey eyes distracted from a steel nerve and a chest-bursting heart. Emily was out to save the world and would let nothing deter her.

Albert reminded her of her own children, despite the fact that her two little ones had yet to be identified as XYZ. It gave her shivers to hear Albert's eight-year-old version of the exact dream she had been having for weeks. Her love of this young boy surpassed any reservation she might have felt about sharing something that may have her seem crazy to the rest of the group.

How could she possibly be having the same dream as this young kid, especially one that recurred almost every night? However, her concern was unnecessary, as the rest of the group immediately offered up that they had all been having similar dreams as well.

A ripple of fear and a flood of questions overtook the group as to how it could be possible. In time, as a collective, they brought themselves back under control, sobered by the knowledge that they were still under protection and surveillance by the FBI. It was understood that this discovery was a secret they would all guard, until they decided how to move forward as a group.

It was in their favor that the FBI had not uncovered a way to effectively monitor their activity. They were able to communicate an overarching sense of belonging and group preservation, especially to Albert. The autonomy with which their abilities endowed them, protected them all from detection. It was only natural that the group's attention was now focused on the dream. Even Jasper, through the haze of his hangovers, could vaguely remember the faceless figure with the illuminated date and time on its chest.

CHAPTER 44

SALIM
10:12 a.m. Quality Inn, Washington, DC

ACROSS HIS CHEST WAS A TATTOO OF KHALID'S NAME IN Arabic, reflected in the bathroom mirror. Dark, thick, wavy curls framed each end—the curtain for the stage. It was the ultimate symbol of total devotion, and an insult to Allah, who considered the marking a sin. His name was the ultimate contradiction, as was how he manifested his occupation.

Salim's name meant peaceful, and in keeping, he always ensured the most painless, humane death for his targets. His empathy contradicted his abhorrent behavior. As the most valued assassin in Khalid's private army, Salim created peace that came with the ultimate sacrifice.

Salim lived as a gypsy would, city to city, hotel to hotel. He had no traceable identity. Khalid and a handful of others were the few who knew his real name. It suited him perfectly; he was able to compartmentalize his job this way. A new city, a new identity, day to day. It helped him leave it all behind. The tattoo enabled him to remember the man who made it possible, the man who had ultimately saved his life. It was total devotion he felt for Khalid—total devotion and love.

Salim's missions were repetitious: a target, a place, a take out, repeat. He never missed. Not one blemish on his record. He was surprised to have received this latest request from Khalid. It was like nothing he had ever been asked to do before. His assignment did not involve a single death, if all went as planned. In fact, quite the opposite. Everyone needed to remain alive and safe—at least the few Khalid was interested in.

Abduction had made its way into Salim's repertoire only a handful of times and, thinking back, he had been asked to kill them all in the end. No, this was a very strange request indeed, even for Khalid. Regardless, as Khalid's favorite soldier, and without hesitation, he set off for Washington, where the FBI were detaining the XYZs.

Khalid's reach was long and wide, his tentacles extending into even the most guarded territory, even the FBI. It was quite easy for Khalid to provide Salim with FBI clearance, even without an actual presence. His hackers could create credentials for practically anything within forty-eight hours.

Salim rolled the security badge over in his hands and laughed. He sat in the back seat of the sedan, picturing himself as a Hollywood actor. He imagined they would love him. No stunt man required. As they neared FBI headquarters, Salim reached for his gun and straightened his tie. He didn't want to waste a moment; the sooner this was over, the better. He would admit only to himself that this one had him worried. He was familiar with single targets and a clean-up crew. He was in and out. it was surgical. People could be unpredictable, especially when they felt threatened. While Salim was banking that his targets would fall in line and take orders, as they would have no reason to question him, he did not like having to leave anything to chance.

He entered through the front, swung open the framed glass door with purpose, and made his way to security. His clearance worked perfectly, other than the quizzical look from the guard, who was obviously trying to place him, until the agent behind him coughed loudly to get the guy's attention.

Khalid walked on toward the elevator as if he had done it a thousand times before. That was the key, to act like you had always been there. Making a mistake was not an issue, but acting like you didn't know which button to push was a huge red flag. However, Khalid's intel was always foolproof.

Salim knew exactly which floor, which room, and which people. He had committed all their faces and respective names to memory, as well as a handful of their personal information should they question his authority.

Emily was the first to notice Salim enter the ninth-floor landing from the elevator. It wasn't that she didn't recognize him that made her feel uneasy, it was the look on the face of the agent who remained in the elevator, travelling up to another floor, that gave her a chill. After 9/11, despite a shitload of conditioning training, a new face, as it were, stood out to people.

Emily was late to rejoin the group in the large meeting room after their routine individual questioning, and had loitered in the corridor. It seemed to be the only break allowed for non-smokers. Seeing this newcomer should have sped up her return; however, she was a sensitive type who proceeded with caution, and she decided to get the scoop before re-joining the others.

Terence, Emily's closest confidant of the XYZs, responded by allowing her direct access through his senses. It was an uninterrupted feed to Salim's instructions in real time. He was here to move them, this new agent—the one garnering untrusting looks from the fellow operative in the elevator. The look of suspicion on his face would not leave Emily's mind, and at that moment, she made a decision that would change the course of all their fates.

If only Ray had been around to question the guy; he was skeptical of everyone and would have easily teased out his subterfuge. Ray could have found him out with no more than two questions. However, Salim's timing during Ray's absence when he was in NYC was no coincidence. Khalid had Ray well within his crosshairs. He just deferred the bullet. That was Khalid's way. He let his enemies do the dirty work as long as possible.

Terence agreed that Emily should escape the transfer if she could. God knows they knew the ins and outs of the building from weeks of detainment. Their badges would not allow them to leave the building, but they did have access to the lobby. She headed to the elevator and began her descent. It would not be long until she reached the security desk.

The agents who had been assigned to the XYZs had been with them for weeks. They were well acquainted with each of the groups' members, and would surely alert Salim that she was missing if he hadn't already discovered the fact for himself.

It took only seconds for Emily to disseminate her intentions to the rest of the XYZ group, and they all rallied in support. Salim's instructions seemed very out of line. Everyone concurred. Unfortunately, his rank superseded the other agents, and they had no choice but to prepare the XYZs for immediate transfer in response to what appeared to be a threat to their safety. It had them all wondering. If they were not safe here, then where?

Salim counted the group and then asked about Emily. The agent didn't trust Salim. He had been interviewing the group for weeks with no real success. Without Ray here to approve the transfer, he was reluctant to hand them over. He knew something was wrong. He had lost a partner in 9/11 and spent a year in Afghanistan. This just didn't add up. It was a gutsy move, but he had to try.

"She's had to leave for a medical examination. She has been struggling with the detainment." His lie received a raised eyebrow from Salim in response.

"That's right; she hasn't been sleeping." Terence came to the agent's defense. Ironically, it wasn't even a lie. None of them were sleeping.

Salim was pissed. They were all supposed to be here. Khalid's intel indicated they had all scanned in. What the hell was he going to do? If he left here without her, he would lose his window of opportunity. Salim knew this examination excuse was bullshit. With seconds ticking by at a pace that seemed like hours, he had to make the call.

Restraint took over his features. "Yes, of course. We will have to collect her after the appointment. Who is the agent with her now? What is his contact info?" Salim wasn't about to give up on this stray little lamb. He was leaving with Emily.

As Emily raced toward the security check-in, the pain overtook her. The XYZ ability to generate a physical response gave them either an offensive or defensive advantage, depending on the requirements of the situation. The guard was immediately in contact with the agents on the ninth floor, while Emily was being assessed by the paramedics on scene in the lobby, following her severe reaction to her manifested illness as it took hold.

He had been right. More people, more problems. Perhaps Khalid had been wrong to trust him with this. He had to find out which hospital they were taking her to. Working this alone, he had no opportunity to leave and collect her. It was killing him, but he knew he had to deliver the rest of the group.

They were all so quiet. Too quiet. It was like they knew something was wrong, but they were in total compliance. It was too good to be true. He sensed something was off but couldn't put his finger on it.

As he escorted them to the armored vehicles Khalid had provided for their transport, he turned to face the ninth-floor agents. "Thank you for your help. I'll take it from here."

The look on their faces told him he had only a few minutes to make his escape before they contacted Ray. They were on to him, but luckily "only a few minutes" would be all he needed. The red tape at the FBI would grant him enough time to make it to the airport, get these people on the private plane, and call it a day.

It would have been another win for him if not for Emily, the one they left behind. Failing Khalid was worse than failing himself. Salim could never live this down.

CHAPTER 45

MALCOLM AND PASCALE
10:43 p.m.   The St. Regis, New York Hotel, NYC

THEY FACED EACH OTHER NAKED. AT THEIR AGE, SHAME AND insecurity seemed a waste of time. They had waited so long for this moment. Anything that stood to encumber their union, the priorities that had prevailed in the past, had finally been defeated. It was as if both their lives had been laid out on a path leading up to this exact moment. There was no time for regret. If only they had pushed everything else aside so many years ago, like carefree adolescents, in total disregard of their mortality.

There was simply now, as they clung to each other while desire ate up the distance between them. The mixture of nervous applications of both perfume and cologne permeated the room and penetrated the crisp white sheets. Gardenia gave way to leather, bitter almond, and vanilla; then a fresh wave of floral would triumph again. The wine they shared in the hotel lounge mixed with the scent of sex and their favorite fragrances was a potent combination. The mise en scène would have been offensive, if either one had been aware. So lost were they in each other that the only sense remaining was touch.

Pascale had been introduced to Malcolm forty years earlier. They had been brought together professionally many times, and had solved many problems. Each one had brought them closer together; however, in turn, either one or the other had escaped from the unacknowledged attraction that always threatened to surface.

They could, and did, talk for hours about any subject, every breakthrough in their respective fields. It was a rare gift to find a kindred spirit, especially in fields where so few had the capacity to even understand what Pascale and Malcolm had mastered.

Perhaps it was only a matter of time, perhaps it was circumstance, perhaps the discovery that everything they ever relied upon had blown up in their face, but this night transfixed them to each other. Whatever time they both had left would not be squandered, not this time, not ever again.

They agreed to share a cigarette, like two young lovers might. Giddy and spent, they both avoided gazing into the mirror, preferring to live out the moment as if they had made the choice forty years prior. Pascale's blush at Malcolm's gaze was made all the more endearing by the wrinkles on her thin face.

Malcolm was the first to break their spell. "I realize this is cliché, but I have to say it. I never thought this day would come."

"Neither did I," Pascale agreed. She would have said more in French, but he would not have understood. In English, it was not worth the effort and far less romantic. She moved over to his side of the bed and put the cigarette between his lips instead.

She continued, no longer able to contain her excitement. Malcolm had been her first phone call immediately following the meeting with Tomas. "What will you do with the boy? How will you keep him safe? When can I meet with him?"

It seemed that the sex had only catalyzed her urgency to learn everything Malcolm had discovered. She was dying to get into his lab, almost as much as she had been dying to get into his bed.

The true reason they had never crossed the line before this day was that, despite the attraction and the intellectual high they reached in each other's company, it was Pascale who always held something back. Many times, Malcolm had discovered her betrayals at worst, and mistruths at best. She refused to take him into her confidence completely. Perhaps he had just given up, deciding to accept her as she was, refusing to fight the attraction any longer.

Perhaps he knew his days were numbered. Perhaps everyone's days were numbered. In any case, he ignored the nagging feeling that always arose, when it came time for them to part, that she would somehow dupe him.

This time would be no different. She had decided even before she had boarded the plane to NYC that she would not share with Malcolm her knowledge of the interstellar object that hovered on the far side of the moon.

CHAPTER 46

MANDOLIN GRACE & ARMAND PRICE

3:07 p.m.   Bryant Park, NYC

HE LEERED AT HER ACROSS THE SQUARE AS IF HE WERE AN elderly nobleman perched offstage in a Degas painting, his arms crossed in front of his chest as he drank in her every move without invitation. She had been a ballerina once, and still looked as if she could be, but his heated expression was not by virtue of lust; it was at the hand of contempt.

Mandolin finally had him. The elusive Dr. Armand Price sat only fifteen feet away from her. She had taken him completely into her confidence at Jack's advice. It was the only way to win him over. Dr. Price lived in a perpetual state of fear. His thoughts cycled through torture, his own death, becoming a hostage, his research being stolen, his family murdered, suicide, and back again.

He blamed Mandolin and anyone connected to her for Camberg's death. These people had no idea the giants they were awakening. He would have never met with her, but the fact that she knew information he had only ever shared with Jack, as well as proof that she and the A-team had discovered XYZ, changed his mind. Armand knew the future would depend on intelligent energy. To discover that it was potentially in use, by our prehistoric alien cousins, was the only reason he agreed to expose himself, despite the risk.

She rose from the table and made her way toward him. It was obvious he had no intention of moving from his seat. The wind was brisk as it danced the red and amber leaves through the wrought-iron obstacle course of chair legs, table legs, and the legs of one livid physicist.

He gestured for her to take a seat as he continually scanned the crowd. His face was drawn, and his grey eyes had sunken into his skull. He looked nothing like the online photo she had found of him a year prior. He found it impossible to eat under the circumstances. His appetite had been lost completely at the news of Camberg's murder.

"I came only to warn you, Mandolin. You have no idea what you are doing, the people you are dealing with. You don't even realize Camberg's murder is on your head." The venom spilled from Armand's lips as he literally spat across the bistro table at her.

The mention of Camberg sent chills up her spine. She would never forget that fateful night he had impersonated the man now sitting in front of her. Nothing had been the same since. It was as if that night had cast a magic spell that unleashed all the destruction that followed. Camberg's death, Jack's death . . .

Perhaps he was right. Perhaps this *was* all her fault somehow. Mandolin immediately regretted this decision. She still felt lost without Jack. It was as if she were flailing in the deep end, with only Cooper to save her now. Cooper made a poor substitute for Jack when it came down to it. He had drawn a line between what was his and hers in this uncharted water.

He was extreme under these conditions. It was 100 percent work when he was in Malcolm's lab, or back at Proteus feigning to continue with Noctural, and 100 percent sex when it was the two of them together at night. Their relationship had become almost exclusively physical from her perspective. Although she suspected that, if Cooper were asked to describe it, he would tell a different story.

He would probably feel they shared everything, and they did, when it came to Cooper. He told her every detail, asked her opinion, and relied on her input and advice. In fact, Cooper had never felt closer to anyone; he couldn't imagine life without Mandolin, despite the fact that he reminded himself daily that their relationship was temporary.

Mandolin reciprocated, for very different reasons of her own. The truth was that she needed Cooper. She was completely lost in a current that continued to pull her under, and the only lifeline Jack had left for her was Cooper. She had long given up attempts to engage Cooper in the details of her life or to seek his advice. She now understood just how important Jack had been, how he knew when she needed him even before she realized it herself.

They were dance partners, she and Jack, and had been dancing for years; she just hadn't realized how critical that dance had become until it had ended for good. Cooper took solace in praising her prowess as an easy alternative to connecting with her. It was much easier than helping her solve her alleged, ever-increasing dilemmas. Perhaps, she was expecting too much anyway. Perhaps this was the best he could offer. She just couldn't help feeling that Cooper was most comfortable living under the pretense of chivalry, under the guise of somebody better.

He was a master at enabling others but never truly committing to their cause. The most important thing to Cooper was Cooper, and if Mandolin had more strength, more resolve, or if she had Jack back in her corner, she would have found a way to disengage, despite the close physical bond they shared.

She re-opened the envelope Jack had left her in the shoebox as soon as she had reached her room at the Empress in Victoria. She held tightly to the key it contained, to the safety deposit box at First National Bank. Once she returned home, it had been her first stop. The deposit box contained an external hard drive and a USB key. Mandolin could only imagine what they contained; however, the instructions were explicit: They were for Armand Price's eyes only. The notebook Jack had left in the shoe box outlined the depth of the business relationship he and Price shared, outlining years of meetings and agendas.

Mandolin's attention was brought back to the present situation as Armand's fury began to seep red from his neck through the features of his face. Her silence added fuel to a fire already in full rage.

"Please understand, Armand, Peter Camberg lied to me. He used your identity to win me over. I never would have met with him, but now I am grateful that I did. You are a smart man, Armand, and now I need to share some information with you that will make me seem as crazy to you as Camberg seemed to me."

Mandolin told him everything: discovering the extent of XYZ, the research with Albert, Irwin's findings, and Jack's murder. His fury was soon replaced by disbelief, as his mind scrambled to make sense of everything he knew and how it all related to what he had just discovered. For the first time in a long time, he felt something other than fear. Even disbelief was preferable to fear.

"Help us, Armand. We need you. You are as safe with us in Malcolm's labs as anywhere else. Please, help us determine if Camberg was right all along. I never wanted any of this. Please believe me." Mandolin's last words rang true. How could they not? She was empty, trying to keep up with her own role in this nightmare.

Mandolin could tell he was considering her offer seriously. On some level, she felt that all these lab rats had wished for this their entire lives: The discovery, real proof, that we are not alone; proof that we are all the perfect outcome of millions and millions of years of evolution; and proof that our ancient cousins had been even more advanced millions of years before. That, in reality, we are our own aliens was the hook that blew their minds.

Armand leaned over to collect his things. Mandolin rose from her seat and ushered him toward her vehicle.

Now the only one left was Sean. She had saved the best for last, so to speak. Mandolin was confident that he would be an ally to her. She was in need of one. After all, his support is what had positioned her in the eye of this hurricane to begin with. It only made sense that he would be the one to get her back to Kansas. He would be her Wizard of Oz, in a sense. If only Jack had been around to hold out a pair of sparkly red shoes instead. If only Jack had been around to warn her.

CHAPTER 47

KHALID AL GAMDI
4:31 p.m. Madison Square Park Tower, NYC

OF ALL THE THINGS AT WHICH KHALID EXCELLED, HIS GREATEST aptitude was identifying an individual's true motivation. It came at a price. Knowing all the sordid details of someone's life took time, money, and effort, but in the end, it was always worth his while. Khalid enjoyed the game, enjoyed holding all the cards. It was like playing God. He made puppets out of people this way, and had being doing it as long as he could remember. It was the single most important skill he had learned from his father: the ability to control another.

Khalid had been following Sean since the beginning of his career. He knew that he was onto something big with Human Pinnacle theory. His entire career had been leading up to it. Sean asked all the right questions, and fortunately for Khalid, wanted more than just the answers; he wanted the glory for himself. Sean was driven by fame. He wanted to be the hero who saved the day. Aspirations such as these made him an easy target for Khalid.

Unlike the relationship with Jon, Khalid had yet to reveal his true colors to Sean. To Sean, Khalid was a godsend. Sean never would have been able to attract the required funding to advance his research without him. Khalid's knowledge about his field was what had initially garnered Sean's trust in him. In Khalid, Sean had found an alter ego, someone he could count on. They had had their share of disagreements, but overall, the relationship had carried on as planned. Sean remained loyal to Khalid and had kept their arrangement a secret, at his request.

As was to be expected, after meeting with Mandolin and Armand, the first person Sean met with was Khalid. He was skeptical of her claims and believed that Khalid was the one person who had the resources to prove them false. If he were honest with himself, Sean didn't want them to be true. Her tale was ludicrous, insisting that she had found the root cause of his theory: that we were all victims to a higher power using intelligent-energy accumulation and as a result had plateaued as an entire species.

Nothing this ridiculous could possibly be true, yet the evidence was ever mounting. Armand Price had been compelling during their meeting, and their story regarding the murder of Camberg made Sean's blood run cold. Perhaps it was science, and everything he relied on as fact, or perhaps it was his pride. Either way, he could not bring himself to believe their story. If anyone was going to discover the answers, the cause of his theory, it would be him.

However, it left him uneasy. He could not help but take note of Khalid's lack of surprise as he relayed their story to him. If Sean had only known the extent of it. Not only was Khalid already aware of the information; he had the majority of the XYZs in his custody and had been behind both murders—Jack's as well as Camberg's. Indeed, none of this was news to Khalid, other than the boy. Until today, he had not been aware of Albert.

Listening to Sean, and feigning interest, took all the willpower Khalid could muster. His instinct was to leave immediately, now that he had the information and had already gathered most of the resources necessary to find out if it were true. Instead, he continued to cajole Sean.

Of course, this was a false claim. Of course, nothing like this could be possible. He needed to coach Sean into keeping communication open with Mandolin. If she trusted Irwin all the better. He had no idea the friends Jack's little reporter had made. He had underestimated her importance until now.

Sean kept gesturing wildly, emphasizing both his relief at Khalid being in agreement with him, that this impossible story could not be true, as well as his disgust that Mandolin would have the audacity to bring it forward. After all, he had made her a star on the forefront of today's most important discovery, and this is how she repaid him? It seemed as if there was no loyalty to be found, as if everyone had their own agenda, their own pretension.

Khalid suffered through his display. It was important to keep him onside; the last thing he needed was for Sean to lose perspective or loyalty. The worst thing that could happen was for him to decide her theory had some relevance and put it forward as his own. Khalid needed Sean to stay the course, to keep in touch with Mandolin, and relay the info back to him. He needed Sean to believe there was no way this theory could be true, and that the best way to discredit the false claims of Mandolin and Armand was to find out as much as he could about what they knew and what else they might be hiding.

It was tedious for Khalid. His mind raced forward, piecing together a plan, as Sean, in his hubris, went on and on, laying claim to every piece of his research that could potentially disprove their claim. It was comical to watch, and Khalid might have even enjoyed it if he were not desperate to leave. How could he have let Jack and this reporter evade him?

Jack had been clandestine, Khalid saw it now. It was incredible the amount of information Jack had been able to hide. He had not given Jack the full credit he deserved. No matter. Khalid would soon regain the upper hand.

He had the XYZs now, and his research team was running them through every test imaginable. Despite the rigorous schedule, Khalid was going to have it accelerated. Now that he knew about Albert's existence, there was no telling how much had been discovered about their intelligence and capacity. Khalid needed to learn all he could about intelligent-energy.

He should have made more of an effort to hunt down Armand Price. At least it was not too late for that. Khalid cursed himself for not making the connection. Camberg had been in place as a decoy for Price. It was not that Price was attempting to distance himself due to Camberg's insane ranting. He had disappeared to keep the secret, because it was true.

Khalid had to keep his head. He had to exploit what he had and then move forward with Price. Salim had done well in capturing the XYZs. The one who got away was of little concern to Khalid. They could reach Emily, if need be. However, the FBI had close hold of her following the mass kidnapping. Still, Khalid felt he had all he required with the rest of the group.

It was Salim who could not forgive himself. Due to Emily now being able to identify him, he had made an attempt to take his own life. Khalid would have none of that. Someone like Salim was indispensable, a true brother. If need be, he would dispose of Emily, but right now, the FBI was reeling, and she was probably scared to death. What Khalid did not realize was the profound communication taking place between Emily and the rest of the XYZ group in his control—an ability he would never be able to replicate or truly understand. If he had, he might have realized just how pivotal her escape had been.

CHAPTER 48

COOPER DELANEY
2:17 p.m.   Malcolm's Private Labs, Genetech, NYC

DEVOTION TO HIS OWN DISCONTENT IS WHAT KEPT COOPER from ever truly being happy. He never stopped long enough to enjoy his success. Before his always-lofty goals had a chance to be fully realized, he had already moved on to the next challenge. So it was with Noctural, only this time the desired result seemed to defeat him.

Not only was his wonder drug failing with Will's test group, it had also stopped working with his original Noctural test subjects. For some reason, the drug had become ineffective for all participants at exactly the same time, regardless of how long each individual had been using it. His only comfort was that none of the other drugs on the market seemed to alleviate the symptoms of insomnia either.

It wasn't just the test groups. Sleepless nights had become somewhat of an epidemic. The subject was popping up in documentaries and every late-night talk show he could think of was cracking jokes about how tired we all were. Insomnia was blamed on everything: exposure to technology, poor food, lack of exercise, and his personal favorite, not enough sex. All jokes aside, there was concern for potential accidents in any circumstance that endangered people's lives: air travel, hospitals, anything that depended on a positive outcome and the capacity of the individual responsible for it. This was the way with insomnia.

No one had enough time to really worry about being tired. The world didn't stop turning after a few sleepless nights, and everyone's story was a little different. Insomnia had a million different causes, with no available cure.

Cooper had all but completely surrendered group testing to Marcus and Rosemary. Working with Malcolm and Ophelia, Cooper had become indispensable, having unlimited access to pharmaceutical testing proved invaluable. They had learned more about XYZ in the past two weeks than Ophelia had been able to study over the past two years. All regulations had been abandoned in a desperate attempt to beat the clock, and hopefully save the abducted XYZs.

Once Ophelia had been made aware that they were no longer in FBI custody, she devoted every available resource to their rescue. Considering the secrets they concealed at Malcolm's labs, any time devoted to Noctural seemed wasted. Ironically, this assumption, like many before it in the past few months, had been made in haste, and unfortunately, could not have been further from the truth.

Jon was having Cooper followed. He didn't know what was going on in Malcolm's labs exactly, but he could only imagine it involved XYZ. It hadn't escaped Jon that Albert was no longer part of the testing at Proteus. The only one missing. It wasn't a coincidence that he was XYZ.

Access to Genetech was impossible without Malcolm's blessing, especially since it was his labs Cooper visited daily. Jon had this much confirmed at least. It made sense. Malcolm was the perfect candidate. He would be in his glory running tests on a new species of hominid. It would be his dream come true.

Jon wanted these minors out of Proteus, and he would have already taken steps to terminate the testing, but he needed to keep an eye on Will, and the more cases of insomnia that were being reported meant all the more reason to come up with the antidote. If things had been simpler, Jon would have been all over this.

With insomnia becoming a global epidemic, he could only imagine the fortune they would make on Noctural. However, Jon was smarter than that. He knew how to find the big fish, and if the tables were turned, he had to admit he would be doing exactly what Cooper was. Ironically, Jon couldn't help him. He knew he needed to distract Khalid. He needed to distract Khalid in order to save them all.

Unless Khalid already knew. Had Khalid already tried to lure Malcolm over to the dark side? No. He doubted it. Malcolm just wasn't the type. If Khalid had ever met his match, it would be in Malcolm. Even if Khalid wasn't directly involved, he may have someone of his own in place at Genetech. If that was the case, it was already too late.

Jon prayed that, if not Genetech in its entirety, then Malcolm's private labs were the fortress he had always imagined them to be. Somehow, Malcolm had been able to rise above any interruption, be it politicians or banks. It was like the world had decided his work was too important to forgo at any cost. He escaped them all, as the "crazy" old scientist hiding away in his lair, hopefully saving us all—saving the world.

Knowing what Jon knew now, this might just be the case. Something else Jon had learned the hard way, all those years ago, was that when the crowd was fixated on the main attraction, it was a good idea to run the other way. You always had to be one step ahead. Soon enough, the show would be over, and they would realize they had missed the ball.

Jon needed to get both Cooper and Will out of harm's way, but once that was accomplished, it was every man for himself. Jon had mastered many things, but none quite as significant as self-preservation. He was a capitalist at heart, and what better way to capitalize than on a global scale? The world had witnessed this many times before, be it war or Wall Street. When things went completely off the rails, you had the opportunity to lose or win it all. An individual's success could only be stifled by their own scruples.

CHAPTER 49

THE A-TEAM
8:41 a.m.   Genetech, NYC

BEAUTIFULLY MACABRE WAS THE EFFECT OF 250 COTS DRESSED in white linens, shrouding all but the face of the body beneath. The rise and fall of the starched cotton fabric against the chests of the participants created waves across the room. It was as gentle and white as newly fallen snow, but left onlookers uneasy, realizing just how vulnerable we all are when sleeping. These intermittent waves were the only thing that differentiated a mass sleep test from a mass morgue.

Malcolm blamed himself. If only he had considered this sooner. It had crept up on him, just as his own terminal case of insomnia had, which persisted still. He had adapted to the symptoms by running on the adrenaline of the discovery of XYZ, and the high of consummating what had until now only been a fantasy with Pascale. He had all but ignored the fact that everyone around him was half functioning, deprived of the sleep on which we all depend to survive. That was everyone but one. So consumed was Malcolm with Albert's testing that it never even occurred to him that Albert was the only one who seemed almost immune.

The mass sleep test had been Cooper's idea. It was actually his comment that had inspired Malcolm's hypothesis. Cooper's jealous rant at the sight of Albert with energy to spare after hours of testing somehow broke through and caught his attention. How could it be that Albert went all but untouched by the epidemic that seemed to be plaguing them all?

Was it a coincidence? Initially, he'd assumed that it was due to his young age, but a call to Will at Proteus confirmed that all his kids were also suffering. Cooper decided to reach out to the original Noctural test participants and found the same was true. The sleep aid was now completely ineffective to the initial test group, despite continued use.

It was like a flash of lightning went off in Cooper's mind as he watched Malcolm take in Albert with true consideration, rather than mere observation. In that instant, he remembered his revelation after the rescue from the avalanche: that it was something unknown, something outside his reach that was pulling the energy, robbing the sleep from Malcolm. He now felt the same shrouded epiphany, that he was close to discovering the truth.

Without an effective sleep aid, the testing had been made near impossible, and they had decided (after much debate) to administer a high dose of benzodiazepine—the highest each participant could safely endure. Will and Catherine were vehemently opposed to the idea, but agreed to the high dose if Cooper and Malcolm could guarantee no long-term adverse effects to their kids.

At this point, they had already crossed so many lines that it seemed they were too far gone to turn back. Although Albert did not require the drug, they administered it to him to remain consistent and ensure the validity of the testing. Secretly gathering 250 individuals for testing at Genetech had proven difficult enough. Cooper and the rest of the group had no desire to repeat the entire process a second time.

It was unfortunate that, due to the size of the group, they could not perform the test in the safety of Malcolm's private labs, but secrecy would have to be sacrificed so that they could produce results from a sample size of significance.

Mandolin came up behind Cooper and placed her arms around his waist, administering a hug from behind. As the days since the shock of Jack's murder passed, sorrow was replaced with a resurgence of their initial attraction. It had caught them both by surprise at first. In the past month, Cooper had all but moved into her apartment. Both of them now observed the same schedule in Malcolm's labs, and had since her meeting with Armand.

Day in and day out, they were witness to Albert's testing. It was during their shared early morning routine that she had noticed that the makeshift electric toothbrush Cooper had purchased to use at her place had all but run out of charge. She couldn't help but tease him, asking why he would bother. What good could that faint buzzing possibly be making to what were surely becoming furry teeth?

His response was to point said toothbrush at her while he made a hissing noise, which was apparently meant to beam her to another dimension. She laughed so hard at this childish response that she doubled over and collapsed to the floor. He couldn't help but be caught up at her response to his antics. It was the first time either one of them had laughed with abandon since losing Jack.

Cooper reflected, after they came back from their hysterics that true happiness is only achieved in the brief moment when one laughs so hard they forget everything else in their life. Meditation, yoga, and every enlightened religion had nothing on that one rare moment. It was like they both realized the other had been there all along, even though neither was able to offer the support or comfort each so desperately needed at the time. Perhaps there was still hope for them. It was like Jack's death had interrupted their courtship, and they finally both discovered that maybe they could go back to where they had left off. Cooper, for one, was more than willing to try.

"Eerie, isn't it?" Cooper said, looking over his shoulder at Mandolin before looking back at the rows of sleeping bodies. "But I have to say, I am jealous. What I wouldn't give to catch up on some sleep myself. Even if it is drug induced."

He gently turned around to pull Mandolin into his arms, as she rested her own tired head against his shoulder. They both knew the reprieve would be brief. All of them were scheduled to attend Sean's follow-up address in the coming week. It was Mandolin's hope that she would have more to share with Irwin following the testing. At this point, they all seemed to be grasping at straws.

As the world spun out of control around them, it was ironic that intimacy for all three couples seemed to thrive. It would have typically left Ophelia and the recent addition of Armand Price to the group as the odd ones out, but Ophelia was fixated on the testing, desperate to learn any news of her abducted XYZs. It took everything in her not to plead with Albert to try to connect with them. With Armand finally able to relax in the high-security facility Genetech provided, he was just happy to be contributing again, contributing to the cause: the greatest discovery in history.

Pascale was an easy addition to the team, and her expertise and connection to Malcolm were immediately accepted without question. Critical to her success was her innate ability to win their trust without divulging almost any information about herself or her agenda. She had made an art of revealing the exact amount of information required, just enough to keep them contained and trusting her—Malcolm included. It was her alone who fully understood the significance of this test, and the possible connection it might have to what lay right on Earth's doorstep.

The sound of 250 monitors created a deafening hum upon entering the sleep quarters on the other side of the observation glass. Rosemary and Marcus had taken to wearing earplugs to ease the persistent hum that lasted hours after exiting the room. They were like kids in a candy store, assisting with the test at a cutting-edge facility; it made the makeshift children's testing at Proteus, although state of the art, seem like a joke.

They had all agreed to gather data for a six-hour test period, capturing each participant's response during that time. A monitor against the west wall pro-jected the data, plotting the entire group's vitals. It was as if they were all under a spell.

An hour and a half into the test, it was Cooper who first noticed the EEG output, with identical sine waves indicating that the subjects were losing double the amount of energy than normal. Energy, neither created nor destroyed, was leaving them, but why and how?

"How can they all be trending identically? That doesn't make sense. The drug wouldn't have the identical effect. It's like they are all having the same dream."

Malcolm moved over to stand beside him, a shadow drifting over his fea-tures. "They are not all identical, son. Not this one." He pulled up the vital monitoring for Albert.

Cooper couldn't believe his eyes. The impact of whatever "dream" the rest of the group was having impacted their vitals to the point that they were losing more energy than if they had been awake. The only one not suffering the adverse effects of this so-called mutual dream, whatever spell all the participants were under, was Albert. By comparison he seemed to be almost immune to its effect—almost immune to the energy loss that was permeating the entire group.

It was Armand who quickly calculated the energy being produced by this spell-like induced-sleep state, never witnessed before. They were like bees in a hive, with all participants fulfilling the demands of a queen.

Armand couldn't believe what he was seeing. "Based on the combined EEG data, total energy accumulated from each test participant, excluding Albert, is equal to 400 watts, the equivalent of a trained athlete. It's no wonder they're exhausted. Each participant is losing energy at a rate four times the rate they would be losing energy if they were awake. If the results witnessed today were occurring in the general population of 10 billion, the total energy loss would be enough to power NYC for over a month." Armand shook his head in disbelief as the room went silent at his revelation.

Malcolm was the first to break the silence, "Provided the energy could be bottled and used. To the best of my knowledge, there is no such technology. Therefore, despite your fantastic observation, which I agree cannot possibly just be coincidence, I am still left with the big questions of why and how?"

It was only Pascale who distanced herself from the group. The rest of them instinctively moved closer together, their physical proximity an indication of their desire to make sense of what they had just discovered. She reached her hand slowly into her bag in order to retrieve her cell phone. She was the only one of them aware of File 710—the only one aware of Ray and just how much this all meant to the FBI.

CHAPTER 50

SEAN IRWIN
10:26 a.m. Orange County Convention Centre, Orlando, Florida

ALONE, SITTING BY THE WINDOW SILL, SEAN READ THROUGH
his notes one last time. His black suit jacket billowed against the steady
stream of air being forced through the window vents of the convention-hall
breakout room. Between the flights, conferences, and office meetings of the
past months, he had become immune to the stale smell of recycled air. Human
Pinnacle Theory had created a frenzy, and his second conference had required
a new venue.

New York could not accommodate the crowds they were drawing, so now
his follow-up address would be held in Florida. It seemed the plenary session
headlined "Sleep is Not a Strategy" had resonated with everyone, from industry
leaders to religious types. All had migrated to Florida, where everything seemed
larger than life, from Disney World to shopping centers, and even the food on
your plate. It was super-sized—the perfect setting for the bomb he was about
to drop.

The insomnia epidemic first reported in North America had been confirmed
worldwide and was currently being exploited by everyone who thought they could
make a buck. There were thousands of snake-oil remedies promoting a cure, brought
to market as quickly as they could be labeled. Everything from potions, elixirs, thera-
pies, and even sleep spas had begun sprouting up in every major metropolitan.

The world had become obsessed with sleep. Finally having hope of a legitimate scientific explanation for what had become the twenty-first-century plague, had all the appropriate individuals flocking to Florida for answers.

Thanks to Khalid's funding, Sean had been able to make huge strides advancing his theory. He argued that the epidemic was just one more indication that our species had plateaued and was arguably on the decline.

The truth was that Khalid needed Sean up on the stage; he needed to divert attention from the real cause of the epidemic. Khalid had his own research to do, and he needed Cooper's access to all the players tucked away in what was proving to be Malcolm's impenetrable private labs at Genetech. His labs were like a fortress. It seemed that nothing came or went without a shitload of cameras and chaperones. His labs made FBI security measures seem like a joke. The irony was that Khalid's diversion through Sean's second presentation would be most appreciated by the FBI. They should be thanking him for this. It was like crowd control for the masses.

Sean's notes blurred in front of him on the page. He had read and reread them so many times they no longer had meaning. His presentation explained the previously understood causes of insomnia, everything from stress to heritable gene variants. It was important for him to break down the molecular basis for insomnia, and why the epidemic currently being experienced was like nothing seen before.

Sean's address explained that explosive population growth had always been the root cause of previous extinction crises, for all species. Unfortunately, we had now gone too far and ruined our own habitat through pollution, over population ... basically through our own greed. Now in the face of our destruction, Sean's message was that, contrary to his own previous hypothesis, we were no longer in a plateau; we are actually in a death spiral headed toward our own extinction.

The impact of pollutants, global warming, and a collection of other issues resulting in the destruction of our own planet had created a mass physical response to all inhabitants, sending out a warning that the end was near. It was a dismal message; however, it was one for which Sean was eager to take credit. He wanted his thirty seconds of fame.

As Sean led the audience through his slides, he basked in the nods of approval and flurry of whispered sidebar discussions. He was too in awe of the crowd's response to notice Mandolin's expression, in stark contrast at the foot of the stage. How could he have betrayed her this way? She had shared everything with him just days before: Camberg's crazy theory, Jack's death, even Albert and the existence of the other XYZs.

She had only agreed to attend the address because she honestly felt he was her ally, and because it was Sean who had brought her into this mess in the first place. Sean alone was in a position to validate what they had learned and win over the appropriate individuals in the audience, alerting them to the fact that our lack of sleep might be the least of our problems, as he had promised her.

Yet as she listened to what he had to say, that the basis of his theory warned that our insomnia was a result of the destruction of the planet and would eventually lead to our ultimate extinction, she realized that he had no intention of drawing a link to energy loss and the potential reasons for it they had discussed. She had shared with him the results of the mass sleep test, and now hated herself for trusting him with it all. She had everything to lose and had not even considered that he could be a foe instead of a friend.

She gripped Cooper's hand even more tightly. Malcolm and Ophelia looked over to her as if to question how it could all be possible. So perplexing was the betrayal that they all stood together helpless, watching it unfold. All except Cooper.

"We are leaving right now." He ushered Mandolin toward the exit and nodded to Malcolm and Ophelia to follow. Cooper hated himself for not being more involved, for leaving it all up to Mandolin. He had been so consumed with Noctural and the XYZs that he'd dismissed the most important aspects of their discoveries, as well as the people and subsequent dangers associated with them.

It was like he'd completely forgotten about Jack, and how Jack and Mandolin had been a team. How could she possibly navigate the waters without him? At that moment, Cooper realized that they were in far over their heads. The group of four had reached the edge of the crowd when the booming voice making a new introduction stopped Cooper in his tracks.

"Please welcome the CEO of Proteus, Dr. Jon Cameron." The words shot through the air like a cannon to Cooper's ears.

The four of them turned in disbelief as Jon took the podium, thanking Sean for setting the stage for Proteus's latest advancement and the cure for the epidemic they all suffered from.

Jon's loud voice rang out, "Ladies and gentlemen, please allow me to introduce Noctural, the Proteus response to chronic insomnia."

CHAPTER 51

COOPER DELANEY

11:44 a.m.   Orange County Convention Centre, Orlando, Florida

COOPER'S HANDS INTERLOCKED AROUND JON'S TORSO AS THE sound of his voice trailed off across the PA system. This was replaced by the hollow thud of his shoulder hitting the temporary stage floor and the synchronized gasps from the audience.

He had made quick work of recovering the distance lost, as soon as he abandoned his plans to leave the presentation with Mandolin and the others and instead joined Jon on the stage without the assistance of the stairs—a decision he would later come to regret as his leg was still tender from the accident. His anger at Sean's betrayal had oscillated to self-retribution then back to anger as he processed Jon's surprise introduction to the crowd.

The flash from cellphones filled the air like a light show, with amateur commentary and instantaneous verdicts from the crowd providing the soundtrack to the live fist fight taking place on the stage. Security was ill prepared for such an event, as the audience demographic put crowd control low on the agenda. As such, each of the guards assigned to the conference were in varying degrees of obesity, evidence of a lifetime's commitment to southern fare. Slow was their progress as they made their way to the stage, eyes wide in disbelief and disappointment.

Time seemed to standstill as all eyes remained glued to the main attraction, watching a fight-club style brawl, literally center stage, that had been long overdue. Sean was the first to react, and he attempted to position himself between the two men, as one of the few people in the room privy to what was going on. His efforts were rewarded with a right hook from Cooper that sent his masseter muscle into spasm. The iron tang of blood in his mouth took him back in time to his shameful youth.

Screams peppered with a few cheers were met with shouts from the security guards, who had just finally waddled their way up to the stage.

Cooper's satisfaction with his quick draw made him vulnerable; whilst resting on his laurels, Jon was quick to take advantage of it. He traveled back in time to his own sordid past, knocking the wind out of Cooper as he returned the favor, planting his face on the stage floor. They engaged in an MMA-inspired floor scuffle as the four security guards visibly argued over what to do next. All of a sudden, the largest of them literally threw himself on both Jon and Cooper in what was, in the end, arguably the most effective strategy available to end the incident. Unfortunately, the corpulent referee left his mark on both opponents: Jon suffered a fractured arm and Cooper broken ribs.

The police were quick to take control of the situation and escorted all seven men to the nearest dispatch. Their vehicles were followed by those of Malcolm, Ophelia, and Mandolin, Sean's wife, Ray, and Jaxxson, as well as Khalid's men bringing up the rear. The procession would have had Jack rolling in his grave.

Cooper was in the hot seat after the conference-security guards indicated he was the one who had initiated the brawl. He sat alone with the detective, the interrogation room a perfect "cop movie" stereotype.

"Help me understand why you would jump on stage to take down the CEO of Proteus? As I understand, you actually work for him. Why did this happen here? Not enough of a crowd at the office for you?"

Detective Barnes overemphasized his aggravation in an attempt to disguise how tired he was, as he half-heartedly flipped through the conference litera-ture. It was incomprehensible to him, as his blue-collar, high-school education limited both his interest and understanding of the technical and physiological nuances of drug receptors and pharmacological half-lives.

"I can't imagine anyone has decided to press charges. so there is no reason for you to detain me. I want to leave." Cooper hadn't given much thought to the fallout when he took the stage and brought down Jon. Not only was he reeling from Sean's betrayal but now, with Jon taking Noctural to market—a drug that didn't even work—he felt like his head had been in the sand all along. He had been played and hadn't even seen it coming.

"You will be walking out that door once I decide that you don't pose even more of a risk than the violence you have already displayed. Do you have any idea what this epidemic has done? Any idea what my job looks like now? It has given license to everyone who ever wanted to fuck around. It's like, 'Hey, I'm not sleeping, so you can't really blame me.' All the crazies have come out to play, and they are either killing someone or blowing something up, and today, I am the one who is here, left to determine just how crazy you are. Ironically, you and your 'Einsteins' are supposed to be solving the problem and saving us all."

Barnes just wanted this to be over. He knew he couldn't hold Cooper for long, and he hated having to continue with this questioning. He had more important things to do than try to rattle the cage of some jilted pharmaceutical Poindexter.

Cooper stood up from the table and his chair rattled behind him, failing to keep up with his unexpected decision to leap off it. "I know you are in there!" He shouted this at the one-way mirror, as he made his way over to it. "Too scared to talk to me face to face? Come out here and face me, instead of hiding like a fucking coward!" Cooper taunted Jon. He wasn't finished with him yet, not by a long shot.

Barnes shook his head and glared at the mirror. Despite his silent warning, a moment later, there was a knock on the door and an officer led Jon into the room. He held his arm tightly. It obviously needed medical attention; however, it was his only sign of weakness. His eyes blazed with fury, and it was not lost on Cooper.

The guards positioned themselves between the two men. Barnes was pissed and shot the guard a dirty look. What the hell had he been thinking letting Jon in here?

"Give us a minute," Jon said to the officer, not even looking at him.

Barnes gave him a look as if to say, *"It's your funeral."* Secretly, though he was glad to be leaving this mess behind. The only thing left to do was tear a strip off the guards for letting him in here in the first place. He had no idea how persuasive Jon could be.

"You are too late, Cooper." Jon took the lead as the door closed behind them.

"Well, that is the one thing we agree on. You take a drug that doesn't even work out to market, while I am killing myself trying to find out why it won't do what you know full well it should. Yes, indeed I am definitely too late. I should have quit long ago. You don't give a fuck, do you? You want every poor soul who can't sleep out there to buy your miracle pill so that you can make a billion on it, and too bad for them when they find out it's all a sham."

Jon glanced over to the window, "Of course the drug works, Cooper. You're just pissed you weren't the one to make it happen. I am so sorry we have to let you go, but I am sure you understand, under the circumstances." Jon raised his injured arm slightly.

Cooper launched Jon against the questioning room wall like a shutter in a hurricane. All the anxiety and fear that once controlled him was lost in an instant.

Jon winced as searing pain shot up through his arm; then he laughed into Cooper's face, inches from his own.

"Tell me what is really going on here! This is too fucked up even for you." Cooper searched Jon's eyes for something that made sense.

Jon's only thought was to protect Will, and that meant protecting Cooper as well. He leaned in toward Cooper's ear, his face purposely hidden from view by the mirror. "You don't want to know," he whispered. The look he gave Cooper then made him back away.

Ray had his arms crossed in front of his chest as he stood behind the viewing mirror. Jon's whisper escaped his detection, but the implication was clear.

CHAPTER 52

ALBERT XAVIER

10:14 a.m.   Malcolm's private labs, Genetech, NYC

WORD-FREE COMMUNICATION HAD ITS ADVANTAGES. WHILE the world seemed to fall apart around them, the XYZs continued perfecting the craft. They had begun a silent coup. The banter that went on amongst them would have left Malcolm and Ophelia little choice but to shut down the testing entirely, but the longer they experienced success at avoiding detection, the bolder their plans became.

The direction the conversation had taken precipitated difficult waters for young Albert to navigate. He was intelligent beyond his years; however, time is required to become proficient at any language, especially one that is unspoken. Albert would catch himself answering back aloud to something he had heard from another XYZ. It seemed an impossible skill to master but he was determined.

His life had changed dramatically from troubled child, in need of daily medication, to gifted anomaly capable of feats his keepers could only dream of. It left him with a sense of wonder but also fear. He felt very alone, and if it were not for Jasper and Emily guiding him through the maze that stood before him, he would have been very lost indeed.

As a novice participant to the captive XYZs' conversations, Albert had learned many things about their circumstances and Khalid. He feared for them, as Jasper and Emily tried everything they could to help pinpoint their location and initiate a rescue mission.

He recognized each of them as easily as he would had they been standing in front of him, something akin to any infant mammal instantly recognizing their mother's call. As he captured their message in his mind, the interaction with each individual was as clear as if he had heard their unique voice. They were a tight group, and as much as he felt sorry for them, he was also struck by how closely they worked together and how they calmed each other's fears.

So different was their approach to the situation than how his own family, specifically his mother, dealt with adversity. Even at his young age, he recognized the advantage of this group cooperation he witnessed every day among the XYZs. There was no talk of blame or regret, only empathy and potential solutions.

He wanted to dedicate himself entirely, to have just as much responsibility as both Jasper and Emily in aiding in their rescue; however, there was something that kept him from participating fully. At first, he thought it was his inexperience, that he was having difficulty receiving the messages from the other XYZs, but now that he knew them all so well, each by their own dialogue and cadence, he realized it was something else. However, his confidence was shaky. Having been a patient for so long had left him doubting himself and his abilities; as such he was reluctant to open up fully.

One night after the testing was finalized, he mustered the courage to question Jasper.

"Do you hear that?"

"What's that you say?"

"Like a bunch of voices sort of saying the same thing. But in a different language."

"Aw, Albie. . . . You just need a rest, little man. I know this testing has been grueling, and I am tired as well. It's just all of the transmitting today. Too many people trying to get their point across. So many voices it sounded like a different language to me as well."

"Yeah, you are probably right. Have a good night, Jasper."

"Good night, little man."

What Albert had just confessed set an alarm bell off in Jasper's head. He was worried about Albert, as he had seen this before in a number of the XYZs in

Ophelia's group. The ones who had experienced it said it drove them crazy, and they had eventually left the group, one way or another.

Jasper rang Malcolm immediately, but his call was sent straight to voicemail. At the moment, Malcolm found himself at war with Pascale following their return from Florida, and the aftermath that persisted.

"Why didn't you tell me about the FBI? How could you keep something like that from me? I have been open and honest with you from the start! After everything we have been through. . . ." The past came flooding back for Malcolm: the games she had played, the lies, and her secrecy. Unfortunately, the future of their relationship had materialized for him, and now he couldn't picture life without her.

Pascale shut down as she always did. At times like this, she was able to detach and hear words without emotion. It all became binary in situations of conflict.

"I don't think we are able to have this conversation at the moment," she said mechanically.

Malcolm had years of practice to know that any protest would get him nowhere. He could pursue this with her, and she might even placate him, make it appear that she was willing to hear him out or even agree with him. However, it was an illusion he had experienced many times over. Exposing her wrongdoing made absolutely no difference.

They had come too far this time, and although this would break his heart, he turned his back on the love of his life and waved at her to leave.

She initially felt surprise. Although her ego was a bit bruised, it was soon replaced by relief. Her nature could not be helped.

His discovery of Pascale's alliance with the FBI was inopportune. Not only did it prevent him from receiving the call from Jasper but it also resulted in him ignoring Will's absence. It was ironic that, at the same time as Malcolm opened the bottom drawer to retrieve a bottle of Dalmore 62 Highland Malt, saved only for occasions such as these, Jon had just removed the cap from the identical bottle in order to pour Will a drink in his office at Proteus. It had been a wedding gift to Jon from Malcolm, one that had long outlived the marriage—a marriage that in retrospect had been nothing but a midlife crisis.

Will accepted the heavy crystal glass without hesitation. He didn't care for the stuff and was far from appreciating the liquor on any other level than the courage it gave him to rat out Malcolm and Cooper to Jon.

Jon took in the information with as much genuine surprise as he could muster. He tried to mimic how he guessed he typically held his face in situations where he was none the wiser. The sad truth was that times like that almost never occurred. That, in itself, gave him confidence that his acting was on point, as he deliberately sat as far forward as his outrageously expensive office chair would allow, in an effort to depict fatherly concern.

Will never suspected that Jon already knew pretty much everything. Rosemary and Marcus were his eyes and ears over at Genetech. Cooper had been too wrapped up in himself to figure that one out. He had become a disappointment for Jon on so many levels. And it was for exactly that reason—Cooper's poor performance of late—that Jon never suspected Will was wearing a wire. It was so outside his younger brother's repertoire and Jon was so intensely focused on Khalid's subterfuge that the thought never entered his mind.

Cooper had flown back from Florida solo, long after the others. He had stayed behind in order to convince the FBI he was on their side—one of the good guys, so to speak. He had plenty of time to himself on the flight back to NYC, plenty of time to recalibrate and take back control of the situation. He hated himself for losing sight of everything, but he never stayed down for long. He was king of the comeback, and this time, it wasn't just his own revenge he sought. He needed to redeem himself in Mandolin's eyes.

Listening in on the conversation between Jon and Will from the comfort of Malcolm's labs, Cooper had to admit he was impressed with Will. He was holding his own, reciting exactly what they had discussed pretty much verbatim. The ice cubes he heard clinking put a smile on his face. Perhaps scotch was Will's performance enhancer as well as his own. Cooper casually listened as Will continued, but it was the key questions for Jon they had rehearsed that were of most interest to him.

Will carefully delivered the first, much-rehearsed question: "How could you do it, Jon? It must have crushed Cooper! How could you sell him out on Noctural?"

"Coop is a big boy, Will. He'll get over it." Jon was smug with the success of the Florida trip. Demand for Noctural was overwhelming; they couldn't keep up with production. Jon was invincible and now, after the incident at the conference, he was under FBI protection. Despite the fact that he knew better, especially where Khalid was concerned, it gave him a false sense of security.

"I just don't understand though. How could you get financing for a drug that doesn't meet FDA clearance, a drug that is essentially a failure?" Will's voice was clear, with no hint of the adrenalin coursing through his veins.

Jon's interest was piqued. Had his brother finally grown up enough to ask the right questions? Was Will capable of more than Jon gave him credit for?

"Little brother, there is always money for the next miracle drug, if you are willing to break the rules." Jon was enjoying the big-brother role as usual.

It was all Cooper needed. He had Jon now, and the admission to bringing a placebo to market without FDA approval. His self-talk was at an all-time high. He was a man on a mission, and the voices in Cooper's head shouted their approval.

The voices in Albert's head had started shouting as well. He found it impossible to ignore them any longer. He had tried to push them away, as he couldn't make out a word, but the steady hum had reached a tipping point, and he shouted back to them in his head, just one word:

"STOP!"

There was silence. It seemed like a miracle. After some time, the voices were back, singing the first few phrases of the familiar Brahms' lullaby in unison. It was the most beautiful choir he had ever heard, filled with hundreds of voices. Perhaps the most beautiful thing about it was that he recognized the language. They were singing to him in English, from the dark side of the moon.

CHAPTER 53

KHALID AL GAMDI
12:20 p.m.   Proteus, NYC

"TELL ME ABOUT THIS COOPER OF YOURS. MY PEOPLE REPORT that he started quite the brawl with you on the presentation stage." Khalid enjoyed putting Jon on the spot. It was one of his favorite things to do.

Jon was considering installing a revolving door. Since Florida, it had been non-stop. Everyone from the FDA to the FBI wanted a piece of him. No one had an appointment; they just demanded an audience. Daphne had all but given up trying to manage his schedule, and Jon himself was starting to get anxious about keeping up with the interrogations, and all the questions that slowly morphed into accusations.

His street sense had served him well. All those foster homes, all that running, had given him a sixth sense he had never truly appreciated until this moment. He knew Khalid was onto him, and probably had been for some time. He also knew that, if Khalid thought he was still useful, he would delay whatever sordid plans he had in store for him. Jon had no choice but to stall until he could come up with a viable plan B—a plan that didn't involve a permanent resignation from his life.

The lack of sleep and the barrage of guests with their arsenal of questions had left Jon disinhibited. He had developed a story and was sticking to it. It would hopefully protect him. Hopefully, it would protect them all.

"He is just an average chemist who thought he should get all the credit for the next big thing. He wanted the glory for creating the next super drug, the pill that will solve all our problems and put everybody back to sleep again." Jon was so tired of this bullshit.

"What is it about you guys in your glass towers looking down on the rest of us? You think you are so much smarter than everyone. There is a term for this in your language. Narcissist. Isn't that right? This is what you are, Jon, a narcissist, someone in love with themself." Khalid loved to toy with Jon; it brought him such pleasure to watch Jon react.

"What do you really mean, Khalid?" Jon was not in the mood. He had no patience left, not even for Khalid, despite the unavoidable risk.

"I mean that the last time I sat here in this chair, you sold me on a sleep aid that was going to make us both rich men. But that was just a diversion, wasn't it, my friend? All of a sudden, I find your boy wonder is in bed with Sasaki, the scientist we have been 'recruiting' for months. How does that come to pass? What in the world would your Cooper want with the world's leading scientist in the field of evolutionary genetics? Please explain." Khalid could sense Jon's annoyance. He had him where he wanted him.

"Why would I know who the hell Cooper, our disgruntled past employee, is making time with? You did not tell me the whole story, but you know what, I forgive you, and fortuitously, I am in the perfect position to get you access to Sasaki through Rosemary and Marcus. Isn't that what you're really after? A way into Malcolm's fortress?" Jon was on the edge. He knew it but seemed almost incapable of effectively deflecting Khalid's accusations.

Khalid sat back in his chair. Jon was and had always been a formidable opponent. That was why Khalid respected him and had made it a mission to ultimately own him.

"Tell me about your people over there. Why do you think you can trust them? Why do you think Cooper trusts them?" Khalid loved the word "trust." With Jon and his type, the minute it was uttered, they would feel obliged to defend their decisions. A lot was on the table when you had to explain why you trusted someone. With a man like Jon, it was sure to be ripe with the snippets from the road he had paved for all three individuals (Cooper, Rosemary, and Marcus) and why they were in his debt.

What came next surprised even Khalid. Due to the stress and fatigue, Jon found it impossible to cloak himself in humility. "I'm not sure I can, Khalid. But that's really not my problem, is it? You would have Sasaki by now, if you had someone on the inside. My people are your best bet. Hell, even Cooper, who is a long shot at best, is better than what you have going on."

Jon regretted his words instantly; the lack of sleep and unending barrage of questions had left him raw. He needed some space, and it would seem that he was not to be granted any for some time. Khalid was the last person he should be taunting, the last person he should ignite.

The thin, strained smile that broke Khalid's lips spoke volumes, and Jon knew he had gone too far. He also knew it was impossible to retract his words—and worse yet to try to explain them away. Khalid was not to be toyed with. How stupid he had been. Will was still over there, for Christ's sake, not to mention Malcolm and that kid.

The look of dismay that crossed Jon's face was not lost on Khalid. He silently congratulated himself on choosing the perfect timing for his visit. Jon was a steady character, but everyone had their limits.

"I'll be in touch, my friend." Khalid stood up and gestured for Jon to receive his goodbye embrace.

Jon felt weak at Khalid's touch, as if life itself was being drained out of him. He had walked straight into the lion's den. He knew Khalid would now stop at nothing to get into that lab. No one would stand in his way, and once he did, he would find out that Jon had known all along and hadn't said a word.

Khalid made his way to the elevator with only one thing in mind: Cooper.

CHAPTER 54

OPHELIA SASAKI
10:41 a.m.   Malcolm's personal labs, Genetech, NYC

SHE HAD BEEN REWINDING ALBERT'S TAPE FOR HOURS, TRYING to decide on her next move. Ophelia had never seen anything like it. The recordings of XYZ conversations she had previously studied were all consistently predictable. As she had witnessed with the rest of her group, the EEG monitor was effectively tracking the brainwave activity between Albert and Jasper. It was all normal, or as normal as brain-to-brain interface between new species of hominids could possibly be.

Albert had been hooked up to the EEG monitor for a marathon of hours each day, so much so that he felt something was missing without the electrode cap covering his head. It was the moment following the EEG spike from the end of the day that caught her attention. She couldn't hear Albert transmitting the command to "STOP" but the spike on the monitor and his corresponding physical reaction as he placed his hands over his ears and squeezed his eyes shut made his intention clear. The spike had come from Albert. That was a given. However, the readings that followed did not make sense. It was like nothing she had ever seen before.

While the XYZ communication did not follow the same patterns a human conversation would typically follow, it was still distinguishable if you tracked it as long as Ophelia had. The fluctuation between the electrical signals that were being sent, as well as those received, were easy to identify if you knew what you were looking for. She had been tracking the ebb and flow of these silent discussions among all the XYZ participants for so long she could almost predict what she would see on the EEG, depending upon the individual, even though she could never fully understand what was being transmitted.

She knew what to expect when Albert smiled or laughed, or when Jasper avoided a direct answer. His facial expression would give away what the EEG would soon portray. While she would never know exactly what they communicated, she had become an expert at decoding a verbal account of their conversation and being able to translate the bits that were left out. It had become her own form of eavesdropping.

However, the reading on the monitor while Albert captured the transmission he had received was off the charts. He wasn't directly communicating with any of the XYZ group. Jasper was off-line, and the time change meant that all of the XYZ that had been captured would also be off-line or asleep, if they were sleeping at all. Even if they had all been communicating at once, which she had also had the opportunity to monitor throughout the course of her testing, it had never been anything like this. So, what was this? Who was Albert talking to? The spikes in the graph scared her. How could he effectively communicate at this heightened level of activity?

Her first instinct was to go to Malcolm, but he had shut himself in his office for hours. He wasn't speaking to anyone following the incident in Florida. Regardless, Ophelia was not sure about following her own instincts any longer. Things were not what they seemed. It was like she too had fallen down the rabbit hole.

She longed for the days when she had full autonomy; she had been granted free reign until the FBI took over, and since then felt like a rat, hiding out in Malcolm's labs. Everything was in chaos, not just here but everywhere. The world was spiraling into a sleepless abyss, and the more time that past, the worse the situation seemed to become. She was experiencing it herself. What had at first been the occasional hour or two of insomnia per night had become a seemingly endless stretch of staring at the ceiling—or, worse yet, a night where she thought she had slept all the way through but woke up feeling more tired than when she lay down.

Everyone seemed to be suffering the consequences of sleep deprivation. It had become the world's latest pandemic, and while it had seemed humorous at first, there were serious consequences involved. Everything from accidents to, in the worst cases, suicides. Chronic lack of sleep seemed to be pushing everyone over the edge.

Until Florida, there seemed to be no help in sight, but now every physician diagnosing a patient with a sleep disorder was prescribing Noctural. As it stood, there were only a handful of people who knew that Noctural lacked efficacy, and she was one of them.

No, this was something she was going to keep to herself. Malcolm obviously had more pressing issues to attend to, and she was used to it. Ophelia seemed the only one capable of giving 100 percent to her work, which meant 100 percent to XYZ, no matter what. So, with free reign over Malcolm's labs for the moment, and a guaranteed night of sleeplessness ahead, she made her way to the Miele coffee maker for yet another espresso.

Life . . . lemons. It was time for some lemonade. At least she had autonomy back, if nothing else. She needed to come up with a plan so that once Albert woke up, she had a solid chance of figuring out what had spiked his EEG, and if luck was with her, recreating the transmission.

CHAPTER 55

KHALID AL GAMDI
6:52 a.m.   Madison Square Park Tower, NYC

QUACKERY WAS ON THE RISE. NOCTURAL HAD INSPIRED EVERY pill manufacturer, candy company, and narcotic dealer to throw their chips on the table. Proteus may have been first to market, but there was a tirade of imitations now entering the new and improved sleep-aid space. For Khalid, it was the perfect frenzy, a global preoccupation to hide behind.

Lost for the talent he required to exploit the abducted XYZ participants, he had pushed the button on Cooper's recruitment, and what better timing than first thing in the morning. The proverbial early bird could already taste the worm.

Security at Genetech was tighter than ever. The level of sophistication required to gain entry to Malcolm's labs was defeating. It was difficult for even for the chosen few allowed to gain entry every day. Khalid had surveillance on the comings and goings of all the players. Of most interest was Armand Price, and of course, Ophelia Sasaki. With everything at stake and time being of the essence, Khalid decided he needed to not go in through the gate but through the gatekeeper, and the best way to do that would be to fool the troll under the bridge with the real deal. In order for him to collect the intel and individuals he required, he needed a willing participant, and he was betting everything on Cooper. Dr. Cooper Delaney would be his man, like it or not.

CHAPTER 56

OPHELIA SASAKI
11:23 a.m. Malcolm's Labs, Genetech, NYC

"TELL ME AGAIN WHAT YOU HEARD. YOU ARE SURE IT WAS singing?" Ophelia had been up all night. It had taken all of her willpower not to wake Albert up earlier, as he appeared to be the only one capable of sleep, so that she could resume testing.

She didn't wait for his reply. Even as the words left her mouth, she pulled the cap over his thick blond hair. Her actions were perfectly efficient and thought-less, as if she were his mother, as she had performed it so many times before.

"I don't know if I will hear it again. It comes and goes. When I hear them, it's really loud, but I can't talk first." His response left her lost for words. Albert was relieved. This was more than any eight-year-old could handle on his own. Even if she didn't believe him in the end, he felt that he had to tell someone.

"That's fine. We'll wait. We'll wait all day and night and then some, if we have to. Do you have somewhere else you need to be?" She asked her question laced in sarcasm, already knowing the answer.

Albert only shook his head in reply. He also knew the answer. He knew it all too well.

CHAPTER 57

PASCALE LAURENT
6:02 p.m.   The St. Regis New York Hotel lobby, NYC

"MALCOLM, PICK UP THE GODDAMN PHONE." PASCALE'S INSIDE voice had failed her, as Ray and Jaxxson's questioning stares magnified her lapse of judgement.

What did it matter anyway? They would go through the back door. Genetech couldn't keep the FBI out any longer, especially now that they could not rely on her as an informant. She needed to report every twenty-four hours, and her twenty-four hours were long overdue. She was tempted to make something up, but fear of being caught up in the end had her thinking better of it. Besides, that was not how Pascale played, and of even greater interest than anything Malcolm had to offer was the FBI via NASA surveillance on the "anomaly" hidden in plain sight, discovered by dumb luck as the second Chinese Chang'e probe landed on the dark side of the moon.

"Men, always so hard to get a hold of." Pascale's attempt to lighten the mood, and perhaps buy a few more hours, was successful in at least putting a polite smile on their faces.

"But never mind him. What activity are you seeing on the probe? Have there been any changes?" Pascale was desperate to move the spotlight off herself and, ultimately, Malcolm.

Ray didn't like it. He wouldn't have said a word but she'd won over Jaxxson, and before Ray could stop him, he blurted out the Coles Notes on their latest update from the space agency.

Pascale reached for the heavy brass handle before the doorman could assist her. As she lit her Gauloises, simultaneously tasting the tobacco and greedily breathing in the nicotine, she had the realization: They were coming closer. She had already heard the same from her team, but what she did not know is that they had already made contact. The transmission and receipt of that transmission could only be confirmed through Albert by Ophelia, and Ophelia had no idea what (or from whom) it was.

CHAPTER 58

COOPER DELANEY
7:47 a.m.   Clock Tower Condo, NYC

THE CONCIERGE ASSIGNED TO COOPER'S LOFT WAS AN AVUN-cular fellow who had procured the appearance of favoring each owner, while in reality following the building statutes to a tee.

"Good morning, Hudson." Cooper had been quick to put himself on a first-name basis with the impeccably dressed attendant. He felt entitled to the familiarity, especially as he owned the penthouse.

"Good day, sir. Shall I have the Tesla or the Porsche brought round? If it were me, I might be tempted to enjoy one last ride with the top down before all the autumn leaves have fallen upon us." Hudson took note that it was late for Cooper to be heading to the office on a work day. Very late indeed.

"Yes, great suggestion, old sport. I will take the Porsche out one last time." They both enjoyed playing Nick and Gatsby. It had become an ongoing challenge between them: Who could better mimic early twentieth-century phrasing? Cooper would never admit it, but he'd tried to watch the movie once or twice and had even started the book so as not to fall out of practice.

Two thoughts crossed Cooper's mind: First, that it was entirely possible this would not only be his last ride in the car for the year but perhaps his last ride in the car ever, and second, that he much preferred the role of abductor than abductee.

As promised, the Porsche soon arrived, the garage attendant loved to bring it up, leaving Hudson no time to finish his account of his weekend's highlights. "Brought round" had become a loose term. Hudson was potentially the only one who still used it, as most vehicles independently drove up to the entrance when summoned, the Porsche being one of the few exceptions.

Cooper made a poor audience, as he scanned the elegant lobby surroundings as if seeing them for the first time. He weighed the odds of a last-minute escape, a distraction that was not lost on the astute Hudson, who kept talking in order to pardon the indiscretion.

In the end, Cooper thought better of it. The look of intent on the face of the man he had just met in his penthouse left no choice but to obey. He had vowed to stay one step ahead, only to find he was now a thousand steps behind. To enter a room in one's home to an intruder is something one never forgets; however, the mention of Jack's final words was what stopped Cooper in his tracks. Salim made Khalid's expectations clear to Cooper, as he sat uninvited and unannounced in Cooper's favorite chair.

CHAPTER 59

THE A-TEAM
8:56 a.m.   Genetech, NYC

MALCOLM RESURFACED TO CHAOS. A COUPLE DAYS' REPRIEVE in his office were apparently all that were required for all hell to break loose.

He continued with his tongue-lashing pointed directly at Ophelia. "How could you take this testing completely off course with no evidence to base anything on? I expected so much more of you. You have some crazy, unsupported hunch, and on that alone, have taken action that has severely compromised the health and well-being of the one person we should all be protecting. Not even an adult, Ophelia, for God's sake. A child!"

Scarlet engulfed Ophelia's cheeks as she could not deny Malcolm's accusations. Her testing of Albert had become desperate and reckless. Selfishly, her only sleep-deprived thought was to have him deliver some proof of her hunch that his communication had been with something or someone off world. Her reckless behavior had now potentially cost them their greatest asset. However, the flagellation would have to wait as the self-proclaimed challenger for greatest asset to the team had just entered the scene, coming to the office an hour late nonetheless.

"Cooper, whatever you have better be worth it. Can't you see we are in the middle of something here?" Malcolm had little time for Cooper on a good day, and made it clear that his patience had already expired. Until that moment, their eyes had yet to meet, but once they did, Malcolm's words all but fell away. He instinctively recognized the look in Cooper's eyes, not because he had seen it before but because undisguised, genuine fear and acceptance of one's own lack of safety was tough to miss. It was a warning, and at the same time, a silent pact between the men to carry on as if there was no danger, because in doing so, they could hopefully save as many as possible.

Without so much as a word, Cooper headed to his office and retrieved his laptop. Once again, he had to fight the impulse to escape, to save not only himself but the two other individuals he needed to convince to come with him.

A desperate fear choked him, one he had experienced only once before, shrouded in a coffin of snow. He pushed it aside, because this time, there was even more at stake—not only his life but the lives of so many others.

He made his way to Ophelia's office and was relieved, albeit in the most horrid way imaginable, that Armand Price stood next to her. They looked up in unison as he entered the room and closed the door behind him.

After ten minutes, the threesome emerged, one as stone-faced as the next. The looks from Malcolm and Albert as they made their way toward the security door were hard to bear. Even harder was Mandolin, calling Cooper's name as she suddenly entered the room. He did not stop or look behind, fighting with himself, fighting the urge to be with her, the urge to escape.

Salim's sedan waited for them in front of the building, and as they drove away, Cooper shut his eyes and tried to block out the sound of Mandolin's voice—a voice he would never forget.

Had he looked back, he would have witnessed her following them out the front doors of Genetech. The questions that ran through her mind were countless, and the fear of being abandoned gripped her as it had done only once before. It was at that moment that a leaf fell from the fall-kissed oak above. It grazed her shoulder and, for a fleeting moment, she couldn't help but feel Jack by her side as her grip tightened on the USB 5 key in her pocket, which she had intended to give Armand only moments before.

CHAPTER 60

HERRIDEN
8:56 a.m.   A Midwestern corn field bordering Lake Michigan

A SUCCESSFUL ATMOSPHERIC ENTRY LEFT HERRIDEN FULL OF excitement and hope. His ship had performed as required and was transmitting his coordinates by the nanosecond back to control. He had secretly been concerned about the effectiveness of the heat shield but now realized he had worried unnecessarily. The modifications had solved the issue, and he was seconds away from his predetermined landing point. Seconds away from his first landing on Earth.

He remembered the time-tested formula for the selection of the optimal landing site: low habitation, low terrain, low resistance to impact, low surveillance, and high potential to hide the ship post entry.

Accelerating through space toward his destination made him realize he was hesitant, but now, as he felt the force of the deceleration from the water and watched the light disappear completely from above, he lost all fear.

The force of impact pushed the ship through the bottom of the lake into the subsurface sediment. It was like being caught up in an avalanche. He no longer had control; the sediment of the lake floor substituting snow. He opened the automated hatch and as water and debris poured into the cockpit, he laughed to himself, gasping deeply. You can't get any more hidden from sight than this.

He left the craft, crawled up through the lake floor, and swam to the surface. It flashed across his mind that it was like he was being reborn—reborn to this planet his ancestors had left behind hundreds of millions of years before. The water was cold, and he shivered as he trudged through the mud toward the shore. The air was dense with humidity and the smell of decaying vegetation. An incredible revelation engulfed him as he realized he was breathing and surviving on an alien planet.

Reconnaissance had demonstrated that a rural location, with minimal population/square meter, just following harvest was the best place and timing to avoid collision or sighting during landing. The dense brush surrounding the lake provided all the privacy he needed, and the timing at dusk increased the likelihood that its inhabitants would be scarce. Had his entry been observed, it would undoubtedly be misinterpreted as a meteor or "shooting star" and be wished upon rather than investigated.

In any case, the opportunity had already passed. His ship was no longer visible, buried beneath the lake floor. Regardless, Herriden performed his detailed investigation of the area for any signs that his entry and landing had been witnessed. Satisfied his arrival had gone unnoticed, he allowed himself a personal account of the surroundings.

He breathed in the air to fill his lungs and felt invigorated; the oxygen content of Earth's atmosphere was almost double that of his home. It was interesting, he thought, as his "home" world had become a misnomer. It was this planet, Earth, that was *actually* his home world—or at least that of his ancestors. Herriden's planet had been completely obliterated; all of them were now interplanetary refugees.

As he looked up to Earth's moon, he felt tears run down his cheeks, a reminder that he wasn't dreaming any of this. He had never experienced a sunset, let alone the beauty of the night sky full of stars, exquisite courtiers in attendance to a full harvest moon. At that moment, he experienced an epiphany, the tragic irony of his entire species, just a few thousand miles away behind the moon, yet so close to home. Herriden recalled the countless debates as their ship gradually made the epic voyage to its current location. The impossible acceptance to which they were forced to succumb—inflicting trauma to these hominid cousins—was innately counter to their nature. Not only were they exploiting the apex species on Earth, who had evolved during their

250-million-year absence, but the homo sapiens were clearly suffering as a result of their unavoidable actions.

As clouds drifted across the lonesome moon, Herriden wondered what would happen next. What would be the impact of their actions, and what would be the consequences?

ABOUT THE AUTHORS

C O-AUTHORS JJ COOK & AJ COOK, MD ATTRIBUTE THE CREATION of this novel—the first volume in the Percivious Trilogy—to the marriage of their unique skills and perspectives.

JJ Cook's background in marketing across a spectrum of industries (including technology, finance, and the arts) brings insight and depth to characters spanning an array of disciplines, ages, countries, and cultures.

AJ Cook, MD's current role as chief of pediatric urology at the Alberta Children's Hospital has allowed him the opportunity to author and contribute to numerous published studies, honing his writing skills, while his experience as a surgeon—as well as the relationships he's developed with his young patients and their guardians—has contributed credibility and realism to the narrative.

They hope this novel—and trilogy—shines a light on something the world seems to have forgotten: altruism, and its impact on society. *"Something that needs a voice now more than ever but also a platform where it will be heard."*

9 781525 565458